To Nikki, with love Liz x

WEB OF FEAR

Elizabeth Russell

First Published in Great Britain 2019 by Mirador Publishing

Copyright © 2019 by Elizabeth Revill

All rights reserved. No part of this publication may be reproduced or transmitted, in any form or by any means, without permission of the publishers or author. Excepting brief quotes used in reviews.

First edition: 2019

Any reference to real names and places are purely fictional and are constructs of the author. Any offence the references produce is unintentional and in no way reflects the reality of any locations or people involved.

A copy of this work is available through the British Library.

ISBN: 978-1-913264-25-3

Mirador Publishing
10 Greenbrook Terrace
Taunton
Somerset
UK
TA1 1UT

Web of Fear

By

Elizabeth Revill

For Tony & Carole-Anne

1

THE SUN SHONE LANGUIDLY IN the early waking hours of a bright spring morning in a nondescript street filled with look-a-like houses from suburbia. The stout wooden front door of a redbrick semi-detached house opened and the brass door knocker rattled as Jan Bernard, a pretty brunette in her mid-thirties, with her hair tied back in a ponytail exited her parent's family home in full running gear.

She stretched her lithe limbs and took several deep breaths as she manoeuvred and twisted her body in some gentle warm up exercises as she prepared for her morning run.

Her breath blew out from her mouth like hot steam and Jan ran on the spot for a few moments, checking her time on her watch and the step counter on her pedometer, before she adjusted her iPod and attached it to her belt. Jan put on her headphones, turned up the volume and jogged off down the path. The tinny sound of percussion instruments filtered through the air with blasts of the singer's full and powerful voice as Jan hummed along to one of the tracks on an Adele album.

The small wooden gate at the top of the path leading from the house to the street squeaked on its hinges as Jan went through it. 'Must get some WD40,' she thought as she reached the road. She tripped and looked down to see her shoelace had become undone so, she stopped, placed her foot on a low wall outside a neighbouring property and retied the trailing shoelace before setting off down the dusty road. She jogged at a comfortable speed along the pavement, keen to reach her usual circuit.

She was oblivious to a pair of shaded eyes belonging to an unidentifiable person sitting inside a black saloon car with tinted windows. As Jan sprinted on, the vehicle started up and pulled out from the kerb following the oblivious runner at a discreet distance.

Jan headed on, crossed a main thoroughfare not yet busy with rush hour traffic and headed toward a green-gated area. She opened the small access gate with ease and ran through the grassland, up a bank to the riverside towpath. It was clear this was a regular route for her and one she negotiated with ease, all part of her early morning routine. Jan was a creature of habit.

On the road, the pursuing car pulled into the kerb of the tree lined avenue and parked. The driver turned off the ignition and removed the key. Lying on the passenger seat next to the driver was a wicked looking knife with a sharp serrated blade. Gloved hands picked it up and secreted the weapon inside the fleece-lined jacket. The driver left the car slamming and locking the door. The shutting mechanism chirruped, almost merrily, in the cool morning air.

The androgynous figure in a dark tracksuit and hoodie scrambled up the bank and surveyed the gently flowing water of the river beneath the tow path and let out a sigh of satisfaction as the water gently travelled onward. It rippled in the bright morning light as it bounced over rocks and shifted the wafting reeds close to the bank.

Jan Bernard could still be seen ahead, running on swiftly. The watcher headed for a small clump of trees on the runner's trail and leaned against the trunk of one to wait. The knife was removed from the inside pocket and carefully held inside the arm close to the body and tightly to the person's side.

This was a popular place for joggers. Many runners of mixed ages and gender chuffed past; some perspiring and puffing, others cool and easy in stride and style. The person, who was indistinguishable as male or female, continued leaning against the sycamore tree and waited.

It wasn't long before the striking form of Jan appeared running back along the track. The figure lying in wait stepped forward, head down and marched purposefully toward her. By now, the other joggers had melted from view. There was no one else in sight, a quick look around revealed there was no one on the path.

Jan had stopped herself from stumbling. She bent over to retie that errant shoelace and her headphones slipped forward on her head. She fixed them in position before getting into her stride once more and passing the anonymous, sinister individual, who had spun around and fallen into step behind the unsuspecting woman.

Jan was struck swiftly from behind, fatally stabbed in the neck. As the blood fountained forth, the air rushed from her lungs and she tumbled head first down the bank and landed face first into the water. The blood seeped into the slow moving river clouding the water around her in red. Jan's body twitched once or twice before finally lying still as the body caught in the reeds and weeds.

Making sure that the job was done properly the knife was quickly hidden and the conscienceless perpetrator jogged away. There was a definite jubilance in the stride almost a skip of glee. A hand punched the air in victory.

Further away in another street people slumbered in their houses as those on regular early shifts rose to face the daily grind and get to work. It was just another ordinary morning. The sun had just shown its face in the sky and garden birds were beginning their morning chorus to start the day.

Small fingers of sunlight poked through the chinks in the curtains attempting to prod the occupants of a comfortable king-size bed to wakefulness but the heavy material of the black-out curtains was mainly doing its job.

The insistent harsh ring of an extraordinarily shrill alarm clock blared out in the bedroom. Attractive Tara Lomas aged thirty-five, groaned loudly and rolled over pulling the pillow over her head to drown out the annoying sound murmuring, "No, no, no." Her husband Steve, athletically built, with a lean washboard stomach hit the off button with a well-practised swipe. He slipped out from under the covers and grabbed his robe from a chair before straightening his side of the bed.

Tara whispered softly, "Come back to bed.... Please?" She removed the pillow from her tousled head and peered at him with one eye open. "It's way too early. You can't possibly have things to do this time of the morning."

Steve grinned at her, "You know what they say, the early bird…"

"I know; I know … I hate worms."

Steve sat on the bed next to her and pulled the pillow away, "It's not for much longer."

"You said that last year," grumbled Tara, flicking a few stray strands of her burnished chestnut hair from her eyes, which immediately flopped back.

Steve lovingly stroked her forehead and removed the rebellious tress, before dropping a kiss on her head, "But, Sweetheart… we want the same things … a new home, a family… We need cash for that. That's why I'm working so hard. To make our dreams a reality."

Tara pouted, "But at what cost, Steve? My body clock is running out. You leave me alone all the time. I miss you."

"I miss you, too." He paused and pursed his lips. "Look, I know it's tough, but we have to look at the bigger picture."

Tara frowned, "But what good is a fancy house if we drift apart?"

Steve smiled and replied, playfully, "We'll never drift apart. We're attached by a silver cord."

Tara sighed forgivingly with a smile, and said in a small tight voice, "I know, together forever. Like otters when they sleep in the water."

"Otters?" questioned Steve bemused.

"Yup. They hold paws so they don't separate in the water. I saw it on Animal Planet."

Steve chuckled and leaned over to kiss her. Tara entwined her arms around his neck and responded passionately. An involuntary moan of pleasure escaped his lips and he whispered, "You don't make it easy for me, do you?"

Tara nipped his neck teasingly, "I don't intend to. You know, there must be something I can do to help?"

Steve's smile left his face as he pulled away, "We've been through all this before. There isn't and anyway with all your schoolwork…"

"I know," said Tara resignedly through gritted teeth and muttered in a cynical sing song voice, "This is for us, a promised promotion, more money, less grunt, work and…" She trailed off wistfully and stroked his cheek before whispering huskily, "Do you have to go, right now?" the promise of fulfilling desire and passion was in her tones.

Steve sat back rigidly and said firmly, "Yes." Tara stopped her wheedling and flopped back defeated. "Come on, Tara. You're tired…"

"Not that tired."

"You're not thinking straight. Let's talk when I get home."

"You mean when I'm fast asleep in bed?" A note of petulance had surfaced.

"Please, Honey. I've got to go. Got a presentation to make. I'll get you some Feminax. You'll feel better soon."

He gave her a swift peck on the cheek and rose as she grumbled and pulled the pillow back over her head, "I'm not pre-menstrual and I'm not a little kid." She popped her head out from under the pillow and poked her tongue out him and giggled.

"Then stop acting like one," grinned Steve. "Principal's office for you, later!"

The conversation was over and Tara knew it. She rolled over and buried her face in her pillow as Steve went into the shower, washed and dressed. He tiptoed out of the bedroom and closed the door softly behind him.

She heard the garage door open. Steve's car reversed out and the door mechanism closed. She swore softly, "Damn! Damn! And damn again! It's no good I can't sleep now," she complained to herself, swinging her legs out of bed. She rummaged in her wardrobe and laid out her running gear deciding that an early morning jog was just what she needed.

2

TARA RAN AROUND THE BLOCK toward the local park, where she immersed herself in the fresh air, clearing her head and she ran for the pure pleasure of running. She passed others walking their dogs before work and her spirits lifted.

"To hell with it!" she cried aloud, much to the amazement of a passer-by. She turned to the stranger and shouted, "Life is for living!" before running back the way she had come.

She soon reached her street where bedroom curtains had been drawn in the rows of houses and folks were setting off in their cars. She called out cheerily to an older gentleman with grey crinkly hair in a pin stripe suit and trilby, who lived a few doors down, "Morning, Mr Markuson." He smiled and acknowledged her congenially. She waved brightly and greeted her next door neighbour as he was leaving his house on foot. "Hello, Mr. Mullis."

He tipped his hat to her, "Morning, Mrs Lomas."

Tara hopped through her gate and began running vigorously on the spot before she started her warm down stretches and exercises. Now feeling fairly puffed out and sweaty, she ripped off her sweatband, opened her front door, slamming it behind her and sprinted up the stairs singing as she went. She reached her bedroom and flopped onto the bed when she noticed the time on the clock, which read 7:45. "No way!"

Tara kicked off her trainers and hurriedly undressed before diving into the shower. Her squeals filled the house as she hit the cold water before the hot. Five minutes later she was out and dressed, tearing down the stairs. She grabbed her briefcase, coat and car keys from the hallway. Her damp hair streamed behind her and she cursed as she struggled to put on her shoes, and hopped around on one foot before she succeeded in gaining her balance and bounced out of the house.

Seconds later she was back followed by the cat, Tilly, meowing plaintively. She dropped everything in the hall, dashed to the kitchen and filled the cat's dish with kitty chow before grabbing everything once more and hi-tailing it out to the garage and her car.

Tara sank into her seat and caught sight of her tangled damp hair and murmured, "No wonder he's not around. You need a makeover, girl." She stuck her tongue out in the mirror, didn't like what she saw and popped it back.

Tara half-heartedly attempted, albeit futilely, to fluff up her hair when her mobile rang, jolting her. She foraged in her bag for her phone and managed to answer before it switched to voice mail, "Hello?" The urgency and panic in her voice was apparent.

"Hya, Baby, it's me. Sorry. Looks like tonight's going to be another late one."

"Oh, Steve…"

"I know; I know but if we want to have a better life and raise a family, we have to make sacrifices…"

She cut him off, "I know; I do, really and you're right, it's just…"

"Look we'll talk about it later. I'm sorry… and about earlier… I do love you very much."

"I love you, too."

"Sorry, Babe, got to run. Don't forget to feed the fish."

Steve ended the call and she growled at her phone. "Grrr! Oh no!" Tara noticed the time again and it was now 8:20. "Bugger!"

She clambered out of the car, raced back to the house, sped to the fish tank and sprinkled some flakes into the top. Her cat watched her inscrutably as she did so, "Now, don't go getting any ideas, you hear? Behave yourself, Tilly." The cat blinked a reply and taking that as confirmation Tara hurried out again and back to her car.

Tara was wearing minimal makeup and struggled to drive safely whilst attempting to brush her unruly hair. A car honked its horn at her and she swerved out of its way finally deciding to throw down her brush and concentrate on what she was doing.

She turned on Virgin radio and listened to Chris Evans' breakfast show in an unsuccessful attempt to calm her down. Finally, she switched it off again as his strident voice became too much to bear for that time of the morning. She usually loved Chris Evans and the banter between him and other regular guests but realised that today she was just not in the mood.

In a third floor apartment in a high-rise block of flats, close to the centre of town a pretty blonde was gazing at a computer screen. She set up a search on a popular social networking site for someone called, "Lee Powell."

The woman, thirty-seven year old, Skye, pulled up a page. There was no profile picture of the person, just a black silhouette. She trawled through Lee's account making notes on a pad, jotting down the names of all the females who had left messages for him.

Skye's eyes filled with tears as she read the jokes and friendly banter, which passed between the visitors to this page and she choked back a sob. "Why, oh why?" she breathed softly to the screen. "Tell me why."

She continued gazing at the screen a few minutes more before recomposing herself and brushed away the tears that had streamed down her cheeks. She stood up and clicked on the computer icon to shut down her PC.

Skye meandered lethargically and miserably to the window and closed the curtains blocking out the morning sun. She wandered into her kitchen and opened the fridge door. A bottle of white wine stared back at her willing her to take it out. She shut the fridge door quickly and leaned against it a soft mewling sound coming from her throat.

Skye fled to her modestly furnished living room and firmly closed the door. The pull of the fridge and its contents was almost magnetic. She doubled over as if winded and tried to suppress the resurgence of her tears. She stood up, crossed to the sideboard and picked up a photo of two children smiling brightly and traced her finger around the face of the little girl with her hair in bunches. She pressed her first two fingers to her lips then placed them on the cherub mouth of the child and then repeated the process with the little boy.

She sighed heavily and sank into a chair burying her face in her hands.

Tara drove into the staff car park of the comprehensive school, where she taught, unbuckled her seatbelt, grabbed her briefcase and flew out of the door. She turned and locked her vehicle before hurrying toward the main entrance. She dived in through the doors and half ran down the corridor. She brushed past teenage students on their way to registration and scooted into a classroom before the last of the stragglers arrived to her tutor group. Names were called and marked present or absent. Tara sat with relief as the bell clamoured and the students picked up their bags and made their way to their lessons. With no formal assembly that morning Tara waited for her English Literature students to arrive.

Tara took a deep breath and steadied herself before facing her fourteen-year old students and smiled as the last pupil sat. She started roll call and was pleased to see that there were no absentees.

Registration complete she waited for everyone to settle before she announced, "Right, text books open to page forty-five."

There was a rustle of books and bags as they complied with their teacher's request and all looked up expectantly, except for a student called Raymond Campbell.

"Come on, Raymond. Where's your book?"

"Haven't got it, Miss." He looked crestfallen and the other pupils laughed.

"Think his dog has eaten, Miss," said one.

"Like it eats his homework," said another.

"All right. That's enough," Tara could see the class could break down. "Here," she offered, taking a book from her desk. "And don't lose it."

Raymond reluctantly collected the book and sat down.

"Heads down, read the passage and answer the questions and then we will go through them together. You have twenty minutes for the task."

The class focused, got down to work and Tara took the opportunity to relax and sort out her work programme for the day ahead. She set her timer for the set period when they would go through the exercise together and while she caught up with her planning she kept an eye out for anyone who needed her help.

Raymond tentatively raised his hand. She rose and went to his side, "What's the problem?" she asked kindly.

"I can't make head nor tail of this, Miss. It's not proper English."

"Of course not. It's old English, Shakespeare. It will become clear when we go through it together. Just give it a try," she tried to encourage him.

One bright spark called out, "He can't understand it cos he can't read." The class laughed and Raymond blushed a deep crimson.

Tara reprimanded them, as she attempted to take responsibility, "That's not only unfair. It's untrue. Now, you get on with your own work and let Raymond get on with his." Suitably chastened the heckler put his head down and started working, while Tara helped Raymond as much as she could before leaving him to continue working alone.

The time seemed to disappear rapidly and it was soon time to go through the answers together, which provoked some heated discussion and perceptive viewpoints from her class. Tara was delighted. She set their homework and checked the time. "You need to finish the sentence you are writing and gather up your books. I'll see you all tomorrow." There was a bubble of chatter that rose among her students as they packed up. She noticed Raymond still scratching his head and studying his book. "Raymond?" he looked up. "Over here, please." She indicated her desk. The boy shuffled across, "If there's anything you are finding particularly tough, come and see me. If I can help, I will," she said quietly.

The school bell rang out. The boy nodded and hurried red-faced from the class.

Thankfully, Tara managed to get through the following lesson with ease before her morning break. Nevertheless, she was more than delighted when the ten forty-five recess arrived.

The bell rang marking the end of the lesson and Tara wrapped up her topic and dismissed her pupils who escaped into the corridor chattering excitedly. Tara grabbed her bag and hurried along to the staff room.

There was a queue in front of the tea trolley and Rona, the plump, pleasant faced dinner lady who served refreshments at break time. For those who didn't want to wait there was a machine dispenser in the back room but the coffee wasn't as good as Rona's and her cakes and shortbread biscuits were just too delicious to forego. Tara waited in line next to her colleague and friend, Lucy Wheeler, a bubbly and slightly whacky but popular art teacher, who wore outrageous paint spattered outfits.

They grabbed their coffee and a homemade biscuit each and retreated to the back of the room to their usual chairs and continued to chat. Tara pouted; "I'm just fed up of being on my own every night. Sounds like I'm whining, doesn't it? I'm not." Lucy raised an eyebrow in disbelief. "Well, maybe I am… a little. I love him so much. Do you know, last night I put on my sexiest undies and waited in bed. I called him upstairs using my most seductive voice and guess what?"

"What?"

"He bounded up the stairs, flopped onto the bed beside me and fell asleep. Can you believe it? I'm supposed to be his red hot wife not his ...."

"Mother?"

"I was going to say, nurse maid. But I may as well be his mum."

"His intentions are good," reasoned Lucy.

"Yeah, I know." Tara mimicked Steve's voice and waggled her finger at Lucy, "Look at the bigger picture..."

"He's got a point," she laughed.

"Hey, you're supposed to be on my side," complained Tara.

"I am." A wicked twinkle came into her eye and she blew out between her teeth before plunging into what she had to say. "I just think you need a little tolerance and understanding... and a little fun!"

"Now, you're talking... Where can an old married woman like me have fun?"

"Nothing dangerous, somewhere to make new friends, find old ones, play games, and chat to like-minded people and all in a super safe environment."

Tara quipped humorously, "I don't think the Pink Stocking Club quite cuts it."

Lucy giggled, "When I said, 'games' I didn't mean pole dancing. No... Friend Finder."

Tara groaned, "Not Social Networking? Facebook, Twitter, Instagram, and all those. They're not for me."

Lucy leaned forward in her seat and chattered on enthusiastically. "It's fun, really. You can find old classmates, teachers, coaches... You don't have to accept friend requests from anyone you don't actually know." Tara looked unconvinced as she sipped her coffee. Lucy turned the pressure up a notch, "Try it. I'll send you an invite and you can set up your page. It'll keep you from getting bored. Really... It's just a bit of harmless, innocent fun."

Tara looked more than doubtful; she wasn't so sure and said so, "I don't know. Sounds a bit risky to me."

"Don't judge now, just try it. If you don't like it, you can always take your page down, delete your account or block someone who becomes a problem and there's no harm done."

"Maybe..."

There was silence between them, while they munched on their biscuits. Tara eventually spoke, "Do you teach Raymond Campbell?"

"Yes, why?"

"I'm just a bit worried about him. He's always forgetting his books or his homework. His uniform's always grubby, he never seems totally clean and he looks half starved."

"I know what you mean," said Lucy. "But he's really good at art. Gets his best marks with me but he does get a lot of stick from the other kids."

"Do you think everything is all right at home?"

"I have heard there's just him and his mum."

"Oh?"

"Raymond is her main carer. She's got MS. Rumour has it he has to clean up, cook and feed her. Not right for a child to have to do that."

"No," said Tara thoughtfully wondering what she could do.

The school bell interrupted them. They hurriedly downed the last of their coffee and brushed the biscuit crumbs from their face and clothes before joining the throng of students returning to class. Tara dismissed the thoughts of Raymond Campbell from her mind and thought about what else Lucy had said. It put an extra spring in her step and with her face set in determination she made up her mind to give her friend's advice a try. "I mean, what harm can it do?" she said aloud.

Tara dropped her briefcase on the settee and chucked her car keys on the table and sighed heavily. She pulled off her coat and dutifully hung it up before moving to the fish tank and sprinkling some fish flakes into the top. She watched them swimming about and nibbling the food. "I must get you some more toys to play with," she mused aloud.

She moved to the kitchen and opened the freezer, "TV ping meal again," she complained as she studied the pack. "Why am I talking to you? I really am going mad. I need a little bit of sanity in my life."

Tara opened the pack, pierced the lid and popped it in the microwave. Set it for the required amount of time and walked to the wine rack. She selected a full-bodied red, grabbed a glass, and filled it. She waited quietly for the ding that would tell her that her meal was ready.

Tara's eyes were drawn to the computer monitor sitting in the corner and sighed, "Do I dare try it? No, Tara be sensible. Eat your supper, watch some TV and mark your books." She pulled out a tray and some cutlery, waited a minute and removed her meal. She peeled back the transparent film and the steam from the piping hot cottage pie almost burned her fingers. "Ow! Darn, I'll have to get the lavender oil on that."

Tilly raced in through the cat flap and looked expectantly at her and mewed. "It's all right. You'll have yours in a minute. After I've sourced the lavender. That's the best thing for burns," she confided in the cat that blinked at her.

Tara picked at her unappetising meal for a few moments before consigning it to the bin and then attended to Tilly who eagerly munched on her pouch of juicy meat morsels. "Darn it, Tilly! Your food looks more appetising than mine!" Tilly took no notice and Tara proceeded to sip her glass of wine. She switched on the TV and flicked through the numerous channels that Sky had to offer before slinging down the remote control.

Tara stared again at her computer. It seemed to be calling her, "Oh, bugger! I give in." She stood up, carried her wine to the desk and booted up her PC. The familiar Google search box flashed onto the screen and Tara typed in 'Friend Finder'.

The search brought up a number of websites and Tara scrolled through them before finding what she was looking for and hit the return button.

The time passed surprisingly quickly, her wine glass was soon empty and the bottle sat comfortably on a small table next to her. She searched out a lot of her school friends and was delighted to find a number of them before she whispered, "I wonder... and typed in the name Lee Powell. A notification told her there were over a thousand people called Lee Powell on Friend Finder. "Oh what?" she groaned.

Two hours later Tara was giggling as she typed her status onto her profile page. She wrote, 'You should never lose your sparkle or shine.'

Almost immediately a reply popped up, which she read out loud. "No, you should always use Mr Sheen." Tara laughed aloud and leaned back in her chair. She picked up the wine bottle and replenished her glass. She jumped as the telephone rang brashly and disturbed her pleasant mood and composure. "Darn it!" she exclaimed before she rose and snatched up the phone. "Hello?" she said almost officiously.

"Hey! Keep your hair on. It's only me." Her friend, Lucy, was on the line, "I just wondered ... Have you seen my request? How's it going?"

Tara chuckled, "No, I haven't picked up your email invite. I thought I'd investigate it on my own."

"And?"

"You were right. I don't know where the time's gone. I might actually be awake when Steve gets in."

"I warn you, it's addictive."

"You're telling me." Tara grinned, "I've already found eleven friends."

"Good for you."

"I tried to find my old athletics and netball coach, Lee Powell, but there were over a thousand people by the same name. That's an impossible search! She could have changed her name, got married or anything."

Lucy chuckled, "You'll have to do some detective work! I'll let you go so you can get started. See you tomorrow."

Tara replaced the handset and returned to the screen. She pulled up the 'Lee Powell' search and began to scroll down, sifting through the names. A list of people with accompanying photographs filled her screen and she scrutinised a number of them, shaking her head as she discounted them and muttered, "This is crazy… I wonder…" Tara selected an area where she believed her old coach might live and her approximate age and chose to refine the search. Six names appeared, but one had no accompanying photo, just a silhouette. The others were definite no-nos.

"So, is it or isn't it?" Tara sat back and then leaned forward again. "Oh well, I've come this far… Come on, Tara; it can't possibly hurt," and she dashed a message off, 'This is a long shot but are you by any chance the Lee Powell, P.E. teacher who coached girls' athletics and netball at St. Mary's?' She hit send and waited with her fingers crossed.

Nothing came back instantly so, Tara stretched and went to the kitchen to make a cup of tea, as Tilly began meowing and rubbing herself around Tara's legs. Tara went to the utility and picked up the cat's biscuits from the top tier of the vegetable tray and filled Tilly's dish. Tilly tucked in and crunched with a loud purr of pleasure.

Tara strolled back to her laptop and could see a new message sitting in her inbox. She opened it, "Sorry, I'm not the Lee Powell you're looking for but I do like sport and I like meeting new people with a sense of humour. I have checked your profile and can see we have lots in common. Perhaps, we can be online buddies. I've sent a friend request."

Tara clicked on the relevant icon and hesitated a moment before deciding as Lucy's words rang in her head, "Don't judge now, just try it. If you don't like it, you can always take your page down or block someone who's a problem and there's no harm done."

"Oh, what the hell," and she clicked accept.

Pretty quickly, another message popped up, "Thanks for accepting. I've posted on your page."

Tara clicked on her page and giggled, as a picture of a cross-eyed owl appeared telling her that 'People who think they know everything are a great annoyance to those of us who do,' and as Eminem said, 'Trust is hard to come by. That's why my circle is small and tight.' BUT as you are a woman I know your mind is cleaner than a man's because the female of the species changes it more often, LOL. So, Tara how the heck are you?'

Tara couldn't help but smile and began to type a reply.

3

THE SUN SHONE BRIGHTLY THAT morning pooling in golden nuggets on the ground where it penetrated through the branches of the trees. The sky was a clear refreshing blue and Tara felt terrific as she made her way to school. She always looked forward to Thursdays as she had two free periods followed by morning break. She sighed happily and just hoped she wouldn't be called upon to cover for another teacher. She was still deliriously euphoric after her session on the social networking site and didn't want anything to dampen her mood.

She giggled to herself as she recalled some of the online quips and banter she had exchanged with her online chat mate. Lee Powell was a very funny guy and he seemed really charming. Tara smiled as a warm glow spread through her.

Tara pulled into the staff car park and parked. She took her time and sauntered to the school building enjoying the feel of the sun on her face. Two students came hurtling around the corner as they played a ragged game of tag and almost collided with Tara, who dropped one of her bags.

Apologising profusely, they retrieved Tara's briefcase, slowed down and proceeded in a more orderly fashion to the school entrance. Tara laughed it off. It seemed that nothing was going to destroy her good humour on such a beautiful day.

Tara almost wished away her two free periods waiting to speak to Lucy. She did manage, however, to finish her marking and get her lesson plans up to scratch for the rest of the week. The more she completed her preparation and kept up to date with everything the more time she could spend on Friend Finder. Lucy was right. Tara knew she would find the site addictive but at least it occupied her time in an enjoyable way and stopped her brooding over Steve and as she had been told before any time spent that she enjoyed was never a waste.

She sighed his name, "Steve" and wondered how he would react if he knew she was interacting with strangers on the worldwide web. She supposed he wouldn't care; after all it was completely innocent. It was a safety net to keep her company on lonely nights. It didn't mean anything. Tara dismissed the thought and headed for the staff room for her morning coffee and to meet Lucy.

She turned a corner in the corridor and came across two students in the middle of a fight. The larger, older, brasher boy was pummelling Raymond Campbell. "Okay, okay, break it up!" She pulled the larger boy, whose fists were flying, back and off Raymond who was now curled up in a ball and struggling not to cry.

A male teacher came striding past and Tara called out, "I could do with some help here."

The French teacher, Ken Ley carried on walking, "Can't stop. I'm too busy. Looks like you have it all in hand." He strode on without so much as a backward look. Tara managed to stop herself from swearing, she wasn't too keen on this master. There was something odd about him. Although, he was relatively attractive in appearance there was just something she couldn't put her finger on. She disliked him even more when he refused to stop and help her. By now, a crowd had started to gather. Some were tittering, others were jeering, spurring the boys on to continue their fight.

"All right, clear the corridor. Everyone go out to break. You two," she indicated Raymond and the bigger boy, "Come with me."

Raymond scrambled up looking shamefaced. The other lad, James Treeves, shuffled after Tara looking sullen. Two bystanders that hadn't cleared the corridor whispered together. "That Mrs Lomas needs to back off. She's asking for trouble. Treeves won't stand for any kind of punishment."

Tara had taken the boys to her classroom. Unable to get to the bottom of the trouble she insisted they both come back at lunchtime and dismissed them. She glanced at her watch, "Darn!" Half of her break had gone so she put a spurt on to reach the staffroom. She wanted to see Lucy.

Breaking her own and school rules she ran to the staffroom and flew inside.

Lucy waved madly at her, she had bought Tara's coffee and saved her seat. She was just as keen to see Tara and wore a bemused expression with a huge twinkle in her eye. "Well?" Tara giggled and instantly felt better. "You're late!"

"Don't ask."

"All right, I won't." She passed Tara her coffee and a piece of millionaire shortbread. "So? Did you track down the elusive Lee Powell?"

Tara winked mischievously, "Wait till I tell you…" Tara grinned and began to relate the events of the previous night concluding, "Anyway, it wasn't her. But we've accepted each other's friend's request," she paused before dropping her bombshell, "But… er… this Lee's a guy."

Lucy raised her eyebrows and murmured warningly, "Tara…"

Tara laughed at her friend's reaction. "Don't worry. We're just online buddies. He's really funny. He makes me laugh and that's just what I need. He's so witty."

Lucy didn't look so sure. She grudgingly replied, "I suppose. I mean, if you hit it off and it's only online then, there's no harm done, is there?" But, she still didn't sound certain.

"Don't worry, it's fine. He seems really nice. In fact, one of the things that impressed me is that on his profile one of his likes was helping other people."

"Aw, that is sweet. What does he look like?"

"I haven't a clue. He doesn't have any pics of anything. I did ask why and he really confided in me about his life. Says, there's a lot more to come. Seems he doesn't like his photos and he found it much easier socialising and talking to someone online than in the flesh. He has very little time what with his work and children. There's no threat there that I can see. And I feel I can really talk to him."

Lucy pursed her lips, "Don't take this the wrong way but do be careful. Don't tell him too much…"

"Why?"

"You don't want to give him the wrong idea. Besides, someone who is afraid to show his face…. He could be the Elephant Man for all you know."

"That wouldn't worry me. John Merrick was a gentle soul. People lay too much emphasis on looks. It's their heart that counts."

"Never-the-less, just be careful."

Tara smiled cheekily, "Yes, Miss!"

Just then the bell blared out marking the end of the morning break. They gulped down their coffee, grabbed their things, darted out into the corridor and joined the noisy throng of students.

Lunchtime came and Tara sat waiting for the two students. Raymond turned up shuffling his feet and looked embarrassed. There was no sign of James Treeves. Tara sighed, "I'll have to speak to your boxing opponent about this. Any idea who his tutor is?"

Raymond shook his head, "Sorry, Miss. No."

"So, tell me, what was it all about?"

Reluctantly, James began to explain. "He called me a retard. Said I was a dirty bugger and my mother was no better. Said she earned her money from turning tricks."

Tara looked suitably shocked. "What?"

"It's not true, Miss. He said, I was a weakling and deserved all I got. I tried to fight back and he just laid into me."

Tara bristled she hated bullying of any description. "All right, Raymond. Go and have your lunch. I'll deal with this."

"I don't have any money, Miss."

"Don't you have any lunch money?" Raymond shook his head.

"Did mum forget to give it you?"

He shook his head again, and looked embarrassed, "No, Miss. I usually skip lunch."

Tara opened her bag and took out her purse and removed a five pound note. "Well, you won't go without today. Here."

"I can't accept this, Miss."

"Yes, you can. Now go and get something to eat. I'll see you in class."

"Yes, Miss. Thank you, Miss." He walked out with his head bowed.

Tara watched him go feeling an overwhelming feeling of compassion. She determined to do whatever she could to help young Raymond Campbell."

* * *

The bar of The Hammer and Sickle was half empty. Tinny music played in the background and the smell of stale beer was in the air from spillages from customers' glasses that had soaked into the busily patterned carpet. The walls were a dingy mustard colour. The few drinkers nursing their pints were a diverse mix of older men in flat caps playing dominoes or cards and two younger men in their mid-thirties.

Mike Piercey, tall, handsome with dark well-groomed hair and wearing clothes that marked him as working in the city took a mouthful of his pint of Doombar. He sniffed, "Don't know why we always have to meet here. The place stinks."

"It's not that bad. And it's the only place close to work that we can get Doombar," chirped Lee Powell.

He was a pleasant faced individual about five foot eight with blonde hair that straddled his shoulders. He wore a pair of glasses that made him look slightly nerdy. The two were in stark contrast with each other. Lee looked more like someone who should be on the beach surfing, while Mike seemed the real city slicker.

Mike took another swig and grinned, "I suppose the advantages do outweigh the flaws. Who's with the kids?"

"What? Oh, Mum picks them up and sorts out their tea and looks after them until I get home. Don't know what I'd do without her. If it wasn't for her I certainly couldn't closet myself away to work when I need to."

The two friends continued to sup their drinks and chat. The conversation twisted and turned from work to home and relationships. Lee listened sympathetically to Mike and the news of his latest conquest that had gone disastrously wrong before piping up himself, "I can't understand why I haven't heard from Jan. She usually calls me once a week and we get together over dinner about once a month and chat over our respective miserable lives."

Mike looked shocked he put down his pint, "Aw, Man…"

"What? What is it?"

"Oh, Lee… you haven't heard?"

"Heard what?"

"I hate to be the one to tell you… Jan Bernard's dead."

Lee looked dumbfounded. The shock came through in his tone as he questioned Mike, "Dead? What? How? … What happened?"

"There's no easy way of saying this so I'll just spit it out." He picked up his drink and took another slurp as if to give him the courage to speak. "She was murdered on the towpath near her house."

"Murdered?" Lee's shock and disbelief was apparent.

"Stabbed, when she was jogging. She fell face forward into the water and drowned. I thought you knew."

"No, man. I've been busy, locked away on the PC writing a new software programme for the company for the past few weeks. I can't believe it… Damn! What a waste. When was it?"

"Last week. I expect the police will want to interview you. They're going through her address book and emails. They've spoken to me already and given me the third degree. It's a tragedy. She was such a special girl. And… I always liked Jan. I meant to ask her out but never got around to it. I sort of buried my feelings because I thought you had aspirations in that department."

"That aside… Why the heck didn't you say something?"

"I thought you must have known and it wasn't something I wanted to bring up this evening, as I know you two were close. Remember, I haven't seen you in a while. The last time we went out for a drink has got to be about two months ago."

Lee nodded and rubbed his furrowed brow; "Can't get my head around this. Why would anyone want to hurt her? I just find it so hard to believe. She was such a great girl, so alive and vibrant, in spite of her terrible relationships. She had plenty of those."

"I know, like me. It was the one thing we had in common, bad choices in the opposite sex… The police are talking to every single one of those losers who messed her about." Mike paused, "Actually, I thought you two might have become more than friends."

"Me, too," sighed Lee. "Me, too." He downed his drink. "Think I'll get back. This news has sort of put a dampener on the evening."

"Sure thing, mate. Sure thing."

The following morning Skye Powell, an attractive blonde, if it wasn't for the dark rings underneath her eyes, marched briskly toward a high-rise office block. It was a clear day. The sun was burning through the light layer of wispy cloud and it promised to be beautiful. The birds in the city were chirruping brightly at the beginning of such an exceptional day. Starlings perched in clusters on ledges vying with pigeons for the perfect spot to watch passers-by and check for anyone kind enough to toss some bread or bird seed by the benches that were set back on the pavement by the avenue of trees. Cheeky sparrows watched from sycamore trees daring occasionally to hop on the ground around a café with some tables and chairs set outside. The planners had worked hard to ensure this part of the city was pleasant to walk through. It had its green spaces that were more than guaranteed to put a smile on anyone's face, but Skye wasn't smiling. She paused on the steps and looked up at the towering building, which dominated that part of the city alongside the many department stores. The sign above the large revolving doors at the top of the stone steps read, "Bartmer Telecommunications."

Skye took a deep breath and bounded up the steps pasting a smile on her face. But it was clear to see that she was unhappy. Her face was gaunt and showed her lack of sleep. She tried to fluff up her soft blonde hair that lacked any sort of style and attempted to look bright and cheerful.

Skye nodded at the woman on Reception busy chatting with the building's Security Officer and headed for the lift. She stepped in with four others and hit the button for the sixth floor. The lift was quiet and its occupants barely acknowledged each other. Skye was almost relieved when the doors slid open on her floor. Skye removed her coat and hung it in the communal cloakroom and walked to her desk, murmuring niceties to those who looked up and smiled. Both sides of the office were filled with men and women wearing headsets working on computers. An office junior moved between stations collecting files and distributing more folders to the workers before returning to a glass fronted office where she filed away the collected reports.

An imposing looking woman, with her hair swept up in a bun, in her mid-forties, sat watching the activities of employees. She was ready to help and answer queries as needed. The nameplate on her desk read 'CEO Marie Yately'. She acknowledged Skye with a friendly wave as Skye settled at her station and booted up her PC. Skye glanced around as calls came in thick and fast and were processed by the other staff. As soon as she was online calls began to be routed to her station.

Skye knuckled down but kept glancing at the clock waiting for her break. She chanced a look at her boss' desk and saw her walking out of the office wearing her coat. Skye scoped around the office and took her chance. She pulled up Friend Finder on her PC and logged in preparing to minimise the page if her boss returned.

Skye typed in the name Lee Powell and pulled up his page. She scrolled down through all his wall posts and public messages and read them avidly. She stopped suddenly at one and with a sharp intake of breath stared hard at a message from Tara, which read, 'You've made my day. I laughed out loud. Until the next time…x'

Skye's face twisted in pain and jealousy. The innocent x representing a kiss seemed to glare out at her until it was all she could see. She studied the thumbnail picture of Tara, who looked far too attractive for Skye's liking.

Skye clicked on Tara's photo, which filled the screen and then accessed Tara's profile page, pulling up Tara's full name and location. Skye hurriedly logged off and sat back in her seat. She stared at the screen as if it would reveal some special secret to her before glancing round again to ensure her boss was still away from her desk.

Skye typed her password and went into Bartmer's directory. Once in she typed the name Tara Lomas. She hit search and up popped Tara's home address, phone number and mobile phone number. She was lucky there were no other people of the same name.

Skye took her notepad and scribbled the information down. Her eyes gleamed with spite. Carefully, she deleted her search and cleared her history before she returned to what she should have been doing, which was working on overdue accounts.

Marie returned to her desk and hung her coat up behind the door. She surveyed the office and noticed Skye sitting hunched up over her desk. She frowned and walked out and crossed to Skye's desk. She could see Skye brushing away her tears and spoke gently, "Everything all right, Skye? Do you need any help?"

Skye sniffed loudly and dabbed at her eyes, "I'm fine, thanks, Miss Yately… Marie."

"You don't look fine. What's wrong?"

"Oh, I just found out my ex is seeing someone else. It's kind of hard to take that's all," Skye sniffed again.

Marie nodded sympathetically and said softly, "I know it's been tough for you, losing your kids and everything."

In her martyrdom Skye turned her huge china doll blue eyes up at her boss and looked pleadingly at her, "It was all lies, Marie. He's so manipulative. He'd make Jesus Christ look like a villain. I made one mistake, one mistake that's all and now I'm being punished forever."

Marie Yately nodded compassionately and gave Skye a kindly smile, "Take a break, Skye. Go on. Go and grab a coffee."

Skye murmured her thanks and rose from her station. She picked up her purse and left the office while Marie looked after her with heartfelt understanding.

4

TILLY RAN TO MEET TARA as she crashed in through the door with a heavy briefcase and an armful of papers. She dropped her burden on the coffee table and flopped into a chair. Tilly's tail stood straight up in the air and was all puffed out in sheer pleasure at seeing her mistress. She jumped up onto Tara's lap and immediately began to purr.

"I know, I know..." sighed Tara petting the cat before setting her aside. "I'm late, you want your supper and I have to feed the fish." She looked at the stack of papers to mark and groaned. "No internet for me tonight but work, work, work."

Tara rose and divested herself of her coat and strolled to the kitchen followed by Tilly who continually rubbed and wrapped herself around Tara's legs. "All right, I'll get your dish. Let me see to the fish first." Tara strolled to the fish tank and sprinkled some flakes while Tilly waited patiently by her empty bowl. "Your turn now, Tilly."

Once Tara had fed her pets she rummaged around for something quick and easy to eat. It didn't take long, some pasta, pesto and grated cheese. 'That would sustain her,' she thought. She hadn't heard from Steve so hoped he would be home at a reasonable time and then glanced across at the mound of work on the coffee table. "It's no good, I better crack on." She spoke firmly to the cat, "And don't go distracting me. I need to get this done. And I don't want you wandering off either. I worry when you go missing on one of your jaunts."

The house was unbelievably quiet and Tara debated whether or not to have some background noise like the TV or radio or even some of her favourite music. "That's no good," she murmured. "I'll just want to sing along." So, she settled on the settee and focused on the task in hand. Tilly jumped up alongside her and proceeded to wash and preen herself thoroughly before relaxing, tucking her front paws underneath her and going to sleep. "Wish I could do that," muttered Tara. "Not a care in the world, no responsibility just eat, sleep and be loved. I could do with some of that."

Tara pressed on with her marking and made good headway. She stopped with four papers to go and yawned. "I want a glass of wine." She wandered to the kitchen and poured herself a large glass of chilled Soave and sipped, "Mmmm. Just what I needed."

As she walked back to her seat, the remaining papers seemed to accuse her of slacking. Her home was abnormally quiet. The odd unknown creak and groan of the house as the heating switched off served to make her shiver and not with the cold. Tara had an unbearable feeling of loneliness seep through her like a trickle of melting ice from a glacial river. She sat down and picked up her papers once more before looking at the clock. It was eight twenty. Tara whispered to herself, "Come on, Steve. Where are you?"

Some minutes later in the ever increasing dark and the stillness of the oncoming night Tara became involved in one of her brightest student's creative writing essay. The girl, Abigail Williamson had drawn Tara into a world of night terrors. Like the old movie 'Rear Window' the student who resided in a remote country property had witnessed a vicious murder in the grounds outside her house, the killer had spotted her and Abigail was describing a frighteningly realistic chase through the countryside on which her life depended.

Tara realised that while reading the evocative passage her spine had begun to chill and the hairs were standing up on the back of her neck. The imagery was such that Tara had placed herself clearly in the story and found she was actually holding her breath. Her eyes moved rapidly as she devoured the next paragraph. She was almost sitting on the edge of her seat when the telephone rang. It blared out sharply, startling her. She thrust down the essay and stood up sighing Steve's name. She picked up the receiver almost relieved that she would hear her husband on the other end of the line, "Hello?" Her own voice sounded tentative in the unusual stillness that had enveloped her like a shroud.

There was nothing, just a weird silence and then the phone line crackled as if filled with static. "Hello?" There was no loving voice to respond on the other end. "Steve?"

Tara shrugged and replaced the receiver. She returned to her seat and picked up her papers settling back into reading the assignment.

The phone rang again.

Tara rose and answered once more, "Hello? ..." There was nothing but a weird silence. Tara held on and listened. She heard the click of a call being disconnected.

She stood thoughtfully for a moment longer without replacing the handset before disengaging the call and dialling 1471 call retrieval. The cultured tones of a woman with an automated response filtered through. "You were called today at 20:42. The caller withheld their number. Please hang up."

"Damn!"

Feeling annoyed Tara slammed down the phone and went back to her task.

The phone began to ring insistently. Tara looked up and not wanting to answer she bit her lip. An uncomfortable feeling of helpless annoyance washed over her and she allowed the instrument to continue to ring.

Irritatingly, aggravatingly and disturbingly it rang and rang. In exasperation Tara jumped up and her papers fell to the floor. She cursed softly and slowly walked to the telephone with its persistent clamouring. She stared at it willing it to stop but then succumbed and picked up just before the answering machine kicked in. But this time she didn't speak.

She flooded with relief when she heard Steve's voice, "Tara? Tara? Are you there?"

"Yes, I'm here," she stuttered.

"I couldn't hear you."

"I've been having some weird silent calls. It just unnerved me that's all. I didn't want to be the first to speak."

"Probably a sales call. One of those multiple dial things. Don't worry."

"Well, I do," said Tara finding the strength in her voice again. "When will you be home?"

"That's what I'm calling about. Should be home within the hour. Get some wine out."

"I've got a bottle open. You better hurry or there won't be any left," Tara said with a giggle in her voice.

Steve laughed, "Okay. See you soon, Babe."

Tara chuckled to herself. She was beginning to feel better. She replaced the receiver and a smile played on her lips when to her horror the phone rang again. She hesitated and then thought it could be Steve calling back so she made up her mind to pick it up. There was nothing, just a hollow silence, a void filled with the whisper of a breath on the other side. Tara slammed down the phone again and pulled the plug out of the wall. This time she was shaking and tears began to fill her eyes.

Tara scurried back to the settee, began to gather her dropped papers and poured herself another glass of wine as Tilly sensing her distress jumped up and nuzzled her as if trying to comfort her. She brushed away her tears and stroked her cat before announcing to Tilly, "This won't do. I have to pull myself together." She set aside the last few papers determining to mark them later or before school in the morning. She moved to the kitchen and began to prepare something for Steve's arrival. She was not going to let him think she'd turned into a neurotic wreck over a few marketing calls.

It was late to be at school. The French teacher, Ken Ley, sat at a computer station in the library. There was no one else around. He stared furtively around him ensuring there were no eyes and no observers. Surrounded by glass windows looking outside and adjoining the corridor it was easy to spot if anyone was approaching the library. He inserted a flash drive into the USB port and began to examine what at first glance seemed to be innocent family photographs. But as the teacher scrolled down the pictures became more provocative.

Ken Ley became sweaty as he viewed more explicit images. His breath came out in short sharp pants like a dog on heat. His eyes grew wider as he devoured the depictions of corrupted innocence, licking his lips lasciviously.

Feeling safe at this computer station, which couldn't be linked to him. He hit a flashing link and was transported to a live chat room, 'Tweenies'. There he scoured the chat room users online and pounced on one of a little girl with an avatar of a cartoon character with golden tresses and began to engage with her claiming to be a twelve year old from a local secondary school.

The sound of footsteps in the corridor broke into his fevered consciousness and he hurriedly broke off the conversation typing that his parents were coming into his room and that he shouldn't be chatting online. He dumped the flash drive icon titled 'Play' into the on screen trash bin to eject it safely and hurriedly removed the memory stick. He logged off and pocketed the USB device. Ken gathered his belongings and left the library walking into one of the cleaners, who he recognised. He smiled at her, "My, you are late tonight, Valerie." He had a winning smile, which immediately put the cleaner at ease.

She smiled back, "I had trouble getting my child care sorted tonight. Almost had to bring Faye with me."

"That wouldn't have been so bad, would it?"

Valerie laughed, "She's going through a difficult phase at the moment, being a proper little madam. Mum managed to come around at the last minute."

"Oh? It's probably just a phase. How old is Faye?"

"She's just turned eight."

"Lovely age," said Ken Ley appreciatively. "So enthusiastic about everything at eight and nine ... Isn't her dad around?"

"Sadly, no. He was bombed in Afghanistan fighting insurgents. His injuries were too great. He passed away almost two years ago."

Ken Ley's eyes sparkled, "Oh, I am sorry... if there's anything I can do at any time. Let me know."

"Thank you. That's very kind."

"I mean it. Have you much more to do?"

"Just this corridor and the library."

"If you like, I'll wait and drop you back?"

"I don't want to put you out."

"It's no trouble, I assure you." Ken Ley beamed at the cleaner, who looked down shyly and began to smile back. His smile was infectious.

* * *

Tara had enjoyed a reasonably peaceful but fruitful day at school. She had met with the school counsellor and made an appointment for Raymond Campbell. She was trying to initiate and set up some level of care package in conjunction with Social Services to help the lad. This was not proving easy. The liaison officer ranted on about budgets and cuts to services. Tara's heart went out to the boy. It was obvious to her that the challenging behaviour he sometimes displayed had its roots at home.

However, James Treeves was a totally different case. Tara made up her mind to check his school records and to speak to his tutor who was currently off sick. She hadn't warmed to the boy at all and that was unusual for her. She found redeeming features in all of her students even the rogues.

Tara gathered together her papers and books and packed them in her school bag. She glanced behind her at the blackboard where someone had drawn some crude pictures and written a few obscenities. Tara grabbed the blackboard rubber and cleaned them off. She slapped her hands together to remove the loose chalk dust, picked up her bag and sauntered to the staff car park.

There were only a handful of vehicles left as most of the staff had left. As she approached her car she noticed someone had tied filled dog poo bags to her aerial. She shuddered and groaned in displeasure. Some sort of school prank, she supposed. "Well, it's not nice!" she exclaimed. She dropped her bags, removed the offending items and wrinkled her nose in disgust as there was a tear in one of the bags from which the smell was escaping. With her arm outstretched she walked to a litter bin by the entrance and dumped the packages. Now, she felt dirty and needed to wash her hands. So, Tara hurried back inside to use the wash basins in the girls' toilets. She used the sludgy brown liquid soap that was used throughout the school, making a face at the very strong disinfectant type scent it gave off.

She emerged from the school feeling cleaner and stopped, "Oh no!" her school bag had tipped up and exercise books and some of her papers were flying around the yard. She hurried across and spent the next ten minutes picking them all up. Tara eventually flopped into the driver's seat and muttered, "Now, that I could have done without!"

Tara switched on her car radio after she started her car and ramped up the volume as one of Eric Clapton's songs, 'Wonderful Tonight' came on. She remembered her mother playing it incessantly as her father used to sing it to her when they danced around the kitchen together. They were beautiful memories. She always imagined and prayed that she would have a marriage just like her own mum and dad who adored each other. Tara sighed as she drifted away on a cloud of reminiscences. Even the growing traffic did nothing to subdue her mood and she couldn't wait to see Steve later. She would plan something really special for him and with loving thoughts bursting from her heart she drove home.

At home the phone hadn't rung and for once Steve was home early. Tara was delighted. The day's events were forgotten and she had taken extra care with her appearance wearing an alluring aubergine slinky dress and was adding the final touches to a good home cooked meal. The scene was, she hoped, set for seduction.

The table was laid, candles lit and soft romantic music played subtly in the background. The lights were dimmed and the tantalising smell of garlic hung in the air mixed with various Indian spices.

Steve was focused on his laptop screen preparing sales charts and spread sheets for his next meeting. Tara looked across at him wistfully as he seemed oblivious to the effort she had put into making the evening special. She shook her head sorrowfully and seeing the steam rising and water bubbling in the pan on the stove, she hurriedly returned to her preparations and began to strain the rice.

She heard Steve swear under his breath as something went wrong with his calculations and swallowed hard. She refused to let his lack of interest spoil the evening. She took a chilled bottle of sparkling wine from the fridge and set it on the table in a cooler and called out; "Come on, sit up. Food's ready."

Reluctantly, Steve closed his laptop and stretched. He yawned loudly and drank in the delicious aroma pervading the air. His mood immediately changed and softened as he eyed his wife appreciatively, "Wow, you look good." Tara smiled. Then Steve saw the table and the array of food. He groaned, "Have I forgotten something? It's not our anniversary or a birthday, is it?"

Tara chuckled, "No. Should it be?"

"Well, you've gone to so much trouble." He took his place at the table and breathed in deeply, "Mmm, now how did you know I fancied something hot and spicy?"

"Give me a yashmak and I'll see what I can do."

"A yashmak?"

"For the dance of course."

"Dance?"

"The seven veils or perhaps you'd prefer a cheerleader's outfit."

Steve began to laugh, "A cheerleader?"

"Well, if it's okay for Madonna, it's okay for me."

"Madonna?"

Now, it was Tara's turn to giggle, "Will you stop repeating everything I say? You sound like a parrot!"

"Ah, but would a parrot have done this?" Steve gazed at her for a moment and took a small box from his pocket. "You're nuts. You know that? Here, I bought this for you." He handed Tara the box, which she opened in delight. It contained a stunning silver bracelet with a small heart charm that said 'I love you.'

She put in on immediately and smiled in pleasure. "Oh Steve, it's beautiful, thank you." She leaned over and wrapped her arms around him and kissed his neck.

Steve pushed away his meal and whispered huskily; "You know, I think I may be more hungry for you." he pulled her down onto his lap and kissed her tenderly before rising, picking her up in his arms and carrying her up the stairs.

* * *

Tara rolled out of bed with a dreamy, satisfied, and extremely happy expression on her face. On the pillow next to her was a note, "Last night was wonderful. Don't ever doubt my love for you. S. xxx."

She picked it up and read it with a gentle smile on her lips. She folded the note up and placed it in her bedside drawer before changing into her running gear. The phone rang.

"Tara?"

"Well, hello, Mr Lomas." She purred in delight at the sound of Steve's voice. The line crackled somewhat as if there was some static on the connection.

"Just wanted to say, I love you. I should be home at the usual time. What are you up to?"

"I'm so filled with energy, I'm going to Rydon Park for my run then I'll have my shower and get off to school."

"You just remember to save some of that energy for me later," laughed Steve.

"I'll have plenty left, don't you worry." The phone crackled again. "See you later." She blew him a kiss down the phone and hung up.

Tara glanced at the clock. She had plenty of time. It was unusual for her to be up so early. She tied back her hair and freshened her face with some cold water before feeding the fish and Tilly. She checked her watch and set off.

Tara was clearly enjoying her early morning jog in the park. She passed some runners that she recognised and acknowledged them with a smile and a wave. It really was a glorious morning in every respect. She loved the feel of the sun on her face and back and she admired the glorious colours blossoming in the park's many flowerbeds.

The clock on the Pavilion chimed and Tara checked her watch once more. It was time for her to return so Tara spun around and began to run back the way she had come. She didn't see someone lurking in the shadows of the trees watching her.

The sun was momentarily eclipsed by a cloud and the warmth vanished from Tara's back. She shivered as she jogged past the trees that led from the park into a thick wooded area. As the sun burst through the fair weather cloud it blinded her in a stuttering light show as it shafted through the branches of the trees.

A figure stepped out behind Tara and speeded up in pursuit of her when a group of runners appeared together coming toward Tara. The figure stopped and pretended to tie a shoelace that had become undone. The joggers who were chattering as they trotted around the green were not moving quickly. The figure stood up and looked around but Tara was nowhere in sight. A hiss of anger erupted from the watcher, who stamped hard on the ground in frustration and dashed off in the direction Tara had been headed.

* * *

Tara had showered and dressed for work. She picked up her car keys and was about to head out for school when the phone rang. Thinking it might be Steve she dashed back to answer and was greeted by silence followed by exaggerated heavy breathing. Tara shouted into the receiver, "Pervert!" and hung up.

Somewhat unnerved she hurried to her car. As she made her way to school she became more and more angry. 'How dare some depraved creep target her with obscene silent calls?' It had to be some nutcase who got his kicks from frightening women. Well, whoever it could be, was messing with fire. Come this evening she would be prepared. She knew exactly what she would do.

5

LEE POWELL WAS SITTING ON the floor of the living room playing a board game with his two children. Discarded toys laid everywhere. There was a lot of shrieking laughter, especially when Lee pretended to cheat and they caught him moving his pieces the wrong number of spaces.

Lee's mother sat on the settee smiling at her son and grandchildren. She rose, "Time for me to be off. Your father must be starving; he'll think his throat's been cut. I'll see you tomorrow to take the children to school."

"Hold on, I'll see you out." Lee scrambled up. "Say goodbye to Nana." The children double rushed their grandma and hugged her tightly.

"Bye, Grandma," they chorused. "Love you."

"Love you, too. See you tomorrow." She extricated herself from their loving cuddle and carefully stepped through the minefield of toys strewn over the carpet. "Lee, I would like a quiet word."

"Sure, Mum." He turned to the children, "You can take my turn for me and no cheating. I won't be a moment."

"It's okay, Daddy. We'll wait," said Amy.

"Anyway, it's my turn," added Peter.

Lee walked his mother to the front door. She gave him a hug and asked, "Have you heard from Skye at all, lately?"

"No. Thank goodness. Why?"

"She's been calling me, asking about the children and you."

"What have you said?"

"Told her the truth that you're all getting on with your life. But she's very persistent. I don't want to worry you but she makes me feel uncomfortable. I'm polite but not over friendly. I thought you needed to know."

"Thanks, Mum. I'll be okay."

"I hope so. I still think she's unhinged. Pity, she was such a nice girl… before… before … you know."

"I know. Thanks, Mum." He waved goodbye to his mother as loud giggles reached his ears. He shouted to his children, "If you've been cheating…"

The phone rang. Lee's daughter, Amy, picked it up, "Hello?" She listened intently to the voice on the other end of the phone and then held it out to her father.

"Who is it?"

"It's mummy, for you."

Lee stiffened and took the phone, "Skye, you shouldn't be calling this number. It's against the court order."

"Lee, please don't be angry with me. I know I shouldn't but you have to know I've got my act together and I just wanted to speak to the kids, to hear their voices, please." There was a noticeable sob in her voice as she spoke. "I still love you, Lee."

"Skye, we've been through all this. We're no longer married. Once you've been clean for five years then there will be a case review and we'll go from there. But, now it's best you don't call again. I'm sorry."

Skye persisted, "Do you know the pain I go through every day and night, not knowing what's happening in their lives or yours? … Not to be able to see them or speak to them?" Lee's children were now standing by their father looking at him on the phone. Their faces were crumpled in worry. Amy bit her lip, all the frivolity from the game had vanished. They both looked serious and frightened.

Lee spoke gently, "I know how tough it must be. But we have to do what's best for the children."

"To be without their mother?"

"Skye, we can't talk any more it's too upsetting for the children. I'm sorry." He replaced the handset and hugged his children to him.

James Treeves leaned against the bike shed with his friend Tommy Porter. He saw Raymond Campbell walk by alone with his scuffed shoes and without a proper coat. He sneered, "There's that scruff, Campbell. Wonder if he did his homework last night?" He called out, "Not got your lady teacher protector with you now, have you?" Raymond ignored him and kept going. "That's it. Walk on. You and I… we've got unfinished business. I'll see you later."

"Leave it, James," said his friend Tommy.

"Why should I? He started it. Yellow belly there, threw the first punch. He shouldn't start something he couldn't finish."

"You did goad him," said Tommy quietly. "Let up on him. I hear he has a tough time at home."

"Proper mummy's boy. If it hadn't been for that meddling teacher, I'd have smashed his face in."

"Mrs Lomas is all right."

"Mrs Lomas needs to mind her own business and I might be just the person to wipe that smile off her face."

The bell rang.

Tommy shrugged, "There's no reasoning with you when you're like this. Come on, we'll be late for registration."

"You go on. I'll be along in a minute. I've got some thinking to do."

Tommy shook his head as if to say, 'sometimes I don't understand you' and he joined the horde of schoolchildren hurrying to class.

James had formed a plan in his head. He worked out exactly what he could do. He would have to wait until after school when everyone had gone. He needed to be wary of the cleaners but felt he could get away with a few pranks that would rattle Mrs Lomas. Oh yes, he was more than inventive. He was sure he could do things that she had never seen before.

Ken Ley sat in the staff room before registration, his face was creased in thought. He took out his mobile phone and accessed his pictures. He studied a picture of an eight year old girl, Daisy, and another of Daisy with her mother, the cleaner, Valerie and he licked his lips. As more staff arrived, Ken altered his screen and switched his mobile to silent. He smirked, and pocketed his phone. As he withdrew his hand his memory stick flew out and scuttered across the floor landing at Tara's feet. Tara bent down and picked up. She looked around for the owner.

Ken Ley, leapt off his seat, put his face up to Tara's and hissed, "Give that back. It's mine." He snatched at the flash drive.

Tara was completely taken by surprise. "Okay, keep your hair on. It just landed at my feet." The teacher stormed out of the staffroom. His face was suffused with colour and twisted into an angry snarl. In amazement, Tara watched him go. Other members of staff stared after the French teacher and back at Tara who shrugged. "Search me. I don't know what's got into him. It's only a memory stick. If you ask me, his reaction was way over the top."

Tara marched to her pigeon hole and picked up her messages, shaking her head in disbelief. "What the hell happened there?" she murmured.

Two days had passed uneventfully and Tara believed that her initial fear had been unwarranted. It was just a blip, some sort of series of silent marketing calls. Maybe Steve was right. She recalled their conversation and his reassurances that although these things were a nuisance and extremely annoying they were nothing of which to be afraid.

Tara groaned and stared at the pile of books she had brought home. Interim reports were due on her examination classes and she didn't feel like working on them. She needed to relax but first there were those that depended on her.

Tara crossed to the fish tank and sprinkled in their allowance of floating flakes. She watched as the fish set the water on top of the tank frothing with their eagerness to get to their food. The pellets were next that sank to the bottom allowing her bottom feeders to gulp down their meal. She studied a baby sturgeon that playfully danced and flitted around the tank. It reminded her of a tiny shark and she wondered how big it would grow. She remembered reading somewhere that fish only grew to the size that their living accommodation would allow. That was good, she giggled at the thought of the little black fish growing into something resembling a great white shark. If it did grow she would need to get a new home for it, maybe release it somewhere safe and suitable like the lake in the park.

Tara glanced at Tilly asleep on the settee. "I haven't forgotten you," she murmured, as Tilly opened one eye and watched her before settling back to sleep. Tara went into the kitchen and finished washing up the breakfast things and filled Tilly's dish with some tasty morsels. At least, she assumed they were tasty, as Tilly seemed to love them. Her duty done Tara returned to the sofa and picked up Tilly to cuddle her. The cat's expression was one of surprise when she was awoken but soon turned to delight to be in Tara's arms and immediately began purring.

Tara enjoyed petting her feline friend and then rose with the cat in her arms and walked to the kitchen setting the cat down by her food. Tilly wrapped herself around Tara's legs, as if in thanks, stretched and yawned before settling down and nibbling with relish at her supper.

The phone rang.

Tara picked up the receiver. Silence. Tara replaced the handset. Almost immediately it rang again. Tara calmly opened a drawer and took out a whistle. The phone continued to ring. She picked it up and was greeted by nothing only a chilling quiet with just a whisper of a breath on the end of the line.

Tara put the whistle to her lips and blew it as hard as she could into the mouthpiece. The shrill blast almost deafened Tara. Heaven knew what it would do to the person on the other end of the line. Tara put down the phone with a shaking hand, disconnected the call and then picked it up again leaving it off the hook.

Tara knew that it would soon begin its siren wail of complaint because it was off the hook but she didn't care. She took a cushion and removed a jacket off its peg and placed them over the phone to muffle the wail that would soon manifest if the other person hung up. If it got too bad she would just pull the plug again. She was hoping that receiving the engaged signal would prove more frustrating to whoever was doing this.

Tara, although unnerved, felt her anger growing. She determined to speak to Steve about it when he got home but for now she had work to do. Then another thought struck her one, which was hard to dismiss. No, she wouldn't alert Steve, yet. She knew she needed to talk to Lucy and with her head swimming full of ideas and wild imaginings Tara marched to the kitchen and poured herself a glass of iced water. She tossed in a couple of slices of cucumber, which made it really refreshing. Feeling slightly better she made a start on her stack of English reports; anything to take her mind off that damned phone.

It seemed her elusive peace of mind was not to be found as the howling on the telephone became louder and appeared almost as menacing as the threat from the silent calls. Tara jumped up in annoyance and pulled the plug from the wall. Her relief was instant.

"You know what, Tilly?" she said addressing the surprised cat that was just making herself comfortable on the settee. "I'm going to expend some energy and have a quick run around the block. I'll feel better and then I can focus on my work."

Tara bounced upstairs and put on her jogging suit and trainers. She hurried down the stairs, scribbled a quick note to Steve and set off into the cool evening air. She checked her mobile phone as she ran and cursed as she opened and read Steve's text, "Sorry, Babe, it's another late one. I'll be back soon as I can. I promise."

Annoyed, she tried to call him back but it just went straight to answer phone. She tried his office number where a man with a gentle voice answered. "Steve? He left the office a while ago, about two hours I think."

"Do you know where he's gone?"

"Someone mentioned drinks at 'The Portobello'. Sorry, I can't help you anymore." The man put down the phone and Tara swore.

"What does he think he's playing at? He should be home with me." Fire filled her belly and she sprinted off wondering what the heck he was doing and her mind was soon running riot. The damaging maggots of doubt had begun to manifest and they were hard to suppress.

* * *

The evening was going to be good. Ken Ley had promised this to himself. He was feeling good and very optimistic. He was reminded of the Nina Simone song of the same name and began to hum the melody. Firstly, he needed to call Valerie and set things in motion. "Valerie? Ken … Just wondering if you are on your own this evening? …. I'm at a loose end I was thinking of getting a takeaway and thought it would be more fun to share it. Have you eaten? … Great… I'll be round in an hour… Of course, she's included. See you later." He ended the call and punched the air. Yes, things were progressing well, very well indeed.

Ken Ley turned up at Valerie's house with a Chinese takeaway meal and bottle of wine. She opened the door and beamed at him. "Thought it would save you cooking and that maybe we could spend some time together, get to know each other better." She opened the door wider and he stepped inside, smiling.

Daisy came running to the door, "Who is it, Mummy?" The little girl smiled happily when she saw Ken. "Hello, Ken. Are we going to read some more of Alice in Wonderland?"

"But, of course. After all it is the best book and one of my favourites."

He was welcomed inside. Valerie began to set the table and took the meal from Ken and popped it in the oven to keep warm. Ken smiled and took Daisy's hand and sat with her on the settee. He picked up the book and began to read.

The next morning Tara looked at the empty space next to her in bed. Steve had got home in the early hours too pooped to talk and Tara was furious. She pretended to be asleep when he came in but couldn't settle and while Steve had snored into oblivion she fidgeted, wriggled and squirmed, occasionally kicking him so he'd turn over and stop his rumbling grunts. This resulted in her not falling asleep until the early hours and now it was time to get up she was shattered and just wanted to sleep. His side of the bed smelled of garlic and booze so he had obviously been out enjoying himself while she was stuck at home with some pervert terrorising her on the phone. She was not happy.

Tara grumbled as she forced herself out of bed and into the shower. She turned the dial to give herself a jet of cold water to wake her up and hurriedly turned it down again when she began to shiver. She murmured, "How these footballers endure those ice baths is beyond me."

Tara hopped out, dried off and dressed. Firstly, she checked the washing basket where Steve's shirt lay. She picked it up and sniffed it. There was an aroma of perfume. Tara frowned as she threw it back and went into the kitchen where a note lay from Steve.

"Darling, so sorry about last night. I was dragged out by the boss and clients to seal a very lucrative deal. I couldn't get out of it and I tried to call you but couldn't get through. I guess you had the phone off the hook. But I will be home tonight with a bottle of champagne to celebrate, as yours truly won the contract. Xxx"

Tara's stomach churned as she read it. Was he telling the truth? She'd never doubted him before. She was confused. She needed to talk. Tara grabbed her things and dashed to her car and headed for school.

The journey whizzed by. She drove like an automaton. The glorious sunshine didn't put a smile on her face and when the floating clouds suddenly eclipsed the warm light the day appeared ominously menacing to Tara. People scurried by on dusty pavements anxious to get to work while others lazily ambled in the growing heat but Tara's confused thoughts only served to fuel the rise of her temper. By the time she arrived at school, her temper had diminished to sorrow and hurt and she was close to tears.

She drove in behind Lucy but they had to park away from each other where they could find a space. Lucy set off toward the school entrance and Tara raced after her, "Lucy! Wait up."

Lucy stopped and turned. She waited for Tara who sprinted toward her with her light military style mackintosh flapping. Lucy grinned, "Still running, I see. Boy, I'm exhausted just looking at you. So, how many miles have you clocked up, girl?"

"Not enough, but that's the least of my problems."

"Oh?" Lucy took note of Tara's strained expression, her bloodshot eyes and the dark shadows beneath, which screamed insomnia or too many late nights. She could see Tara's emotions were running close to the surface and that she was really distressed; her eyes were welling up with tears. "What's happened?"

Tara gulped in an attempt to quell the sobs that threatened to rise. She swallowed and tried to control her trembling voice, "Steve didn't get home until really late last night. He stunk of garlic and booze; claimed he was with a client."

"But you said he's trying to …."

"Lucy, what if he's having an affair?" Tara interrupted, her tears beginning to manifest.

Lucy put her hand on Tara's shoulder to comfort her friend and said gently, "Not Steve. He loves you, Tara."

"But…"

"You were there for him when his brother died **and** when he changed careers. Think back to when your grandma passed, he was a tower of strength. He never left your side at the funeral. Besides… he's not the type and you know I'm a pretty good judge of character," she added pointedly.

"But I didn't finish. When he was out I received several hang-up calls. I could tell someone was there a couple of times but they wouldn't speak."

"You're still getting those calls?"

Tara nodded, "They really rattle me. Then, when he comes home after being out with someone else and claims it was work… Oh, I don't know, I just imagined the worst."

"It probably was work. You know he's trying to do his best for you both."

"He bought me this. Why? Is it guilt maybe?" Tara showed Lucy the bracelet. Steve had bought her.

Lucy admired it, "Wow!" She pursed her lips, "Listen to me, all I'm saying is that Steve deserves the benefit of the doubt. It's not like him, honestly."

Tara didn't look convinced. Eventually she sighed, "I know. It's just that all

I could think of was that old movie, Fatal Attraction. It gave me the creeps."

Lucy laughed, "You have an overactive imagination, Tara Lomas. Come on, we'd better hurry before the bell goes." As if on cue the strident bell announcing the start of the school day bellowed out and the two women hurried into the school building.

Tara's problems had only just started. Once roll call was over and her tutor group had departed for their lessons Tara went to the blackboard to set her tasks for the first lesson. She picked up the chalk and tried to write on the blackboard but nothing would come out, not a mark. Puzzled she tried with a different colour all to no avail. By now her English students were drifting in and settling at their desk. They sat watching her efforts to write on the board. She ran her hand down the board. It appeared to be covered in some sort of surface dressing. She rubbed at the board with the board eraser... nothing.

By now, the class was beginning to titter and Tara's temper was rising. She spun around and addressed them, "Do any of you know what is wrong with this board?" The class shook their heads and whispered together delighting in the fact they couldn't start work.

Raymond Campbell tentatively put his hand up. Tara rounded on him, "Yes, what do you know about this?"

The class laughed as Raymond replied, "Nothing, Miss. I was just going to say, try turning the board over. The other side maybe okay to write on."

Someone shouted out, "Sneak!"

But Tara quelled the rising hysteria with her hands, "Enough! That's not a bad idea, Raymond. She selected two of her brawniest boys to do the job. "Jake, Tristan come and turn this over, please."

The two boys came up front and disengaged the board and switched it over to the other side and then reclaimed their seats. Tara picked up the chalk and bingo! It wrote across the surface with ease. She turned to Raymond and asked, "Are you sure you know nothing about this?"

"Yes, Miss. It wasn't me but I've seen it done before. I think someone has polished the blackboard with French chalk."

"Tell-tale," shouted someone else. Raymond went quiet.

"Thank you...." She waited for the class to fall quiet. "And the next person to shout something derogatory will be in at lunchtime to wash this board and clean it up."

"What does that mean?" muttered a boy called Luke Carpenter.

"Look it up in the dictionary. I suppose you are capable of using a dictionary." Tara said. There was an audible groan from Luke and another lad called Philip Bull. "Right, Luke Carpenter and you, Bull. You have the job of cleaning this board at lunchtime."

"Oh, what?"

"You were warned. And if anyone can tell me who did this I will pass the job onto them." No one spoke. "As I thought, now you can start work on this new assignment."

The subdued class began working and worked solidly until the bell went marking the end of the lesson.

Tara called Raymond Campbell to her desk, "Before you leave, Raymond, a quick word." Raymond shuffled to her side. "I wanted to thank you. If it hadn't been for you the lesson would have been a disaster."

"It was nothing, Miss."

"It most certainly was. Speaking up took courage… Are you, all right? Is everything okay at home?"

Raymond shrugged, "Same as always, Miss. No change there."

"Listen, if ever you want to talk. Or if there is anything at all I can do to help, just say, will you."

"Yes, Miss. Thank you, Miss."

"Okay, get off to your next lesson if anyone tells you off for being late, blame me. Understood? What have you got next?"

"Art, Miss."

"Then get along. I understand you are very good at art. You don't want to miss it. I will speak to your teacher."

Raymond shuffled away and Tara's heart went out to the lad. She had to try and find out if there was any way of helping him without making waves. She determined to speak to Lucy later and she would visit the school secretary to see if he could qualify for free school meals. The boy looked half starved.

* * *

As usual, Tara stood at the sink washing up a few dishes left over from breakfast. Her face was thoughtful as she mulled over her conversation about Raymond Campbell with Lucy earlier in the day. They had hatched a scheme to involve an art prize that would provide equipment for the winner. Money could be sourced from the school fund and Raymond stood a good chance of winning. Tara had been to see the school secretary and discovered that he did indeed, qualify for free school meals but his family had never applied. Tara took it upon herself to access the forms and arranged to see the lad the following day. She was determined that if need be she would visit him at his house.

They had gone on to talk some more about it at lunch before launching into Tara's problems at home and the pranks at school. Lucy had almost managed to reassure Tara that she had nothing to worry about. The jape with the blackboard was just that … a cheeky trick by a student meant in fun. They both admitted that it was quite funny and if Tara had been in a better frame of mind, she would have laughed along with the students.

Tilly was asleep on the sofa and the house seemed unusually quiet. The sound of the crockery being stacked on the drainer seemed abnormally loud. She stopped and wiped a sudsy hand over her face flicking away a tendril of hair from her eyes. Just for a moment she seemed suspended in her own bubble of time, lost in a myriad of thoughts.

The telephone rang.

Her head snapped round. She bit her lip; her gaze drawn toward the instrument that was shouting for attention, demanding to be answered.

The phone appeared to have a life of its own as the ringing seemed louder and more insistent. It seemed to increase in volume with each jangle, which she knew was impossible. Tara couldn't avert her eyes, as the sound appeared to reverberate around the house penetrating her mind, tightening her nerves to screaming pitch.

Tara gasped and came to. She dried her soapy hands and tentatively moved toward the noisy interruption. She edged nearer slowly, slowly and reached out her hand to answer it.

It stopped.

Tara heaved a huge sigh of relief. She was about to return to the dishes when the phone began to ring again. She snatched up the receiver and listened.

"Tara?"

Relief flooded through her as she heard Steve's voice, "Steve!"

"What? What's wrong?" his voice was filled with love and concern.

Eventually she burst out, "It's these horrible calls."

"If you mean the last one that was me. You didn't pick up."

"No… I was afraid to. I wasn't sure if… Steve, it's really getting to me." She bit her lip again but so hard this time that she tasted blood.

"Aw, darling I'm sorry. Listen tonight's client has had to cancel. Thought we could have a little 'us' time. I promise… Just you and me and a bottle of wine…"

"Oh, Steve. That would be great." A smile had entered her voice. She attacked the washing up with renewed vigour.

* * *

Tara sat alone at a table set with fresh flowers, candles and place settings for a romantic dinner for two.

She looked at her watch for the umpteenth time.

It was 8:35.

Tara rose and blew out the candles, then angrily gathered the unused china and returned it to the cupboard.

The phone rang startling her. She jumped and almost dropped a plate. Tara set the dish on the counter top and walked to the living room handset and answered, "Hello? ... Who is this?"

There was a long pause followed by a sinister click as the person terminated the call. Tara nervously stared at the receiver before replacing it. She steeled herself, picked it up and dialled a number and waited. It rang and rang insinuatingly. With a shaking hand she put it down once more.

The kitchen door creaked open.

Tara listened terrified, as footsteps approached. She froze.

Steve appeared in the living room doorway.

Tears streamed down Tara's cheeks, "I just called. Why didn't you answer?"

"I was already home."

Tara trembled. She was visibly shaken and went on the defensive, "But you could have answered instead of sneaking in the house."

Steve set down his briefcase and loosened his tie. He put his hands up as if in surrender, "Whoa! I entered the house through the garage. The same way I always do," he complained.

But Tara was running scared and her words came out in gushing complaint,

"You should have known after last night that I'd be scared here alone. But, no... you're out doing... whatever... after promising me you'd be here. Leaving me alone all hours of the night."

Steve removed his suit jacket and slung it on the settee. He emptied his pockets of change, keys, receipts and his wallet onto the desk. He tried to apologise to her, "Look. I'm sorry. I didn't mean to scare you."

"Well you did," said Tara petulantly.

Steve was now becoming frustrated at what he saw as an unwarranted outburst. "I said, I'm sorry." He paused as he studied his wife's hurt expression. "I'm beat. It's been a long day."

"And night, I'm sure," she said caustically.

"Listen, I don't feel I have to explain my every move to you. There was an emergency at work."

"And no one else could deal with it?"

"No!"

"Or maybe there was someone else working at it with you?"

"If you don't trust me after six years…"

The phone rang interrupting them.

Tara said icily, "Go ahead. You answer."

Steve strode to the handset and picked it up. "Hello? Lomas residence."

There was dead silence.

"Hello? Who's calling?"

Nothing.

Steve slammed down the receiver and swore, "Damned telemarketers." He moved to the stairs and said cursorily, "I'm going to call it a night."

Tara stopped him her voice filled with chilling accusation, "Who were you with tonight, Steve?"

He spun around, "If you must know, I lost our second biggest client tonight. Does that make you happy?" He didn't wait for Tara to reply but turned his back and stomped upstairs.

Tara threw herself onto the sofa and sobbed.

6

THE IRIDESCENT LUMINOUS DIAL ON the digital bedroom clock read 12:25 and ticked softly. It was the only sound in the room apart from Steve's deep breathing.

Silver shafts of moonlight filtered through the chinks in the curtain pooling in an unearthly shimmer on the thick pile of the carpet.

Tara lay next to Steve on the bed. He was sleeping soundly. Her eyes red from weeping were wide open as she reclined somewhat rigidly beside him. She didn't want to move for fear of waking him and she listened to the odd sounds of the house as it creaked and groaned in settlement in the night as radiators cooled and the chill breeze whispered eerily through the gaps in the windows.

Her heart thudded loudly in her chest and increased rapidly as the telephone disrupted her thoughts.

His sleep disturbed Steve fumbled for the receiver. He raised it to his ear and murmured sleepily, "Hello?"

The phone crackled.

There was an empty but menacing silence. He heard a soft click as the receiver was replaced. Groggy from sleep he leaned up on his elbow and switched on his bedside light. He blinked in the brightness, which hurt his eyes.

Tara rolled over and whispered, "Who was it?"

Steve groaned, "Another hang up."

Tara said firmly, "I've had enough of this. Tomorrow we're changing to an unlisted number." In need of comfort she snuggled into his back. "At least you were here this time and heard it yourself. You know I'm not exaggerating."

Steve turned and took her in his arms, "You're trembling."

"I can't help it. It's freaking me out."

Steve held her close and nibbled her ear. He said quietly, "Let me deal with it. I promise I'll sort it." He nuzzled her neck. "I'm sorry about tonight. You know I hate to fight."

"Me, too."

"You should know there's no one else. Never could be." He began to kiss her and she responded with equal ardour and fire. They kissed more passionately and tenderly but as Steve caressed her they fell into a frenzy of lovemaking.

The phone rang.

This time Steve leaned back and tugged the phone plug from the wall. He returned to her waiting arms and they moved rhythmically together as one, enjoying each other's bodies and their loving union.

* * *

The early morning rays of sunlight pushed through the curtains and stroked the couples' faces willing them to open their eyes and welcome in the new day. Tara traced her finger down Steve's back a tender smile playing on her lips. She moved closer and tucked her body into his, as her lips brushed the nape of his neck. He began to stir and rolled toward her with a satisfied expression on his face. He kissed her gently.

"How did you sleep last night?" asked Tara.

"Like a baby," he sighed, as he traced her lips with his fingers. "And you?"

"I don't think I moved once."

There was a comfortable pause between them as they each explored the other's face with their eyes.

Suddenly the alarm blared out shrilly startling both of them and Tara giggled.

Steve reached out and slapped the off button. He groaned, "Five o'clock. It never gets any easier."

"I just wish we could sleep in like the old days."

"Yeah, at least until seven."

They both laughed. Tara took the opportunity to snuggle in his arms, "Wait till we have a baby. Then we'll really reminisce about our old sleep habits."

"Ha! I bet. Won't be long now and boy am I going to enjoy working at getting us pregnant." Tara kissed him sweetly, tasting his manliness. "You know, I have an idea for getting Chalmers and Associates back on the client list."

"The client from last night?"

"Yeah." He looked deeply into her eyes, "If I can get them back then all our dreams will come true and happen much sooner."

"Then you'd better get onto it, Mr Lomas."

They kissed again, entwined in each other's arms and their passion began to rise. Steve let his head fall back on the pillow. He murmured, "You're making it very hard for me to leave."

Tara twisted her fingers through his chest hair. She sighed, "Good. That's the idea. Maybe you'll be home early tonight."

"I'll do my best."

She nuzzled his neck and upper body breathing in his manly aroma.

"In the meantime, don't answer the phone until we get caller ID and an unlisted number. Just let the answer machine pick up the calls." Tara leaned up and disentangled her fingers from his wiry hair. "Oh, how I love your chest…"

"Ouch!" Steve batted her hand away.

"It'll mean a new phone."

"Don't worry. I'll take care of everything. It's hard for you in class and everything and I don't want us to leave it till the weekend. It needs to be done now."

"I know." Tara smiled and took Steve's face in her hands and interrupted him with a gentle kiss. He eventually tore himself away from her, albeit reluctantly.

"Spoilsport!" she teased. He laughed, replaced the covers his side of the bed and dashed to the shower. Tara sighed contentedly and lay back, a dreamy expression on her face. "Go on, then" she murmured, "Leave me for the office and the shopping channels," and she closed her eyes.

* * *

Steve sat at his desk in his small but efficient looking office with expensive equipment and gadgets on the counter top over his cupboards. The telephone directory was open in front of him as he talked on the phone.

He twisted his pen relentlessly in his other hand, clicking the button off and on that released the pen while he listened before checking his watch and groaning. "Yes, I understand all that," he complained in an over patient tone. "All I want is to place the order." He paused as he was forced to listen to more sales talk. "No, don't put me on hold, please." Music began to play. He rolled his eyes futilely until the sales person came back on the line. "Hello? ... Yes, that's right. If the package deal is better let's go with that." Steve nodded as he made notes on a message pad. "555-899-2643? Got it. And the unpublished number will be effective immediately? ... Thank you. Oh, I almost forgot. Is it possible to prohibit calls from blocked numbers? ... Yes? ... Great. That should do it. Perfect ... Yes, same bank details. Terrific. Thanks for your help."

Steve replaced the receiver and grinned. His tummy growled, he needed something to eat and then he'd text Tara. 'Hopefully, the new account should put a stop to the nuisance calls', he thought. "But just in case, I think I'll call the local police and put them in the picture." Steve picked up the phone again and dialled the emergency services.

* * *

Skye Powell drove through the tree lined street. The roads were mottled with alternate shadows and pools of gold as the sun filtered through the foliage and gleamed behind scudding clouds. The effect was like a magical light show of sorts.

She swung her car into a petrol station forecourt, pulled up outside a payphone, which were few and far between in this digital age and stopped. She leaned across and scrabbled in the glove compartment for a scrap of paper, which she took with her to the public phone booth. She snatched up the receiver, inserted a pound coin and dialled the number scrawled on the note. She waited, her eyes glittered dangerously and her foot tapped in agitation as she mumbled, waiting for the call to connect, "Come on, come on."

An automated voice shook her, "The number you have dialled is not recognised. Please check and try again." A single tone followed the message. Sky was incensed, her face suffused with colour and she pressed the return coin button. In an absolute rage, she hissed into the receiver before slamming it down, "Think this'll stop me, Bitch? I've dealt with others. I'll deal with *you*."

She slammed down the phone in fury and her face was now white with anger. Skye got back into her car and raced off the forecourt. Her tyres squealed as the rubber burned and the vehicle belched out black smoke.

Her heart raced and her eyes filled with tears of spite and rage. She hiccupped a strangled sob and cursed loudly. The look in her eyes bordered on demonic as they played with a manic light and she talked to herself encouraging her to move to the next stage of her vendetta. "You don't know who you're dealing with Tara Lomas, think you're safe? You're in for a shock."

The car screeched down the road toward the town. She passed a police car that pulled out into the traffic and moved alongside waving her into the kerb.

Skye took a deep breath and tried to regulate her breathing. The copper stepped out of his car and approached Skye's vehicle. The window slid down.

"Would you mind stepping out of the car, Miss?"

Skye complied and smiled sweetly, "So sorry, Officer. What have I done wrong?"

"You seem to have been driving somewhat erratically."

Skye was quick thinking and cunning, "I haven't got my driving shoes and my foot caught under the pedal. I was trying to free it. I am so sorry."

"Where are your driving shoes?"

"In the hall at home, I was late and just forgot to put them on."

"Then I suggest you remove your footwear and drive without them."

"I thought that was against the law?"

"It's against the Highway Code but not the law; much better to be safe, Miss. We don't want you causing an accident."

"No, Sir. I'll remember that. These shoes are not made for walking or driving," she quipped.

The policeman managed a feeble smile and nodded. "Now get back in your vehicle, I'll watch you out into the traffic."

Skye had another retort on the tip of her tongue, but thought better of it as she got back in her car. She had wanted to ask the copper to move away first so she would know where he was. She sniggered to herself, took off her shoes and waved one, out of the window to show she had obeyed, before tossing them on the seat next to her and easing out into the flow of cars.

She thought she handled it quite well, considering her mood. She did not want to attract any undue attention and she drove in exemplary fashion into work. At the next set of traffic lights, the cop car turned off in another direction and Skye heaved a sigh of relief.

* * *

There was a distinct chill in the air as Tara made her way from class to the staff room but she was positively glowing. Her freshly washed hair glistened with a healthy sheen and there was a confident spring in her step as she walked briskly with her head held high.

She marched through a tide of students many of whom smiled and acknowledged her before she nipped into the staffroom for her coffee break. She waved brightly at Lucy who had saved her a place and sat hunched over a steaming cup of coffee.

The room was awash with teachers and inconsequential chatter but a stolid few sat with their heads buried in books or papers. Ken Ley seemed to have his eyes glued to his phone, grunting non-committedly to any attempts at conversation.

Tara managed to get her elevenses from Rona who encouraged her to indulge in one of the freshly baked delicious cupcakes. Tara wove her way through the others to get to her seat. She sat down with a sigh and a big grin.

Lucy eyed her friend, "I must say you're looking heaps better today. Good weekend?"

"Thanks, hon. Yes. I expect my early morning runs have something to do with it. If I don't get one in I'm fit for nothing."

"It's more than that," said Lucy enquiringly. "You and Steve must be getting some nookie?" laughed Lucy.

"Maybe," said Tara mysteriously.

"I knew it! You just have that look, a satisfied look."

"Yes, and finally getting some decent sleep. Ever since Steve changed our number and made it ex-directory, things have been so much better."

"I'm glad. Oh, and don't forget to give me that new number."

"I won't."

"So… you and Steve," pressed Lucy.

"You're so cheeky," smiled Tara. "But, I can honestly say we seem to be getting our heads around everything and sorting stuff out. Steve realises he needs to lighten up on his work load."

"That's terrific… Dare I ask about Mr Powell?"

"I haven't had much time for social networking recently, just the odd message. But, I'm sure I'll get back in the swim."

Tara's mobile began to vibrate and sent out its bird tweet whistle alerting her to a text. She fished it out from her pocket and clicked on the message box.

"What the…?"

Tara's face drained of colour, her shoulders drooped and she almost spilt her coffee. She passed her phone to Lucy who read the shouting message on the screen: 'DOES YOUR HUSBAND KNOW WHAT YOU'RE UP TO?'

Tara immediately texted back, "Who is this?" But the text bounced back as undeliverable. Lucy watched her friend, her face grave. "How can that be?" said Tara. "I'm replying to the number that sent the message. It doesn't make sense."

Lucy returned the phone, "Probably, someone's idea of being funny. It's just a senseless, very bad joke."

Tara's hands were trembling as she returned the phone to her pocket. Her voice became uneven and slightly tremulous, "After everything else that's happened? I don't think so." Tara murmured, "How can it be a duff number?"

"That's easily explained," said Lucy. "I know there's an app you can use to mask your number so it comes up as something completely different; some sort of spoof number service."

"Well, it shouldn't be lawful. Think of the trouble that could cause."

The friends fell silent and Lucy reached across and took Tara's hand. She squeezed it reassuringly. There was a rumble of thunder in the distance and rain began to fall. It tamped on the windows and began to sheet down, bouncing like ball bearings on the ground.

Tara looked across at her friend, "A storm. Maybe it's a sign of what's to come."

Lucy said nothing.

Tara walked back to her classroom and was surprised to see the class all seated there with expectant faces. She called the register and settled them down. After she'd returned their marked books she announced that she would go through the questions with them and picked up a piece of chalk. There was a collective excited whispering that ran through the form.

She turned back to them. "What now? You haven't polished the black board again, have you?"

"No, Miss," they chorused innocently.

Tara turned to the board and went to write when another giggle was heard. She steeled herself and began to write the first word. The chalk whizzed, popped and banged as she did so, startling Tara and the class who had collapsed into laughter.

"Very funny!" exclaimed Tara as she examined the end of her chalk. "Someone has gone to a lot of trouble to disrupt the lesson." She picked up another piece but it produced the same effect. Tara could see that someone had drilled into the end of the chalk and filled it with a type of gunpowder and re-plugged the end. After the initial shock she was forced to laugh and turned to the class. "If you put as much energy into your work as you have into your pranks you would all have A stars. I must say, though, whoever it is has been very inventive. I salute you." She gave them all a mock salute.

Tara couldn't hide her smile when she picked up the box of coloured chalk, which hadn't been tampered with and began to write with a yellow piece. Her classroom was calm once more.

With peace restored, Tara moved up and down the aisles stopping to engage with students and offering help when needed. She approached Raymond Campbell's desk. For a change he seemed to be totally immersed in what he was doing. "Raymond?" He looked up at her, "Can we speak after class? I have something to tell you." He looked somewhat embarrassed but inclined his head and returned to his creative writing essay.

Tara could see that he was something of a loner but believed he kept himself to himself from self-consciousness. She knew he needed a friend but how could she engineer a friendship? Most students ignored him and didn't even attempt to befriend him. It would not be an easy task. But, Tara had a few ideas. She needed to talk to Lucy.

The final bell sounded and her class rose from their seats, "Hold on. Wait!" she ordered. "Hand your books in before you leave. For homework, I want you to prepare a plan for a play on the theme of 'Friendship'. If you want to, you can work with a partner and devise a short play on the subject. It should have drama, conflict and resolution. Keep the character list small. Remember this is just a plan, an outline of what you expect to happen. We will start work on them next week. Right, off you go." There was a flurry of excited chattering from some who clearly enjoyed the prospect of writing a play and groans from others who found this type of task difficult.

Once the classroom was empty, Raymond sidled up to Tara's desk. "You wanted to see me, Miss?"

"Yes, Raymond." Tara stood up and closed the door before returning to her seat. The boy looked at her expectantly. "I have been thinking a lot about your situation." Raymond bristled. Tara continued, "I spoke to the school secretary and she assures me that you qualify for free school lunches but haven't put in a claim." Tara fished in her bag and removed the forms and handed them to him. "Mrs Graff has filled in all the necessary details all you have to do is to get mum to sign it."

Raymond glared at her as he was forced to take the application, "Why don't you stay out of my business? I don't need to be humiliated or have your or any other do-gooder's help!"

Tara was aghast but stopped him before he left the classroom. "Raymond! Wait. Let me explain." The boy looked sullen but stopped and turned back. "No one is patronising or humiliating you. I just want to help. I know things are tough for you. This will guarantee, at least, that you will have a hot meal inside you. No one need know that you are on the free school list, if that's what you're worried about. You will have a ticket like everyone else. I have made certain of that, I promise you. You will look like anyone else getting your lunch. Please, ask mum to sign it. You don't have to hand it back to me, just take it to Mrs Graff. She will do the rest."

Raymond appeared somewhat calmer at this explanation and shuffled his feet nervously. He looked up red faced, "Sorry, Mrs Lomas. It's just at primary school we had to give our names to the canteen staff and sign a free register. Everyone knew and I got so much stick because of it. When I got here I decided I'd rather skip lunch than go through that ordeal."

Tara smiled kindly and said softly, "It's not like that here. We have a different system. Students pay for their lunches on a Friday and are given tickets to hand in at meal times. They receive tokens as change if they don't spend the full amount and can add them to another meal. I will make sure you have your tickets on a Friday like everyone else. Why not try it out? Get mum to sign, please."

Raymond nodded and stuffed the forms into his school bag. He slouched to the classroom door and turned, "Sorry, Miss."

"That's all right. Have a good weekend."

Raymond nodded his head again and ambled out into the corridor. It pained

Tara to see him like this. She knew the lad had pride and didn't want his self-esteem damaged further. But she believed she had made a good start on helping him sort out his lunches, at least. Time would tell. She hoped after the weekend he would bring back the signed forms and they could start afresh.

* * *

In a corner of the library at a computer sat Ken Ley. The screen was filled with the text of a French novel and he was setting a series of questions. He made some notes on a foolscap notebook next to the mouse pad. His phone vibrated, interrupting his thought processes. He removed his handset from his pocket and read the text message. 'See you later. I have prepared a special meal. Daisy is looking forward to seeing you and hearing some more of Alice in Wonderland.' Ken smiled smugly. Things were going well, very well, indeed.

He paused a moment and scrolled through his collection of photographs on his phone with a strange smile on his face, before leaning back with a sigh of satisfaction. He set the phone next to him and tried to concentrate on the task in hand. As was his habit he patted his jacket pocket reassuringly but the expression on his face changed. He thrust his hands into his pocket and removed his keys, wallet, a handkerchief, a pack of gum and a single condom. He turned his pockets inside out as panic gripped him. Ken stood up and returned the items before feeling in his inside coat pocket and trouser pockets.

Ken's hands trembled as he logged off and packed his briefcase. He examined the floor around him and under the computer station. By this time, he had attracted the attention of the librarian who was striding toward him. "Is everything all right, Mr Ley?"

He blustered, "Er… yes, thank you, Miss Parsons. I seem to have misplaced my memory stick. It has all my sixth form work on it."

"Oh, no. I will keep an eye out for it. Is it marked?"

"Um, no… it had a red cap on the end."

"Very well. If it turns up here I'll put it in your pigeon hole." She smiled at the French master. "I'm sure it will turn up. What a nuisance though. I hope you don't need it today."

"No… er no. I have a backup one somewhere. I'm sure I'll find it. Thank you, Miss Parsons." The librarian returned to her desk.

Ken Ley picked up his things and left the library in a hurry. He needed to retrace his steps. His heart pounded as he struggled to think where it could be. What if the flash drive could be linked to him? If it fell into the wrong hands… it didn't bear thinking about.

Ken studied the floor of the corridor as he walked. He entered the language centre and rummaged through his desk. Nothing. He peered on the floor underneath his seat. It wasn't there. Ken fled back to the staff room and examined the floor where he usually sat. It wasn't there. He slammed his hand on the wall and his eyes were drawn to the pigeon holes and something attracted his attention. He strode to the unit. There in his slot sat the distinctive memory stick with its red cap. He grabbed it and looked all around him. A member of staff must have recognised it and put it there for him to collect, but who? Who knew he had one with a red cap? He paused and then hissed between his teeth, "Tara, Tara Lomas." He would check that out first thing Monday morning.

7

SKYE SAT AT HER COMPUTER scrolling through a list of overdue accounts to print off. She hit the print button and glanced furtively around her. Everyone seemed to be engaged on his or her task. Quickly, she pulled up a fresh window and typed in a new number search for Lomas.

Behind her in the office Marie was circulating, stopping briefly to speak with employees at their desks. Skye continued to keep an eye out for her boss. But, just as the list appeared on the screen Marie crossed to Skye who immediately hit the delete button.

Her boss looked curiously from Skye to her screen that was now blank. "Sorry, Marie. I hit the wrong button."

"Oh, okay." She appeared to accept the explanation and continued, "Skye, we're going to take a quick break for a short meeting."

Skye's heart was thumping but she nodded, "Sure."

As Marie moved onto the next person, Skye cleared her search history, sighed and logged off from her computer. Her knees were shaking, she whispered quietly to herself, "Close call." But her demeanour had an aura of flintiness and she promised herself; "I'll finish this later."

There was a flash of lightning outside.

Skye picked up her notepad and pen and moved to the conference room where the meetings always took place. The employees took their seats. Marie's voice droned in and out of Skye's consciousness as she doodled on her pad drawing a succession of stout black boxes around the page and blocking them in before striking through them in an aberrant fashion. The girl sitting next to her turned to stare but Skye's steely gaze fixed on her until the female was forced to look away.

There was another crash of thunder and rain began to lash against the windows of the office as the sky turned dark.

The meeting finally drew to a close. People rose up to move back to their work stations but Skye still sat there unmoving. Marie came across, "Is everything all right?"

Skye forced a smile, "Yes, of course. I've just not been sleeping too well lately that's all. I'll get back to work."

"Is there anything you need to go over?" There was another flash of lightning. The storm was moving closer and it lit up the room with its jagged light. Skye's face plunged into shadow making her look haggard and possessed.

"You don't look too good, Skye. Is there anything I can do?"

"I'm okay, just tired. Like I said I've not been sleeping too well." She forced a smile.

"Have you understood the company requirements and new code of practice? Do you need me to explain anything?"

"No, thanks. I'm fine." Skye rose to return to her computer not having a clue about what had just transpired. She glanced about her and stopped at one of the other worker's desks, "So, what was that all about?"

"Don't ask me," replied a young bespectacled man. "New code of conduct rules followed by the usual pep talk, as if we needed it. Only good news was about our bonuses."

Skye didn't feel it right to ask but agreed. She assumed that she obviously hadn't missed anything important. Now, she needed to get Tara Lomas' information and get it quickly, while Marie was involved with another co-worker. She picked up her printed list of default payers and settled at her PC and pretended to study it.

Skye felt as if a tight band constrained her chest. There was just too much activity around her to allow her to continue with her search so she continued doing her job and what was expected of her. She knew she'd have her chance soon.

Ken Ley glanced about the staffroom on Monday lunchtime looking for Tara Lomas. He had missed her at break time as he had been on duty. He spotted her eating sandwiches with that art teacher friend of hers. He swallowed hard and forced a broad grin on his face as he rose and crossed to where the two friends sat. "Hya," he said nonchalantly. "Thanks for returning my flash drive. Got all my sixth form work on it."

Tara looked up, "No trouble. When I saw it, I knew it was yours by the red cap. I just managed to stop a lad from making off with it."

Ken forced another smile as his mouth went dry, "Er… Out of interest, where was it?"

"What? Oh, it was on the floor outside the Language Centre. Two kids were fighting over it until I rescued it."

"I see, thank you. Hope no one accessed it. It's got all the test papers on it. If it fell into the wrong hands, someone could make a mint from selling the questions."

"Well, no harm done." Tara smiled brightly at him. He gave her a quick wave and returned to his seat, his hands were still shaking.

* * *

Three days had passed uneventfully. There were no more tricks at school and Tara had begun to become more relaxed at home. Her morning jogs helped and Steve's attention was comforting. There was still, however, a niggling feeling of doubt, which rose to the surface every now and again but she tried hard to suppress it. As she and Steve sat at the dinner table her face was pensive.

Tilly rubbed herself around Steve's legs as he finished eating. He lay down his knife and fork and bent down to fuss the cat, which set her off into a loud rumbling purr.

Tara peered at her pet and mused, "Cupboard love. She wants feeding."

"And I thought it was because she adored me," he protested.

"It's either that or she's so unused to you being home this early she's making her mark on you not to forget us."

"As if I would… So… All quiet on the Western Front?"

"Seems to be. Changing the number appears to have worked. Makes me feel so much better."

"Looks like the psycho has given up."

"Apart from that text."

"It was only the one. Maybe, Lucy was right; a student prank."

"Maybe." But Tara's expression showed she was not so sure. "But I'm not going to talk about it now and spoil our evening. For once you're home early and I'm going to make the most of it." Tara set down her utensils, rose and wrapped her arms around Steve's neck and planted a kiss on the top of his head.

The telephone rang. Tara froze. The bile rose in her throat and she felt sick.

Steve jumped up and answered, "Hello? ... Oh, hello, Mum ... Yes, we're fine." Tara immediately sighed in relief. She steadied herself, sat and listened to the conversation. "Sunday? Let's see ..." Steve cupped his hand over the mouthpiece, "Mum wants to know if we can make lunch on Sunday?" Tara nodded. "Great. Yes, that's fine ... Do you want us to bring anything? Something to drink, perhaps? ... We sure will. Yes, okay. See you at one."

Steve replaced the receiver. Lunch at Mum's on Sunday. That will save us cooking."

"Us? I like that. I'm the one who slaves over the hot stove, not you."

"I know. But you're so much better at it than me," he grinned. "And now let's feed this cat before she starts covering me in her fur. These are my best work trousers."

As soon as Tara moved toward the kitchen Tilly followed and raced past her with her tail straight up in the air.

Tara chuckled, "You know, it's so good to feel comfortable in our home again."

Steve looked adoringly at her and nodded in agreement. "I think that deserves a glass of wine, don't you?"

* * *

The day was gloomy as the sun played hide and seek behind the growing clouds that had begun to roll intrepidly across the heavens threatening rain. Skye hurried from the car park and through the revolving doors of Bartmer Communications. The Security Guard on Reception looked up in surprise, "Blimey, you're in early."

Skye nodded as she dashed toward the lift, "I didn't get everything done yesterday and don't want my pay docked. My bonus is at stake."

The guard acknowledged with a smile and wave, "I know what that's like. Good luck. Hope you get it all done."

"Oh, I will," said Skye confidently as she stepped into the lift and ascended to the offices. Skye used her pass to access the main office and hurried toward her desk. She placed her bag in the drawer and looked around. There was no one else there. Good. She cursed as the door opened and a co-worker, Aubrey, entered.

He headed straight for the coffee machine and called out, "Want one?"

"Not yet, I've got some stuff to finish first."

"Okay." Aubrey made his drink and crossed to Skye's desk. "What you doing?

Skye groaned inwardly and gritted her teeth, "I've just got some work to finish, don't want Marie on my back," she said through tight lips.

"Anything I can do to help?"

"No." Her answer came too quickly and Skye backpedalled. "No, thanks." She said in a more conciliatory tone. "Something I've just got to do. Tell you what, let me get on, and then we can have a chat and I'll have that coffee."

Aubrey shrugged and smiled good-naturedly, "Okay, but I'll help you if you need me to, the offer is there."

"Thanks." Skye forced a smile and waited till he'd moved away. She logged onto her PC and worked quickly before anyone else arrived. Skye ensured Aubrey was not observing her and ran a search for new unlisted numbers that were ex-directory for 'Lomas'. A list appeared. Skye quickly scanned the list; then hit the print button. She hurried to the printer, retrieved the list and returned to her desk. She stuffed the paper into her bag and murmured, "Ha! And you think you're so smart."

"Pardon?" called Aubrey just as Marie entered.

"My, you two are keen," said Marie. "Must be the promise of extra money." She smiled brightly and moved toward Skye's desk.

Skye hurriedly closed down her windows and engaged in work related chatter with her boss. She was anxious to get Marie to move away, whilst trying to appear interested in what Marie was saying. Although the sensitive page had been deleted, in her panic she had neglected to remove her search history. She shoved her bag in her desk drawer and closed it with a slam. Marie moved onto her own work space. Skye smiled brightly and called out, "I could do with that coffee now, Aubrey. Thanks."

"That was quick," he raised his eyebrows.

"I must be losing it. I could have sworn I had two contracts outstanding. I must have done them on automatic pilot." Skye sighed and smiled as Aubrey handed her a mug.

Marie joined them at the coffee station, "I'll have one, too, if you're offering."

Skye smiled, "Of course, anything for the boss."

"Now, don't go overboard," said Aubrey. "I can see she's wrangling for employee of the month," he laughed.

Skye grinned and passed her boss a steaming mug of coffee with a look of extreme satisfaction on her face.

8

THE DRAB WEATHER WAS BEING swept away by a strong west wind. The clouds bowled across the sky leaving a clear ceiling of stars. Tara and Steve snuggled up on the sofa together to watch some television. Tilly rubbed herself around Steve's legs, arching her back and giving her special pretty multi-toned hungry meow. Steve leaned down to fuss her and she purred in delight. "I swear that cat is talking to me," said Steve. "She has such a variety of sounds, some even sound like 'hello'. There's another that I'm sure says, I love you." Tilly tried to bat Steve's hand with her head and mewed again.

"Told you, it's cupboard love. She wants feeding," said Tara.

Steve grinned and studied his wife's face with tenderness in his eyes. "She'll have to wait. Besides there's some chow in her dish." Steve paused and his tone turned serious, "So, is all quiet on the Western Front?"

"Seems to be. On the Telephone Preference Service, changing the number and using a call blocker seems to have worked." She sighed, "Makes me feel so much better."

"Looks like the psycho has given up."

"Apart from the text."

"It was only one. Maybe Lucy was right, a student prank." Tara's expression showed she was not so sure as Steve continued. "Still, it was a strange thing to put." That sort of text could cause huge problems in a relationship but not with us. We are so much stronger than that."

By now, Tilly had got fed up with her efforts and wandered to her bowl and began munching on the dried food. The couple watched the cat in silence, momentarily lost in their own thoughts.

Once Tilly had eaten her fill she proceeded to clean herself up before returning to the settee and jumping up alongside them. She soon curled up in a ball and promptly went fast asleep.

"I wish I could do that," said Tara wistfully.

"You'll soon be back to normal. Now that lunatic can't get at you anymore."

"What if it doesn't end, Steve?"

"It will," he paused; "There's something I haven't told you." Tara looked up anxious faced. "Nothing to worry about but after I changed the number I called the police. A complaint has been logged so if the maniac does ring again. There is a formal record of this frightening behaviour."

Tara nodded in understanding, "Better to be safe than sorry," she agreed. She glanced across at the dinner table where the remains of their romantic meal were still on the table. Tara groaned, "I need to clear up," She started to rise but Steve pulled her back down.

"No, you cooked. I'll clear up. It's only fair. You have been really attentive to me and deserve a break. Now, cuddle up and let's watch the film. I know you like Tom Sellick and the Jesse Stone series. Heck, you've read all the books."

"Mmm, I have to admit the thought of Tom Sellick does put me in a sexy mood."

"That's what I'm counting on."

"He can put his shoes under my bed anytime," she teased.

"I think that maybe a step too far. Perhaps I ought to grow a moustache…. Or maybe start drinking whisky, heavily."

"No… I don't think so. It would affect your performance."

"How do you know? Aren't you willing to try?" Steve held Tara lovingly and kissed her. "Don't know what I'd do without you. If you ever found someone else… I don't know … I'd be devastated."

"Not going to happen," said Tara in between kisses. Steve pushed her back on the settee much to Tilly's discomfort who jumped off the couch and stared accusingly at them her sleep disturbed.

The phone rang. Its strident ring jangled for attention demanding to be answered. Steve and Tara stared at it briefly before Steve picked up the receiver, "Hello?... Hello? Who is this?"

Steve waited for a reply. There was nothing. Just an ominous silence. The phone clicked as someone on the other end curtailed the call. Steve slammed down the phone and swore in frustration. Tara had turned white. She tried to control the trembling that had manifested in her hands.

Tara's mobile was sitting on the counter top and it pinged indicating she had received a text message. Their loving mood was now truly broken as they exchanged a worried look. Tara moved to rise but Steve stopped her with his hand, "No, I'll get it."

Steve retrieved her phone and pulled up the message. It read: 'You're playing with fire, BITCH!' His face was creased in a mixture of concern and anger as he reached for the landline.

He dialled call retrieval and received the message, "You were called today at 21:05. We do not have the person's number to return the call. Please hang up."

"No call back number."

"But, how? We have a call blocker."

Steve immediately called the police.

Tara's face was frozen in shock but a steely determination had entered her eyes and she held out her hand for the phone, "I should deal with this."

But Steve shook his head and put the phone on speaker. "No, let me... Hello? This is Steve Lomas. I spoke to one of your officers earlier." He pulled out the scrap of paper from his top pocket. "They gave me a reference number, 64211."

"Is this an emergency, Mr Lomas?"

"It sure as hell is. We need an officer over here, now."

"Hold the line, while I pull up your details …" There was silence while the dispatcher accessed the report online. Steve paced impatiently around the room, as Tara listened biting her lip. "Ah, yes…. Harassing phone calls threatening your wife, Tara. Is that correct?"

"Yes. We've done what we can and the pervert is still getting through."

"Has anyone physically harmed your wife, Mr Lomas?"

"Not yet. But I'm afraid…"

"Unfortunately, we cannot stop nuisance calls. Why don't you try calling your provider tomorrow, as we suggested, and change your number."

"We did that. Look, our number's ex-directory. We have a call blocker yet we're still receiving silent hang up calls and threatening text messages on her…"

"I'll file another report. If the problem persists contact your local police not the emergency services."

The call was disconnected. Steve slammed his hand on the counter top in frustration. "Damn it! Just what do we have to do?"

Tears welled up in Tara's eyes and she fell back on the sofa unable to suppress her escaping sobs as Steve looked on helplessly.

At school James Treeves had collared his friend Tommy Porter. They had taken position behind the cricket pavilion on the school field. James was lighting a surreptitious cigarette, "Have you heard the rumours?"

Tommy looked puzzled, "No, what's up?"

"I heard that old Ken Ley has all the sixth form exam work on that memory stick of his. The one with the red cap."

"So?"

"So, if we can get hold of it and copy it we can make ourselves a bundle by selling the exam papers to grateful sixth formers. What do you say?"

"I don't know, James. Isn't it risky? How are we supposed to get the stick from him?"

"Easy, peasy. He carries it in his jacket pocket. A few distraction tactics and like the Artful Dodger, I can pick his pocket."

"And who's going to do that distraction stuff?"

"You, Tommy boy. You." Tommy looked unconvinced. "Think of the money." James rubbed his hands in glee.

* * *

A few more days had passed with no further calls but the damage had been done and Tara was looking rough. She routinely sprinkled fish flakes in the tank. Her glazed eyes were red from lack of sleep, her face was pinched and pale in spite of wearing makeup. She looked exhausted and had clearly lost weight.

The house looked as if it could do with a good clean. Tara just hadn't the energy or desire for housework but she knew she would have to pull herself together and clean up at some point.

Tara shook her head and gave herself a stiff talking to, "Come on, girl. Snap out of this fog. You mustn't let this crackpot win. Rise above it. What can I do?" She snapped her fingers and moved across to her computer and turned it on. "A little distraction is needed, I think."

Tara waited until 'Friend Finder' loaded and clicked on her home page. She scrolled down to see what had been happening in the online world. As she did this her eyes began to widen in horror as she read a torrent of severely abusive messages.

'You're nothing but a slut. Your days are numbered, whore.'

Tara hit the power button and the screen went black. She sat there visibly shaken and frozen. She refused to let tears prick her eyes and swallowed hard. She remained there in silence and deep in thought before coming to a decision.

Tara switched the power to the PC back on and re-opened the last window of Friend Finder. She studied her contact list and saw that Lee Powell was active online and immediately began to type a private message to him.

'This isn't funny, Lee.'

His reply was instant, 'Sorry?'

'These messages. They're frightening me.'

'I don't know what you're talking about. What messages?'

'No? Then check my home page.'

Puzzled Lee clicked on Tara's page. He gasped in horror at the brutal messages and immediately typed, 'Tara, it's not me. I swear. This is hideous. You need to call the police.'

The response bounced back, 'I have.'

Tara hit the message off button. Filled with fury she was about to delete her page and close her account but then stopped. If she needed evidence of a stalker then this was it. Instead, she pulled up her privacy settings and personal information and set about restricting her page and public access to any information except for real friends that she knew and not friends of friends and definitely not for the general public. She then took a screen shot of all the hateful and abusive comments, reported the posts to the admin of Friend Finder and then deleted them. It took a little time but eventually she succeeded and switched off her PC. She felt violated and dirty as if she had done something wrong. She flushed guiltily as she thought of Steve. She hadn't told him about her online activities believing it was just innocent fun and then the thought struck her that all this horrid abuse and the nuisance calls had only started after she had joined Friend Finder. Had she done the right thing with the screen shots? Keeping the messages would enable the police to check into them and chase down the maniac's IP address, wouldn't it? Or perhaps she should have completely deleted the account "Bugger!" she exclaimed.

Tara felt she had to do something. Not doing anything would only leave her brooding. She decided to set to and clean the house. She went to the broom cupboard and took out the vacuum cleaner. She would start now, better to be busy than fall apart.

Lee Powell sat in his comfortable room staring at his computer in disbelief. How could Tara believe he had something to do with those awful comments? Poor woman she must have been beside herself. He reached for the sandwich sitting next to him on his desk and was about to take a bite but changed his mind. He stood up and placed a tea towel over it to stop the bread going dry. "I need something else," he said aloud staring at his empty wine rack. "I also need to try and fix this."

He moved toward the telephone and stepped on a toy. The high-pitched shrill squeak of the bath time toy made him jump.

He picked up the phone and dialled, drumming his fingers on the desk as he waited for the phone to be answered, "Mum? I need to go out. The kids are in bed asleep. Can you sit for a while? I won't be long…. Yes, sure … How long? Great. See you in ten minutes."

Lee tiptoed upstairs to check on his children. Assured they were sound asleep he went back down, put on his jacket and picked up his car keys. He glanced at his watch as he heard a key in the lock and his mother came in and gave him a hug. She took off her coat and sat on the sofa and switched on the telly.

"I'll be as quick as I can. Promise. There's something I must do." He gave her a swift peck on the cheek and left quickly. His mother asked no questions but just smiled, flicked through the channels and settled down to watch an old episode of Heartbeat.

The night was uncomfortably dark. The moon and stars were obscured by low cloud that bubble wrapped the sky. There was hardly a breath of wind, just the occasional movement of a gentle breeze. The houses in the street were cosy and locked up tight with only a muddy glow of electric light escaping from gaps in the curtains and under badly sealed doors.

In the shadows outside Tara and Steve's house stood a sinister figure in a hoodie. A camera was focused on the front window of the Lomas' house where the drapes were open and a light announced that someone was home. The woman inside could be seen clearly. She was alone and paced the living room seemingly unable to settle.

An expensive camera was raised and several pictures were taken in quick succession. The sound of the camera shutter barely broke the cloying silence around the figure.

A woman walking her dog strode past and the figure cringed back into the bushes that grew and belonged to the house opposite Tara's. The woman waited patiently for her pooch to do what was expected and cleared up the offending mess in bag and tried to encourage the animal to continue on their walk. The curious creature was reluctant to move on and tugged at the owner's lead. The canine tried to enter the driveway of the house where the invader lurked and let out a series of short barks. "Come on, Poppy. You'll have the whole neighbourhood up. Shush. Poppy. That's enough sniffing... Poppy!" The owner yanked on Poppy's leash and Poppy eventually gave up her investigation of the shrubbery, obeyed her mistress and trotted after her. There was a slow release of breath on the night air, which mingled with the soft whisper of wind that had begun to sough in the trees.

The sinister sentinel stepped out from cover and took more photos before stepping back into the shadows and continuing the obsessive silent night vigil.

Tara couldn't concentrate on anything. She had papers waiting to be marked and a meal to prepare. Every now and then she would pace the room feeling unbearably uneasy. She felt extremely vulnerable and the serpentine twisting fear that coiled in her stomach manifested into an uncontrollable trembling. She stepped to the window and looked outside. She stood there motionless for a full minute or more and shivered. "I can't live like this," she whispered. "It's not life, it's purgatory."

The malevolent observer took full advantage of Tara's careless actions. The camera zoomed in on its target and took several shots in quick succession achieving close-ups of Tara's worried face. The persistence of the intrusive camera continued and seemed to photograph Tara from every angle and her every movement.

Tara couldn't shake off the feeling that somehow, she was being watched. She grabbed the heavy curtains and pulled them together blocking out the threatening night. Once this was done she felt better and strode determinedly to the telephone and pulled out the plug.

Tilly mewed to be let out. "Why can't you use the cat flap?" But Tilly just mewed again. Tara opened the back door, closed and bolted it firmly against any possible marauder. She leaned against the door, closing her eyes, her chest was heaving and she sighed again.

The indistinct figure swore softly in exasperation as the curtains closed. Escaping the protective cover of the shrubbery opposite, the figure boldly crossed to the Lomas house and safe that no one had seen or observed the stalker's actions attempted to circle the house and find another point of entry or place to capture further looks at the occupant.

Tilly now out and free padded curiously toward the malign watching figure, laid back her ears and hissed before bounding off on her own night hunt.

9

IN THE PLAYGROUND JAMES TREEVES and Tommy Porter were kicking a ball around. "I heard it was hysterical," said James. "It was worth staying late and polishing that board. Just wish I could have seen her trying to write on it."

"Yes, it was definitely clever and the exploding chalk was brilliant."

"Yeah, but she found that funny, too. I need to do something that will really upset her."

"Why don't you just leave it? You've had your fun."

"Oh, I'm only just beginning. This is just the start."

The bell for morning registration blared out and the two boys made their way to class. "Remember, after Maths we begin our next top secret operation. Should be a blast!" Think I know what I want to do when I leave school."

"What's that?"

"Join the Secret Service. This is all good experience."

Tommy laughed, "Ha! You as James Bond? I don't think so."

"No? You just wait and see."

James and Tommy had raced from their respective Maths classes and were now lounging against the wall of the corridor in the Language Centre. Tommy had a basketball under his arm. "Now remember when Mr Ley comes out for break you start bouncing the ball. Let it bounce into him. Don't let any other kid take the ball. He should come out after the rest of his class that's when you bounce and I will do the rest." James held up another memory stick that he intended to switch with the real one.

"Okay. You know I'm likely to get a detention for this?"

"Suck it up. Think of the money."

Just then the bell sounded out. Mr Ley's classroom door flew open and the pupils streamed out laughing and joking. A few minutes later Ken Ley emerged and Tommy began bouncing the basketball. His voice boomed out, "You boy, stop that. Give me the ball." Tommy steadied his nerves and threw the ball, which hit the teacher in the chest. Mr Ley grasped the ball and continued regaling Tommy as Treeves skirted around the back of the master. "What's your name, Boy?"

"Tommy, Sir. Tommy Porter."

"You can report to my room at one o' clock if you want your ball back."

Tommy had the good grace to bow his head and look shamefaced, "Yes, Sir. Sorry, Sir."

James nodded his head at his friend that he had switched the sticks and he turned tail along the corridor and hurried to the stairs. Mr Ley continued on his way to the staffroom holding the ball.

Tommy began to run after his friend. Mr Ley roared after him, "Don't run. Unless you want a detention to add to your misdeed."

"No, Sir. Sorry, Sir," Tommy called back over his shoulder as Mr Ley tutted.

James and Tommy raced off to the library, "We need to copy this info and get the stick back to him asap," said James as they sat at a vacant Mac computer. James fired it up and typed in a programme search.

"Have you got the new USB stick and the carbon copy clone app to download?" asked Tommy.

"Got the stick. Doing the app now. Read me the instructions," said James shoving a handwritten list at Tommy.

"Okay," said Tommy slowly. "Once you've downloaded the Carbon Copy Cloner app, attach your external drive via USB or Firewire."

"Done."

"Launch the Carbon Copy Cloner."

"Okay," James said, as he clicked on it.

"Select the source and destination."

"Hang on.... Okay.... Next?"

"Pick the type of clone from the drop down menu."

"Yes. I've selected..."

"Lastly, click on clone."

They both watched the blue line travel across and a ping to show the files had been cloned."

James removed the sticks carefully and put his cloned copy into his inside pocket. He waved the other one at Tommy. "Now to get the original back. We don't want to arouse any suspicions. Come on." He logged off the computer and the pair left the library.

"How do we get it back to him?" asked Tommy. "I can't use the ball again."

"No… and he's not the most affable teacher. Let's get to the Language Centre and we'll think on the way."

The two boys hurried down the corridor, across the yard and into the block that housed the Language Centre and ran up the stairs. As luck would have it when they rounded the corner leading to Mr Ley's classroom he was emerging with a pile of books and papers. Tommy crashed into him, the papers and books went flying. He immediately apologised. "Sorry, Sir. Let me help you with that."

"You again!" the master roared as he stooped to pick up the scattered papers. Both James and Tommy helped gather all the books, but each time James tried to switch the sticks he just couldn't quite manage it. "You boy," the master yelled at James. "What are you hovering around me for?"

"Nothing, Sir. No reason. I just want to help that's all." James' face looked panicked. Tommy rose and tapped the master on his shoulder to pass him the books and papers he'd collected. The master swung around and James was able to make the switch. He dashed off down the corridor but was stopped by the master's voice. "Stop!"

James skidded to a halt. Mr Ley strode toward him, "Name?"

"Treeves, Sir. James Treeves." He was trying to be respectful.

"What have you got in your hand?"

"Nothing, Sir."

"Show me."

James palmed the stick and opened his hands. There was nothing there.

"This is a warning. If I see either of you acting the fool around here or anywhere else. You will both have a detention."

"Yes, Sir. Sorry, Sir."

"Now get to class."

"Yes, Sir. Thank you, Sir."

The two boys scooted off as fast as they dared and dashed into the playground. "Now what?" asked Tommy.

"I'll come around to yours and we'll get the test papers up and print them off. Then we advertise!" He grinned broadly. "This could set us up nicely for the holidays, Tommy boy."

"I can't do tonight. I've got a cricket match and my parents are taking us to Gran's house on Wednesday. Only days free this week are Thursday and Friday. We'll have to make it on one of those nights."

James didn't look well pleased, "Time is of the essence."

"Why can't I come to you?"

"Because our printer is on the blink and my mum asks too many questions. Your mum doesn't interfere. Besides you have the whole set up in your bedroom. Ours is all downstairs. Okay, we'll make it Friday. I'll be there at seven."

Tommy nodded. He could see the sense in why James couldn't do it at home and the two went off to their next lesson.

The following night, a police car was lying in wait outside Lee Powell's house. The officers inside had been waiting a while and tilted their seats back to relax. One murmured, "I hate hanging about. Tires me out doing nothing."

"Me, too," said his colleague. "If the chap hasn't turned up in…" he glanced at his watch, "Say, fifteen minutes, we'll call it a night. We'll try and catch him again in the morning early."

The other nodded his head in agreement and yawned. "I don't fancy waiting here longer than necessary. Sounds like a plan. Besides, I'm hungry." He patted his rumbling tummy before reaching up to adjust the driver's inside mirror and spotted someone turning the corner. In the dull lamplight it was hard to see any facial features. "Hold up… this could be him." They watched and waited.

Lee quickened his step as he rounded the corner and saw the car sitting there. Uncertain whether they waiting for him or not, he was glad that his children were staying with his mother. In his hand he carried something in a brown paper bag.

He strode to his front door and as he inserted the key in the lock he heard two car doors slam. He turned as the police officers approached him.

"Mr Powell? Mr Lee Powell?"

"Yes?"

"Is it all right if we come in? We need to speak to you."

Lee nodded and entered his house. He led the male officers into his open plan living room and gestured for them to sit. "Please sit down."

One officer removed a squeaky ball from the seat and smiled, "Got a dog?"

"No, it belongs to Amy, my daughter."

The officers nodded and settled themselves. One took out a well-used notebook and pencil ready to take notes. The taller of the two men explained, "We're investigating the murder of Jan Bernard. We understand you were friends and would like to ask you some questions."

"Of course, anything I can do to help."

"Firstly, in order to eliminate you from our enquiries could you tell us where you were on the morning of Tuesday the 15th?"

"I haven't a clue. Can't even remember what I did yesterday let alone then. Hold on and I'll check my diary." Lee ventured to his desk and skimmed through the pages, "I was here, working on a software project."

"Can anyone vouch for that?"

"Er... my mother came around 8:35 in the morning to collect the children and take them to school for me. She returned afterwards at approximately 9:00 and prepared a meal, I'm not good at remembering to eat when I'm working," he added sheepishly.

"And she can verify that?"

"Yes, of course, mum is often in and out as she helps me with child care."

"We will need her details."

Lee recited her address and telephone numbers.

"Other than that, you were alone?"

"Yes."

"What about earlier?"

"Earlier?"

"Before your mother called?"

"I was getting the kids ready, dressed and breakfasted."

"So, you didn't leave the house?"

"No."

"We're given to understand that you and Miss Bernard were more than just friends?"

"I would like to have been. I suppose you could say we were working toward that... I'm still struggling to get my head around ... it." Lee couldn't bring himself to say the word 'murder'.

"Do you know of anyone she had trouble with? Someone who had it in for her? Wanted to hurt her?"

Lee shook his head, "No, Jan was a lovely girl. We consoled each other about our terrible choices in relationships."

"She'd had some bad ones? Could any of them have wanted her dead?"

Lee shook his head, "I honestly don't know. I didn't know any of them personally."

The police continued to interrogate Lee asking searching questions about his relationship with Jan. It was over an hour before they left and Lee felt exhausted by their visit, even doubting and questioning himself. He raked his fingers through his long hair, picked up the phone and rang his friend Mike, "Fancy a pint?"

"Do I ever? When?"

"Tomorrow?"

"Sure thing. Meet you in the Hammer and Sickle? Around six? Are you okay? You sound weird."

"Nothing a pint of Doombar and some good company won't fix," said Lee. He replaced the receiver but didn't look as confident as he sounded and walked across to his PC. He booted it up and sat there for an extraordinary amount of time staring at a blank screen. His mind was not on his work. Eventually, he logged off and rose. He took the Merlot from the paper bag and placed the bottle of red wine on the table and grumbled, "Don't even fancy a glass now," he said aloud. "Looks like another sleepless night."

The phone rang. Lee looked at the telephone, an uneasy feeling creeping through hm. He didn't want to talk to anyone. He got up and pulled the wire from the socket and the ring tone ended.

Lee sat morosely, with a beer in his hand, across from his friend Mike. He was already on his third pint. The pub was starting to get busy with people stopping off for a drink after work and there was a cheerful buzz of chatter in the bar but that didn't appear to lift Lee's spirits. In between swigs of ale he continued with the whole sorry tale of the previous night's events, "Anyway, you were right about the cops. I just got back from the Off-Licence and they were waiting. They gave me an absolute grilling. Made me feel really guilty like I was in some way responsible."

"I know what you mean. I felt the same way," said Mike sympathetically.

"Made me think, I can tell you. I expect they'll be back with more questions if Tara reports me."

"What?... Who's Tara?"

"Just an online friend. Tara Lomas. Never even met her or have any intention of meeting her. We exchanged a few jokes. She was fun and made me laugh… totally innocent."

"Then, I don't understand…"

"She suffered a load of harassment and abuse. Cyber bullying and threats. Horrible stuff on her timeline and she thinks I'm responsible."

Mike snorted in derision, "You! Stuffy old Lee who lives for his kids? By the way, where are they?"

"Mum and dad have got them for the week while I finish this programme." Lee took a swig of his beer. "I hate the thought that anyone would think I could do something like that." Lee stopped and took another mouthful of beer. His eyes began to fill with tears. Mike waited until Lee had composed himself once more.

"And?" asked Mike. "I know you. There's something you're not telling me."

Lee took another swig of his drink and looked his friend straight in the eye. "I've been thinking… You don't imagine Skye's got anything to do with this do you?"

"Skye? Well, she was pretty cut up after your divorce."

"Ha! Isn't that the truth? Nearly cut me up and the kids."

"Na, she wouldn't have done that for real. Threatened to maybe…"

"You're forgetting I had ten stitches. She was like a wild animal."

"That was the drugs. Not the real Skye."

"Maybe, maybe not."

There was a lull in the conversation as both men pondered on the events. Mike seemed to consider his next words. "Tell you what, I'll go and see her. She still trusts me. I'll see what I can find out, but I can't believe it's her."

"And you trust me. Keep your bachelor status. If I could turn back time I'd never have married the witch. Hindsight's a wonderful thing."

"But you wouldn't have had two great kids."

"I suppose and then it wasn't all bad."

Mike left his friend Lee with his head buzzing. He made his way home to his flat and opened his laptop. He logged onto Friend Finder and being curious did a search for Tara Lomas. He found what he thought was the right person from the list of suggestions and clicked on her page. There was little to see except her profile picture and no posts available to view. He gave a low whistle she was a very attractive woman. He logged off and went to his address book to seek out Skye's details and tried to call her but there was no reply. He shrugged and whistling cheerfully, he set about preparing an evening snack.

Tara could barely drag herself from her bed. She was unable to sleep through the night and once she had risen to pop to the loo she found it impossible to get back to sleep. She was lucky if she managed two or three hours a night and the strain was telling on her face. She had survived registration and first lesson, which was private reading but was unable to focus on the work she needed to do. Her next class would be more demanding. Tara chewed on her pen, unsure whether she was ready for her lively English class.

By the time the pupils had filed in for their lesson Tara looked extremely tired. She faced her class of fifteen year old students but soon became energised by the varied discussions that developed from examining their homework based on their selected exam texts. Her demeanour improved markedly after they had gone through the best methods of answering the test questions. She encouraged them all with a smile and a short burst of applause. "Well done, all of you and I mean it. I am most impressed with the way you have tackled the revision test papers. Now, let's take another look at this speech from The Tempest. Turn to Act One, Scene Two." There was a rustle of pages being turned as the class found the selected page. Tara looked around her class, "Okay, this is not so difficult." There was an involuntary groan from some students and Tara laughed. "I promise you, you will all get a clearer idea of what is being said after we have read it. Karl read the first sentence please."

Karl looked up in horror, "No, not me, Miss, please."

"All right." She surveyed her class again, "Robin?"

Robin smiled in delight and read with relish, "As wicked dew as e'er my mother brushed with raven's feather from unwholesome fen drop on you both!"

"Now then, what does that sound like?"

A few students shrugged but Karl piped up and said tentatively, "A curse?"

"Right. What does this show?"

The class was interrupted by a knock at the door. The students looked up curiously as another older pupil, Jolene, came into the room carrying a long box. "Excuse me, Mrs Lomas. This has arrived for you." Jolene handed Tara the box, which she set aside on her desk.

"Thank you, Jolene." The girl smiled and left the class and Tara continued with the lesson. "Now, what do those lines show of Caliban's character?" but the students were more interested in Tara's gift.

Robin bravely suggested, "Aren't you going to open it, Mrs Lomas?"

There was an immediate chorus of approval from students who urged her to open it.

Smiling good naturedly Tara decided to humour them especially as she was more than curious herself. "Oh, very well." She detached the ribbon and tape from the lid, which she then removed. She recoiled in horror stifling a scream.

Some students rose from their seats to peer at the contents and turned away in disgust, others screamed. The room fell into chaos before Tara struggled to replace the lid on the box, which contained a bouquet of dead flowers that harboured a dead rat that was covered with wriggling maggots.

After the initial shock, silence fell on the school room. Tara rose and, in an attempt, to regain calm, picked up the offending box. "I won't be long. Please look at Caliban's speech and try and translate what Shakespeare intended and we will go through it on my return." Although unnerved, she tried to appear more confident and calmer than she was inside. She swept from the room and the still silent class, but once she had gone there was a flurry of whispers among the pupils about what they had just seen.

Robin stepped from his chair and watched at the door as Tara marched along the corridor toward the secretary's office. It was clear to anyone she passed that she was fighting to prevent the tears pouring from her eyes. She was trembling and both sickened and furious that her place of work should be defiled in this way.

Moments later Tara sat opposite Mrs Graff, the kindly school secretary. The offending box lay on the desk between them. Jolene, who had been summoned, sat next to Tara. The poor girl was in floods of tears after a brutal verbal attack by Tara. Jolene pleaded with the teacher, "Please believe me, Mrs Lomas, I had no idea what was inside. I didn't know. I didn't open the box. You have to believe me."

Mrs Graff interrupted, "She's telling the truth, Mrs. Lomas. The… gift box… was delivered to the office. Jolene happened to walk by and I asked her to take it to your classroom. She couldn't possibly have had time to tamper with it and I know that Jolene would never pull a prank like this."

Tara shook her head vehemently, "I'm afraid this is more than a prank."

Mrs Graff raised her eyebrows, "It is, indeed, a horrible thing to do but I know that Jolene is not to blame."

Tara pursed her lips, "I accept that and I apologise to Jolene." She nodded at the girl, "Please return to class." Jolene gratefully accepted the apology and escaped from the situation. Tara turned to Mrs Graff, "I will need any information that you have on the delivery, please; which florist it came from or the company, anything at all." Tara stopped and tried to regain her equilibrium. "And now I must return to my class."

Mrs Graff nodded sympathetically, "I will see what I can find out."

Later that morning, after the box of flowers incident, Tara sat with her friend Lucy in the staff room drinking her coffee. "This break couldn't have come more quickly for me," finished Tara after explaining everything that had happened to her friend.

Lucy took another sip and said after a pause, "You know, Tara, you may be right. This could have something to do with Friend Finder. You need to tell Steve."

Tara shook her head slowly, "I can't. I honestly can't."

Lucy leaned forward, "You have to. Look, you haven't done anything wrong. For heaven's sake Steve will understand."

"I don't want to mess things up. It's been so good between us, telling him about Friend Finder could jeopardise everything."

Lucy was insistent and said firmly, "Tell him tonight." Tara looked unconvinced and more than a little worried. "Listen, it's probably just cyber bullying. Some sickos get their kicks out of terrorising others. But, if it isn't and you really do have some nutcase of a stalker, Steve needs to know. Either way, you can't go on like this."

Tara sighed disconsolately, "I hear what you're saying and I understand but just how do I tell him?"

"Just tell the truth. After he's heard about what happened today surely, he'll listen? It will be all right. I'm sure it will"

"I wish I could be as certain as you."

The end of the school day couldn't come quickly enough for Tara. Rumours were spreading around the school and the story of the so called prank had spread swiftly amongst staff and pupils alike. Fortunately, Tara was mostly a very popular English teacher with a reputation for being firm but fair, someone who always listened to students and had high expectations, which they usually reached. So, sympathy was with her and by the time four o'clock had come she had already received a massive amount of support, which buoyed her up.

When Tommy Porter heard about it he wondered if it was anything to do with James Treeves. All James would do was tap his nose and say, "Wait and see. It's for me to know and you to find out. You have to admit it was a blistering trick."

"I thought it was pretty nasty, really. I don't think she deserved it. I like Mrs Lomas. She's one of the better teachers."

"You're biased. You'll see… I'll drive her from this school."

Tara sighed with relief when the final bell rang out. As she packed up her equipment she began to imagine how she would broach the subject of internet chat buddies with Steve and prepared what she had to say a dozen different ways. This made her feel a little better about her confession that was to come.

She arrived home in something of a daze and chastised herself for hardly remembering the journey. It was as if she had driven like an automaton, again. "You need to get back in the right head space." She lectured herself aloud as she drew into her driveway. Tara banged the steering wheel in frustration. "I shouldn't have to do this," she exclaimed. She sat in the car a moment longer before steeling herself to get inside and do the normal usual things she would do after school. This was *not* going to affect her. She wouldn't allow it. Now the decision was made she felt better and left her vehicle.

Once inside, she fed the fish and Tilly before preparing the evening meal. She asked her Amazon Echo, Alexa, to play her 'My favourites' playlist and the music reverberated around the room. She sang along with some songs and her spirits lifted as she tried to vanquish the memory of that hideous 'gift'. She continued to rehearse in her head what she would say to Steve and decided it would all sound better after a delicious meal and so laid the table specially. She put some wine in the fridge to chill and started to peel some onions. Soon the kitchen filled with the tasty aroma of fried onions. Already, Tara was feeling more positive and the tantalising smell of the garlic and onions was making her feel hungry. This was good, she decided, as she hadn't felt much like eating lately.

10

SO FAR, TARA'S PLAN WAS working well. In excellent humour and feeling pampered Steve sat cuddled up with her on the sofa. They each had a glass of wine and the residue of Tara's culinary efforts lay on the table, which Steve had promised to clear.

After much prompting Tara had launched into the description of her day and the horrific flower delivery. Steve was shocked and attempted to comfort her and sympathised, "Darling, how awful for you. I can't imagine how you felt and in front of a class of kids, too. Just horrible. It seems like someone has really got it in for you. We are going have to find out and put a stop to these bizarre antics once and for all."

Tara snuggled into Steve enjoying his protective arm around her, "Lucy says it's just cyber bullying but…"

"But?" questioned Steve.

"The dead rat was real enough. I can't get the image out of my head with all those horrible wriggling maggots."

Steve kissed her head affectionately in comfort and thought for a moment, "You know, Lucy could be right. Some whack job getting a kick out of frightening you…. Maybe the rat was a student prank that came at the wrong time."

"Maybe…" Tara weighed her words carefully and changed her expression to one of sorrowful guilt before admitting, "Steve, I've done something really stupid."

Steve was all attention and sat upright and held Tara's face in his hands, "What? What is it? Come on, Hon, you know you can tell me absolutely anything."

Tara paused and bit her lip, "Can I really? I am so scared. I don't know how to tell you. Things have been so good between us recently. It's the one positive that's come from this. I don't want to spoil things." Her eyes filled up with unshed tears that threatened to course down her cheek. Tara twisted her face away from Steve's gentle grasp.

"Hey, Babe, come on… Now, you're frightening me."

Tara brushed away a tear and took Steve's hand. "You know I love you more than anything? And that I would never do anything to deliberately hurt you."

"Tara, what is this?" His tone was anxious and concerned.

She gulped, "It was something totally innocent and meant nothing." As she continued Steve began looking more unnerved. She took a deep breath, "I've been passing time on the Internet, chatting with old friends and…"

"So?"

Tara tried to justify herself, "You were never home and it was just a bit of fun." Steve's face seemed to darken and became more serious in the candlelight. "I joined a site called 'Friend Finder'. It was Lucy's idea. She thought it would help me while away the evenings when I was alone. I hunted for my old netball coach from school, Lee Powell. There were hundreds of suggestions, I found one that seemed to fit and let him friend me."

"Him?"

"Yes, a guy. It wasn't my coach, as I'd hoped, but someone else."

"A guy," repeated Steve. His tone had changed.

"Yes, I don't know him. We've never met or anything. It is all totally innocent, I promise you. Just some light hearted banter. But, now…."

"Now?"

"I'm wondering if all this is anything to do with him." An uncomfortable silence spread between them and Steve sat back. "I needed to fill the void … You weren't here… I was lonely…"

Steve rose and from his expression and demeanour he was deeply hurt, and said in disbelief, "So, you hooked up with some guy?"

"Steve, it was nothing. We've never met. We only talked. It was just a bit of fun. You have to believe me."

Steve walked toward the door, "I'm going for a walk to clear my head. I need to think."

Tara looked after him unable to speak as her throat was so constricted with anguish. She looked completely devastated. Her heart began racing again. It was a sickening feeling that was becoming all too familiar.

Steve walked through the suburban street. The dim glow of street lamps lit his way. There were few stars that night and the moon seemed shrouded in cloud only making a fleeting appearance when a gust of wind moved them on. It was as if he was on automatic pilot and unaware of his surroundings. He plodded on listening to the two voices in his head arguing about how he should feel and what he should do. One half of him reasoned that Tara hadn't done anything wrong. The other half suggested that her intentions might not have been so snow white. He knew it had been tough for her with him working all hours. She was bound to get lonely. His other voice pressed on, why couldn't she be satisfied with her women friends to talk to online?

The noise from a bar attracted his attention. He looked up at the name, 'Razzamatazz Bar'. Music filtered out into the street. The music was cheerfully exciting and folks were engaged with each other. It was busy with party revellers laughing and joking. He remembered he and Tara had visited the bar quite a few times in the past. Had he really walked that far? He decided it was just what he needed to buck him up. Another drink would make him feel better. Company around him would improve his mood. Maybe there was someone he knew in there? Steve crossed the road and entered the lively bar.

He pushed through the noisy throng toward the counter and waited in line to purchase a drink. He scanned the bar not recognising anyone but spotted a couple leaving a table in the window and hurried to grab the table and a seat.

The neon lights of the bar flashed its name outside on the street and invaded the window where Steve sat casting varying coloured shadows across his face. He downed his first drink and slung his coat around the seat to keep his place and returned to the counter. This time he carried two drinks back to the table.

He sat nursing his red wine and again slugged it down, before picking up the next one, which he sipped more slowly. His knuckles showed white on his fists as he gripped his glass. He sighed heavily and the sigh resembled more of a stifled sob than an outbreath.

Steve took out his mobile phone and scrolled down to his home number. He went to hit the call button but changed his mind as one voice in his head forced him to rethink. He returned to his screensaver, a picture of a smiling happy

Tara. His mouth twisted in anguish and he slammed it down. He rubbed his forehead in despair before draining his glass. Steve was looking more and more morose.

He stared across the bar and caught the attention of the bartender and signalled he wanted another drink. The barman finished polishing the glass he was wiping and set it on the counter and poured Steve a fresh drink.

Tara couldn't sit there being miserable any longer. She stared at the half full bottle of wine and was tempted to pour herself one but decided against it. She rose and paced the room. She didn't see eyes staring at her from the darkness watching her through the chink in the curtains. She glanced at the clock and murmured aloud, "Where the heck is he?"

Unable to stay in the house alone. The twisting churning in her stomach had become unbearable. She snatched her coat and picked up the car keys. She had to do something or try and find him.

Tara went to her car after securing the house and reversed out of their double garage. She zapped the overhead garage door, which closed behind her and drove down the street. Steve was nowhere to be seen.

So, she cruised onto the main road and headed for the car park nearest to the town's night life. 'I expect he's walked down town for a drink or company…' she thought. Suddenly, she cursed and thumped the steering wheel. "I should never have told him. Stupid, stupid, stupid!"

Tara drove into a vacant space, she had plenty to choose from, and parked. She pulled a hankie from her purse and blew her nose before pulling down the sun visor to reveal the mirror and checked her makeup. She applied some lipstick and dabbed a little concealer underneath her red eyes before getting out of the car.

She locked her vehicle, popped the keys in her bag and began to stroll through the half empty, badly lit car park. Her bag swung on her shoulder as she walked moving in time to the metronome click, clack of her steel tips on concrete. The sound echoed strangely in the night air. A soft breeze gently moved the ends of her scarf and although a warm night, Tara shivered. For some reason she felt uneasy and so she picked up her step.

As she approached the vehicle entrance, car headlights flooded on and blinded her. She shaded her eyes from the bright glare. A car engine revved and the vehicle moved toward her. Its lights continued to dazzle her and she stopped. The car edged closer, threatening her with a roar of repeated revs. Now, completely unnerved, Tara began to run.

She raced half stumbling with her heart pounding. Her breath was coming in short sharp gasps as she struggled to breathe. Panic had well and truly taken hold of her and she was hyperventilating. Tara reached the corner of the block and stopped. She held her side that hurt painfully with stitch and seemed unable to move on until the appearance of the car, which sidled up beside her, forced her to move. She pulled off her shoes and, in her confusion and terror, began to run.

The malevolent vehicle slowly cruised alongside her, taunting her, menacing her as she staggered along the road. Any moment Tara thought she would trip and go sprawling or that someone would leap from the car and take her captive. The terror she felt was unbearable. She began to sob as she turned the corner into the busy street with its rows of clubs, bars and cafés. The lights and music that blared out from various establishments made her feel better. This was where she should be in a street full of life, bright lights and people.

Tara grabbed another mouthful of air when she spotted the lights of the bar Razzamatazz with its jangling music and people spilling out onto the street. Tara got her second wind and sprinted to the door, which she pushed open and gratefully tumbled inside the busy bar. A young Scotsman caught her by the arm and steadied her to stop her falling, "Say, Lassie, are you all right? You look as if all Hell is on your tail."

Tara nodded and managed to blurt out, "I'm fine, thank you. Just had a bit of a scare." She leaned down and replaced her shoes before looking around the bar and spotted Steve at a table. She pushed her way through a crowd of people to reach him and flopped in the seat opposite him. Her hands shook as she placed her bag on the table and she trembled violently. "Oh, Steve, I'm so scared."

Steve was about to make some cutting remark but then he saw Tara's frightened face and could tell that she really was terrified. In spite of the alcohol he'd consumed he became alert and concerned, "What is it? What's happened?"

The words tumbled from Tara's lips interspersed with sobs, "After you left I knew I couldn't stay home. I had to find you. I couldn't let you leave like that." Tara gasped for breath and endeavoured to speak more calmly. She paused as she tried to steady her voice.

"And?" prompted Steve.

"A car... a car in the parking lot... Turned its headlights on me and followed me. It kept revving its engine like some rabid monster. Steve, I'm sure it's the same creep that's doing this."

Steve's tone was filled with compassion, "Oh, Baby..." he reached across and took her hands.

Tears had begun to spill down Tara's cheeks, "You know I love you more than anything."

"And I love you." He kissed her hands. "I got upset that's all. Jealous really. That should show you how much I care. I couldn't bear the thought of you sharing laughter with someone else." He paused as he gently stroked her face.

"But what about the car? What do we do? What if it's outside waiting for me?"

"Don't worry about that now. We'll work something out. Let me get you a drink. You need one." He smiled and tried to lighten things, "Why don't you go and freshen up? You've got a nose like Rudolph."

Tara gulped and half laughed. She was looking calmer. She picked up her bag and rose to go to the Ladies room. Steve pushed his way through the bar. People were arriving all the time to this very popular place. He purchased a drink for Tara leaving it on the counter while he examined his change.

Steve crossed to the juke box and selected a couple of CDs. He didn't see the person who'd just come in and was hovering by the bar; the person who dropped something in Tara's glass. The tablet fizzed for a moment dissolving rapidly. No one else appeared to notice either.

Happy with his song choices Steve retrieved the drink and moved back to his table as a tender love song began to play.

Tara had entered the quiet ladies' toilets and peered at herself in the mirror. She splashed some cool water on her face and patted it dry with a paper towel. She was now much composed. She began to fix her face, to hide the dark shadows under her eyes and her red nose before finally reapplying her lipstick. She fluffed up her hair and checked her appearance once more. She was feeling and looking much better. Ready to face the world and Steve, she stepped out and fought her way back to the table.

Eyes followed her every move and watched her as she sat.

She smiled brightly before taking a sip of her drink. "They're playing our song," she almost purred.

"I thought it might cheer you up. The song says it better than I ever could." Steve smiled back at her caressing her face with his eyes.

"Oh, Steve." Tara sighed happily and took another sip of her drink.

"First thing we'll do when we get home is call the police. I'm not having you threatened like this."

"What good will it do? They didn't do anything last time."

"No, but this time you've got a lead. Give them all the information you have on this Lee character. Tell them about the car that followed you. Stalking is recognised now as a serious business."

"It might not be him…."

"Then he won't mind, will he?"

Tara acknowledged this and looked lovingly at her husband's face, which began to blur. His voice became distorted and echoed around her head and mingled with the music. Tara couldn't understand what was being said. She could see Steve's mouth moving but his words were garbled as if underwater. She shook her head trying to clear her mind. The music drummed a beat in her head, which was now pounding. The cacophony of sound felt like someone was playing with the volume control turning it up and then down. In quick succession. She started to sweat feeling clammy and woozy.

Steve stopped as he noticed the change in her. She looked distant and disorientated, "Are you okay?"

Tara didn't understand and rose unsteadily to her feet. Her head was swimming. She grabbed her purse, I just need to splash some cold water on my face. I feel strange…."

"Then we must get back." He glanced at his watch. It was five minutes past ten. "It's probably the fright you had."

Tara was confused. She had no idea what Steve was saying and she thought she was going to be sick and needed to get to the restroom. She zig-zagged her way across the bar, through the crowds and struggled to get to the Ladies. It was as if she was drunk.

Tara stumbled into the loo and made it to the wash basin and turned on the tap. The water whooshed out sounding extraordinarily loud. She leaned over the sink holding on with one hand to stop the room spinning and splashed her face with cold water.

She was overcome with an urge to be sick. She clutched her shoulder bag and headed for an empty stall but collapsed on the floor inside. There was a surge of music as someone opened the door to the restroom and that someone approached the cubicle. Surgically gloved hands grasped Tara and pulled her inside. The door was bolted. Tara was now in a trance-like state and barely conscious. She groaned before she passed out completely.

The hands opened Tara's coat and stripped off her skirt, which was stuffed into the toilet bowl. Her purse was rifled through. The gloved hands removed Tara's lipstick and uncapped it. The word 'whore' was written in capitals on Tara's forehead.

Tara's car and house keys were removed from the bag and impressions taken of them in a flat tin that contained modelling clay. The keys were then replaced in Tara's bag.

The perpetrator froze suddenly as the door opened and a gang of giggling women entered. They talked and joked loudly. Still the stalker remained hushed and still until the gaggle of women had done what they had to and left. Once all was quiet the perp climbed onto the toilet seat and clambered over into the next stall and left quickly.

Steve continued to sit sipping his drink in the busy bar. His eyes were fixed on the door leading to the corridor where the toilets were situated. He twirled his glass, as he thought and then looked at his watch again. It was now ten thirty five. Tara had been gone for thirty minutes and in the light of all that had happened he was now very concerned. It was a packed bar and anyone could have been responsible for the threats against Tara.

Worry seeped through his body and a fluttering of panic manifested in his stomach. He rose and pushed his way through to the counter. The music belting out in the bar was particularly loud as someone had selected a number of heavy metal songs. He tried to attract the bartender and shouted above the music. "Excuse me…"

The tall barman finished serving two women, giggling hysterically, with their umpteenth cocktail and approached Steve, "Same again, mate? No? What can I get you?"

"No, no… My wife went into the ladies' toilets half an hour ago. She hasn't come out. Can someone check for me that she's all right?"

"Sure thing. I'll get the owner. He's out back."

Steve waited impatiently, tapping the counter with his fingers. A balding middle-aged man emerged from the back office and the barman went back to serving customers.

"What's the problem?" said the man brusquely.

Steve explained again and the owner nodded, "This way." Once in the passageway the music faded except for the thumping bass notes and drums beating out.

They entered the corridor and made their way to the toilets and the owner knocked on the Ladies' door. "Hello? Anyone in here?" he waited. There was no response so they entered. The owner looked around, "No one here, pal." The owner was embarrassed to be there and anxious to leave but Steve stopped him.

"Wait. Let's check the stalls."

They walked along the line of cubicles and pushed open the doors, which were all empty except for the last one that was locked. The owner and Steve looked at each other and Steve crouched down on the floor and peered under the door.

He saw Tara slumped there minus her skirt. He shouted out, the distress apparent in his voice, "Tara!" he turned to the owner, "Call nine, nine, nine."

But the owner objected, not wanting any trouble, "Now, hang on a minute…"

"Call nine, nine, nine, damn you! She's been assaulted."

In shock, the owner dialled the emergency services on his mobile phone. He had started to sweat and grumbled, "This could ruin my business."

"Damn your business. This is my wife. What sort of a reputation would you have if you did nothing?"

The owner nodded, he could see Steve was making sense. "Hello? Police? This is Razzamatazz Wine Bar. We have a serious incident here and need an ambulance immediately."

Steve instructed the owner, "You can't let anyone in here. She mustn't be disturbed."

"But…"

"No buts, if someone needs the loo, tell them to use the Gents."

"But…"

"You have to keep people away from here. This is a crime scene, now."

The owner looked toward the door, "I can hear the sirens. I'll go to meet them." Steve nodded and turned his attention back to Tara who was still unconscious.

Crowds of people stood outside the bar where two police cars were parked, their flashing lights reflected in the front window and mingled with the neon lights, which provided some sort of light show spectacle. Partygoers and customers had left the now silent bar in a reasonably subdued fashion. Each person from the premises was being checked out by two cops who stood at the door. They verified customers IDs and noted down their personal details.

Paramedics examined Tara who was now conscious but confused and shivering miserably. Steve watched as the doctor, also there, checked out her vitals.

The bartender was at the bar being interviewed by a female officer who had introduced herself as Cheryl Dixon. "I can't tell you much," insisted the barman. "I didn't even notice the woman going into the toilets."

"What about her husband?"

"He's been sitting there most of the night."

"He didn't visit the restrooms?"

"No. He just walked a path to the counter and back to his seat. Nowhere else."

"Are you positive about that?"

"Absolutely. He has been in constant view all night."

"You can say that categorically? Even with this amount of people present?"

"Yes. His table is reflected in the mirror behind the bar and I was keeping an eye on him. I won't serve anyone who has had too much to drink."

"Was he drunk?"

"No, but he'd had a few."

The questioning continued. The frustrated owner of Razzamatazz was receiving an equal grilling from another officer.

Officer Dixon had all she needed from the bartender and crossed to where Tara had been brought and now sat. "How are you feeling?"

"Sick, groggy. My head's swimming. I can't remember anything. Everything's a blank."

Cheryl Dixon turned to the doctor, "What have you found? Have you anything we can use?"

The doctor stood up, "We'll know more when I get these blood samples back to the lab but off the cuff I'd say it looks like GHB."

"The date rape drug?"

"I'm afraid so. But she has no need to worry about pregnancy or STDs. She hasn't been raped, just grossly humiliated."

"Maybe the perp was interrupted," said Officer Dixon.

"Maybe," agreed the doctor. "But for the moment it's, as I said, an assault with a bucket load of degradation."

Steve who had been listening protested, "But that's just as horrific."

Tara found her voice, "Too right. What are you going to do about it?"

Cheryl Dixon was calm and reassuring, "Mr Lomas, I suggest you get her home. She should take some time off work. This has been a harrowing experience. We'll be in touch as soon as we know anymore. We've taken samples of the lipstick print but it looks like they used her own lipstick to write the obscenities and the case is clear of prints except for Tara's."

"I'm in no fit state to drive and neither is Tara so, how do we get back?"

"It's all right, my colleague and I will give you a lift." She helped Tara to her feet and they proceeded to the bar's entrance. Tara needed steadying as she swayed from the effects of the drug.

Nobody spotted the hooded figure standing on the other side of the street in a shop doorway. The street lamp was out and as revellers passed, the person stepped back into the shadows and held up a mobile phone. The camera took a burst of pictures and filmed Tara leaving the wine bar with her husband and the police. There was a snort of derision mingled with satisfaction that Tara looked violated and without dignity.

As Tara was helped into the police car. The figure stepped out from the shop doorway and marched off down the street in the opposite direction.

11

STEVE STEPPED INTO THE BEDROOM with a cup of tea for Tara. He pulled back the curtains to let the daylight in and reassured her, "I've squared it with the school and told them you won't be in for a few days, maybe more. I've explained it all to Lucy who is really concerned about you and she promises to stop by. When I don't know."

"Thank you." Tara's voice was husky. She took the tea from Steve and sipped it. "When is it going to stop, Steve? I am really frightened."

Steve nodded sympathetically, "I know, Sweetie." He paused as he struggled with his own feelings then continued, "I have to go to work now but I won't be late. You rest up and don't answer the door to anyone. Promise me?"

"What about Lucy?"

"Well, obviously if Lucy turns up you can let her in. But don't open the door to anyone you don't know. Stay put. You'll have Tilly for company. I will bring your car home. I've got a workmate picking me up. He's going to drop me off at the car park. I've got your keys. Oh, and I'd stay offline, too, just to be on the safe side. I'll leave the answer-phone on so you can monitor any calls. Now, will you be okay?" Tara nodded. "When you're up to it, tell the cops about this Lee character. I hate to leave you and I won't be late. I promise." Steve took her in his arms and hugged her before kissing her goodbye. The fear and worry was etched in his face. He walked to the door and blew her a kiss, as a car tooted its horn outside. "Now lock up after me." Tara managed a lame smile and then he was gone.

Tara sighed heavily, "This won't knit the baby a bonnet," she said aloud. It was one of her mother's favourite sayings and made her feel close to her. How she wished her mum was alive now. However, she knew it was no good moping around. She had to do something. Staying in bed with or without the TV playing would just make her feel worse. Besides she had work to do. "Come on, lazy. Get up!" Tara gave herself a stiff talking to. It made her feel less alone. "Besides," she quipped to herself, "What better class of conversation than with oneself?" She even managed a smile.

Tara rose and had a quick shower. The water invigorated her and made her feel very much alive. However, she was still a little confused. No matter how hard she tried to remember what happened she couldn't. "That way madness lies," she murmured. But feeling more refreshed she dried herself off with a warm fluffy towel, which was soothing and put her 'comfies' on, as she called them; a pair of elasticated waist jogging bottoms and a sweatshirt. She towel dried her hair deciding to let it dry naturally, finished her tea and trotted downstairs.

Firstly, she checked all the doors and windows ensuring they were secure before stumbling to the kitchen and making a couple of slices of toast. The smell of the bread browning always made her feel hungry. Once it popped up she slathered it with butter and a dollop of marmalade. Just the look of it set her taste buds going.

As she munched her eyes lit on her PC but Steve's words reverberated around her head, "Stay offline, too, just to be safe." Tara crossed to the computer and pulled out the power plug. The action made her feel better, more decisive and assertive. She glanced at a pile of books that needed marking but decided she couldn't face them yet and sat on the couch. Tilly immediately jumped on her lap and began to purr. It was so comforting to hear her furry friend purr and stroking the cat soothed her. She switched on the telly and became involved in watching an old black and white movie that was on the Talking Pictures channel starring Cary Grant and Ingrid Bergman.

She soon became immersed in the action. 'Notorious' was a dramatic tale full of drama, romance, sinister characters and unlikely plot developments, Tara thought it was one of Hitchcock's best early films. There were some great scenes of unbearable tension in the second half of the movie, which Tara had reached. She was sitting on the edge of her seat when the doorbell rang.

Tara stifled a scream and physically flinched in alarm at the sudden noise. Tilly who was fast asleep mewed plaintively as Tara removed her from her lap. Tara edged tentatively toward the front door and called out, "Who is it?" before peering through the peephole.

A delivery man in uniform stood at the door with what appeared to be a very large box wrapped in gold foil. "Delivery for... Tara Lomas." The man read the card.

Tara dithered. She didn't want to open the door and called out, "Just leave it on the step." The man shrugged and stooped down leaving the box on the floor. Tara went to the window and pulled back the curtain to watch as the man placed the package down and returned whistling to his van. Tara scrutinised the van. It was plain white with no transfers or logo so it was hard to say where it had come from. She watched the van pull away and moved back to the front door. Cautiously, she drew back the chain and gingerly opened the door, snatched up the box and hurriedly shut and secured the door once more. Her hands were shaking and her heart pounded.

Tara took the gift into the living room and pulled back the gold wrap to reveal an oversized box of chocolates. She smiled, lifted the lid to examine the various flavours and centres and set the box on the desk before picking up the phone and dialling Steve's number. He answered almost immediately. "Tara?"

"You really do know my weakness," cooed Tara.

"Sorry? What do you mean?"

"The chocolates, silly!" She picked up a heart shaped strawberry one and went to pop it in her mouth.

"What chocolates? Tara, what are you talking about?"

Tara stopped and threw down the sweet in horror, "What? Steve are you serious?"

"Deadly. Don't touch them. You haven't eaten any, have you?"

"No, but I nearly did."

"What? Thank God, you didn't. Who brought it?"

"Some guy just delivered it."

"Does it say where it came from?"

Tara picked up the wrapping and looked it over, "No, there's nothing. Not even a store name."

"Remember everything you can about the guy, the van he drove, anything at all and call the cops. I'll be home as soon as I can."

"Right," Tara's hand was shaking as she replaced the receiver. Firstly, she double checked all the doors, locks and windows. They were secure. All the time she talked to herself, "Medium height, short dark, brown hair. Um...

medium build... Think Tara, think." She rummaged in her bag and pulled out Cheryl Dixon's card and dialled the number, "Hello? Officer Dixon?"

Tara poured out her heart, talking at speed, so much so, Cheryl Dixon had to urge her to slow down. The officer took down as much detail as possible and managed to extract even more information about the van and driver before saying, "I'll be with you in about thirty minutes. Keep all your doors locked."

Tara waited anxiously for Officer Dixon and her husband Steve to arrive and as advised she kept all windows and doors locked tightly. Tara just couldn't settle and half expected her tormenter to begin calling her again. She hesitated, should she pull out the phone plug? She wouldn't turn on her mobile phone as she dreaded the abusive texts that had plagued her.

Tilly could feel her mistresses' nervousness and as Tara paced Tilly rubbed herself around her legs and meowed plaintively. Tara eventually succumbed to her cat's attentions and stooped down to fuss her. "You know, Tilly, sometimes I wish you were a dog, who would growl and bark if there was an intruder or someone prowling around the house." It seemed Tilly didn't think much of this idea and padded across to her dish and mewed again. Tara took her dish and filled it with some Iams cat biscuits. Tilly purred in appreciation and tucked in.

Tara sighed, and walked to the window and looked out across the drive and her front garden. She couldn't understand why someone would target her so viciously in this way. Was it this so called online friend? It was certainly strange all her problems had started since she had joined Friend Finder. She glanced across at her computer lying idle and switched off. She wasn't at all tempted to log on. Far better to live on in ignorance than be scared witless again, she thought.

Tara drew closer to the window and looked longingly at the road outside. It was a perfect day for running and she missed her early morning jogs. There was a gentle breeze, the sun was rising in the Simpson sky with its mottling of clouds, as if an artist had splattered white paint on a blue canvas.

Tara felt imprisoned. She could understand how prisoners could go stir crazy. She was getting close to that feeling herself. "Do something, Tara," she told herself sternly. "You need to be occupied." She stared at the pile of exercise books on the counter that needed marking but they didn't appeal. She needed total concentration for that. Magazines lay on the coffee table but they didn't interest her either, nor the latest paperback by Dean Koontz an author she loved to read.

Tara plonked herself on the settee and picked up a Sudoku puzzle book. 'ideal,' she thought. 'I can pick it up and put it down and with a bit of luck I might even get involved in it.' But, her eyes kept wandering to the clock and she watched the hands click around but even time seemed to be on go slow.

In despair, Tara lay on the sofa and closed her eyes.

Officer Dixon pursed her lips, her eyes registered sympathy with Tara, now standing close to Steve who had a protective arm around her as she wrapped up her report. She indicated the box of chocolates, "We'll run a check on these, it may take a few days, In the meantime, I recommend you stay home and off the internet." Tara rolled her eyes. "A police patrol car will be on duty day and night, cruising the area, just in case. I'm also putting in a request for a permanent police guard until we've caught whoever is doing this." Cheryl Dixon waited for a response.

Steve prompted Tara, "Darling?"

Tara finally nodded, "I understand what you're saying. I do. But in the meantime, I'm not just waiting around for something else to happen. I'm going to get motion sensor lights fitted outside. If someone prowls around the house, we'll know about it. And so, will they."

"Excellent idea," said Officer Dixon.

"I think however, I will do the buying and get a professional to do all the fitting. I don't want you placed in any danger;" said Steve.

"What about video cameras? That'd work," said Tara.

"Yes, we'll fix this," Steve agreed, as he pulled Tara in closer and tighter. "I'll get onto it right away."

Officer Dixon was satisfied with this and left the Lomas House. It was only after she'd gone that Tara remembered that she hadn't breathed a word about Lee Powell. She made up her mind she'd mention it another time. However, she was still reluctant to do this as she firmly believed that it was nothing to do with him.

True to his word Steve trawled the internet for Security firms, checking their website validity, Companies House, researching their backgrounds, before looking for genuine recommendations. He then progressed to sitting on the phone to find which one of his shortlisted firms could do the work almost straight away or better.

It was a long haul.

An official from Safe Call, the winning company, who fitted their security lights and cameras, handed Tara his work sheet for her to sign. "That's it, Mrs Lomas. If a mouse as much as washes its whiskers the floodlights will come on. And the mailman better smile when he delivers, it will all be caught on camera." Tara beamed in delight and signed the form with a flourish.

There was a new spring in her step as she felt so much better. She felt more secure at home and things with Steve were improving all the time. Tara believed that something positive and good had come from something negative and bad. She hoped it would prove to be a turning point in this hideous business.

Almost like a child with a new toy she was keen to test the effectiveness of the installation even to the point of putting Tilly outside on the front step and watching the indoor monitor to see what the cat did and if the equipment was as good as promised.

Tilly was not so happy and stood on her hind legs pawing the door and mewing for it to be opened. Tara was gratified that both the sound and pictures were transmitted inside and the alert indicating movement had been triggered. Tara laughed in delight and opened the door to readmit Tilly, who ran in with her tail twitching. She didn't like being put out and made her feelings known. This only made Tara giggle even more. She crouched down and fussed her pet, "You know, Tilly you can always let yourself in through the cat flap," but Tilly was not in a forgiving mood and walked away effectively turning her back on Tara, who shrugged and shook her head bemused. "Guess you won't be wanting any treats, then?" she said aloud. Tilly took no notice and proceeded to wash herself.

Tara walked to the cupboard and removed a small container of cat treats, which she shook. Upon hearing this Tilly changed her mind and ran to her mistress, her tail straight up in the air and fussed around Tara's legs. Tara rewarded her with a handful of Dreamies, which Tilly proceeded to eat.

Tara sighed, for the moment it seemed to her that all was well in the Lomas household.

James rang the bell at seven o' clock prompt. He was at Tommy Porter's house whose mother opened the door. She called out, "Tommy, James is here," before turning to James and smiling, "He's upstairs in his room. Go on up." James pounded up the stairs two at a time and Mrs Porter returned to the sitting room.

James went into Tommy's room. He was already at the computer. "Have you got it?"

James grinned and waved the stick, "Have I ever?" He looked back at the bedroom door. "Perhaps we should put the lock on, just in case."

"We'll be all right. Mum won't disturb us."

James raised an eyebrow. "There's always a first time."

"Okay." He slipped off his seat and slid the small bolt across. "Anyway, I suppose it's best in case my snooping sister comes in."

"Exactly," said James settling himself down next to Tommy who was now back at his computer. He inserted the offered flash drive into a USB port and they waited for the icon to appear on screen before clicking on it to open it.

"Funny thing to call it... Play..." said Tommy. They waited for the file to open. Their mouths opened in surprise as what appeared to be family photographs filled the screen.

"Scroll down. It must be further on."

"Or else, we've got the wrong memory stick," said Tommy.

As the page rolled up both boys' expressions turned to one of horror as hundreds of pictures of nude young children appeared on screen. The two friends looked at each other, "What the heck have we got here?" said James.

Tommy continued to scroll through the images that became more lewd and disturbing. There were some video symbols on the page. Tommy clicked onto one, which revealed Ken Ley engaging in a sexual act with what appeared to be a little girl of about six. He looked at his friend, James, whose eyes were wide in shock and disbelief, "What the hell have we stumbled on here?"

James finally came to and rubbed his hands in glee, "A nice little earner, Tommy boy. Better than exam papers. We'll have this pervert in our pocket for good."

"How?"

"Blackmail."

"No, James. We need to report this. These are just little kids. It's horrible and it's wrong."

12

THE ENVELOPING DARKNESS OF NIGHT fell over the city. On the other side of town in a dimly lit sitting room brimming with shadows, as the drapes had been drawn against the evening and the invading moonlight, was an odd scene. Under the window was an altar, covered in a purple cloth. Incense burned and an overhead soft light bathed a shrine with an ethereal light. Two fake candles with an electric flickering flame were placed at each end. There were photographs of Skye, Lee Powell and the children in happier times. Rose petals were scattered on the cloth and a small posy of fresh flowers was placed at the front with a wedding and engagement ring tied with a tiny red ribbon and a pottery heart.

Skye sat stock still, on a stool in front of the home made memorial. She stared longingly at a picture of Lee before reaching out and picking it up. Her eyes scrutinised every part of his face before she traced her finger around his lips and kissed them. Her eyes filled with tears and she choked back a sob.

The doorbell rang breaking her daily ceremony. Skye sniffed back her tears and was suddenly alert. She tiptoed to the door with its peephole and peered at the person that was interrupting her ritual.

She saw Lee's friend, Mike standing there with a crazy grin on his face and a raised eyebrow.

Skye yelled out, "Go away! I don't want to see anyone." She leaned against the door struggling with her emotions.

Mike gently tapped on the door and used his most persuasive tone, "Come on, Skye. Let me in. I bring gifts." He said trying to chivvy her up. Skye turned back and fixed her eye to the spy-hole again. She saw Mike waving a bottle of wine and a giant pizza box.

Skye was ever suspicious. She brushed away her burgeoning tears and demanded, "Why? Why do you want to see me?"

"To catch up, have a chat. Come on! I can't pig out on my own. The wine I can drink but this pizza will get cold." He added in a sing-song voice, "It's your favourite… Pepperoni and pineapple."

Skye sniffed and said, "They don't make that. Anyway, my favourite's mushroom."

"Got that, too."

"Oh, hell."

"It's one of those new sliced ones with a different topping on every slice, so I knew there would be one you liked."

Skye hurriedly wiped her eyes and removed the chain from the door. She took a deep breath and opened it. Mike strolled in and blinked in the lack of light. He set the pizza and wine down on the dining table. "It's dark in here. You should open the curtains, let some light in." Mike strode to the window and took hold of one curtain.

Skye snapped, "Leave it! I like it this way."

"Or at least put a light on…" But as Mike looked up he saw the bulb had been removed from the central ceiling rose. He bit back the words ready to fall from his lips and forced a smile.

Mike's eyes gradually adjusted in the gloom and he saw the shrine set up to Lee. He indicated it and shook his head sadly, "Come on, Skye. You can't carry a torch for Lee forever."

Skye's expression froze. Her voice became petulant, "Marriage is for life. Till death us do part. Isn't that what they say? That's what we vowed, in church, before God. Doesn't that mean anything?"

"Not today. Marriage lasts until the love flies out the door. Come on, Skye. You need to get a life, and move on. Forget him."

"I can't. He's got my babies."

Mike dragged out a chair from the table and sat. He opened the pizza box. "Got a corkscrew? And glasses?"

Unable to help herself Skye laughed, "It's a screw top."

"So, it is. Come on, cheer up! Let's dig in." Mike helped himself to a large slice of vegetable pizza with pesto. The smell was tantalising. Skye put two glasses on the table and took a slice of mushroom topped pizza.

Mike decided to take his lead from Skye. He didn't want to push her. He would let her talk. Skye returned with glasses, which were filled and plates that caught fragments of melted cheese that dripped from each slice.

They sat in silence, munched on their chosen portion and sipped their wine. In Mike's eyes Skye appeared to be gradually loosening up and becoming less guarded.

He winked at her and she flared up, "What's all this about? You didn't come to see me about my health."

"I told you. I've been concerned."

"Why? I don't understand why…" Skye protested.

"I've always liked you, Skye. You know that. It could have been us if you hadn't met Lee. I just wanted to make sure you were all right. Nothing more. No hidden agenda."

Skye sniffed and studied Mike's face, an odd glint in her eye. They continued eating in silence.

Tara sat at her desk, going through bills and writing cheques. She sighed heavily. Although concentrating on paperwork took her mind off her problems it also exhausted her. She leaned back in the chair and stretched, yawning loudly. "You need a break," she told herself.

She foraged in an open bag, full of pick and mix sweets that sat on the desk hunting for a piece of chocolate fudge. She found one, popped it in her mouth and groaned in pleasure at the taste, as it almost melted in her mouth.

Savouring the chocolate, Tara rose and moved to the window and peered out at the poorly lit street. The phone rang. Tara jumped in alarm and shivered. Her heart was pounding, she stared at the instrument and its offending ring and waited for the answer phone to kick in.

"Tara, pick up. It's Lucy."

Tara breathed a sigh of relief and dashed to the phone. She answered, "Lucy! Thank goodness. I'm about to go out of my mind. Can't go for my morning jogs. I'm a prisoner." Tilly rubbed up against her leg and enjoyed Tara's attentions as she reached down and scratched Tilly behind her ears. "If it wasn't for Tilly I don't know what I'd do."

"Too bad you don't have a dog. At least you could take it for a walk. That'd be safe if it was a big dog!"

Tara eyed the bag of chocolate and sweets on her desk, "I could use some exercise. I'm so bored I've turned to comfort foods."

"That's not good. Listen, dig out your favourite fitness DVD and I'll stop in after school, tomorrow. We'll get you moving again."

Tara smiled brightly. "I'll be here, heck I'm not going anywhere. It'll stop me going stir crazy. Thank you! It'll be lovely to see you. Now, tell me what's been happening at school?"

The giant pizza in the box had almost been eaten. There was one slice and a few crumbs left, together with bits of crust that the topping hadn't stretched to, which remained. The bottle of wine was a quarter full. Mike shared the rest between him and Skye who was now visibly more relaxed. The food and drink had loosened her tongue and enabled her to open up. Mike was taking full advantage to learn everything he could from Skye in order to help Lee.

He asked casually, "Why is it you think that Lee's dating? He hasn't got time with work and the children. He hardly ever goes out; rarely sees me and is married to his work and the kids." Skye snorted derisively. It was clear she didn't believe him.

Mike continued, "Like I said, he only just manages to see me once in a while. I'm his best friend. I'm his 'date', if you can call it that. If you should be mad at anyone, be mad at me."

Skye responded quickly, "Shows how much you know. He's got someone, all right, Tara Lomas."

"Never heard of her."

"He met her on Friend Finder."

"Oh, her! You've got that wrong. He's never even met her. She's a chat friend or was, not anymore."

Skye paused and looked in disbelief at Mike. She downed a mouthful of her drink. She looked a little tipsy as she rose somewhat unsteadily. She appeared to have to focus on her words as she spoke. With her glass in her hand she crossed to her bedroom door and beckoned Mike, "Is that so? Come with me."

Mike attempted to turn the chat that had suddenly become serious into a joke, "Skye, this is so sudden. I don't sleep on first dates…."

Skye was insistent, "I'll prove it." She pushed open her bedroom door and went inside. "Come on."

Mike rose looking puzzled but followed her inside. He tried to disguise the shock he felt when he stared around the room. His eyes were first drawn to a large cork board on one wall. It was covered with photos of Tara, phone numbers and addresses; the name and address of the school where she taught and her home. It was clear from the pictures that they had been taken without permission. There were shots taken in quick succession that had been captured from outside her house. Some were of her standing in her living room; others in her garden and on the road and on the paths where she jogged. Skye had defaced some pictures with a red pen, one had a large knife with a serrated edge sprouting blood droplets attacking Tara's eyes. Another had completely torn out the woman's eyes.

Mike shivered. He suppressed his distaste and tried to appear unfazed. He gazed at a different wall where there was another memo board that was smothered in vile messages full of spite and venom. Her computer that sat in the corner had 'post it' notes with email addresses and passwords stuck all around the screen. Next to the PC was a pile of photographs of Tara and a few computer print-outs of all her details together with copies of timetables of her daily routines.

Mike was stunned. It took him a while to find his voice as he tried to take in exactly what he had walked into. His voice betrayed his utter shock, "Skye, what is this?"

"It's her. The bitch." Skye almost spat out the words. Her eyes glittered dangerously.

Mike tried to calm what appeared to be becoming an alarming situation, "No, Skye. You've got it all wrong."

Skye stared sullenly at Mike but said nothing as he picked up the photos of Tara and studied them. He turned to Skye, "She reminds me of someone … Now, who?" He paused, then clicked his fingers, "Got it! Jan, it's Jan Bernard."

"Another whore." Skye's face had taken on a malevolent light.

"Skye, you have to give this up before it gets serious. You don't want to be hauled off by the cops. If they caught sight of all this you'd never get your kids back."

Skye tried to impress her view on Mike, "No, you don't understand. It's all her fault. She's poisoned Lee against me… I'm just getting my own back."

"Skye, listen to me, you need help. Professional help."

"What do you suggest I do? Hire a hit man?" she said sarcastically.

There was a lull in the conversation as they both surveyed each other. "Mike broke the silence, "I've always been fond of you. You know that. Don't do this to yourself. You can get better. Look, I'll help you."

"What makes you such an expert?" Skye retorted angrily. "You've never been able to hold down a serious relationship. Your last girlfriend told me you were off your head. She called you nuts." A muscle in Mike's cheek began to pulse. He slowly moved toward her as Skye continued, "You think I'm mad, delusional…"

Mike did his best to placate her, "No, no. I know you're hurt. I can see your pain. You're heartbroken and that pain is eating you up. It's making you do things you wouldn't do normally."

"I want her to suffer. Suffer like I have. I loved Lee, Mike. Loved him like my heart would burst and he does this to me, parades some tart all over the internet." The pent up emotion burst out and she began to cry.

Mike pushed a stray strand of hair from her eyes and said gently, "It's not like that. He stayed with you through it all, the drugs and drink…"

"I'm clean now," she said softly. Her rage appeared to have abated.

"Yes, but after the outburst with the knife when you nearly killed him and the kids…" Mike tried to reason with her.

"I'm different now. I've changed. Promise me, you'll talk to him. Please, Mike, promise me."

"I'll do what I can."

"I want to see my kids, please." Skye was hanging onto her glass so hard that the glass shattered. Red wine spilled down her front and mingled with her blood, which dripped onto the floor.

"Quick get into the bathroom. Hold your hand under the tap; you need to flush any glass fragments away. Hurry, now. I'll see to this." He indicated the broken glass and red stains on the carpet.

Skye weaved her way to the en-suite bathroom. Mike could hear the sound of the water whooshing into the sink. He moved toward the kitchen but stopped and paused in front of the computer screen to study the pictures of Tara. He picked up a copy of her details and examined them before stuffing them into his pocket. Mike looked at one of Tara's timetable of activities and after a moment he pocketed that, too. His face took on an odd expression and he chose one of the photos from the pile and secreted it into his inside pocket before hurrying to the kitchen.

Skye was running her hand under the cold water tap. She could see the lacerations the glass had made to her palm and had to probe to get one sharp shard from her finger. She flinched at the stinging pain. The accident and action of the water had the effect off sobering her up. "She called out, "Mike! What now?"

Mike returned carrying a cleaning rag and the carpet solvent, Resolve. He went into the bathroom and put the items on the washstand. He took Skye's hand and winced as he noted the gash and cuts on her palm.

Skye indicated the Resolve and quipped, "Hope that's not for me."

"No, it's for the carpet." He managed a smile. "Have you got a first aid kit?"

Skye indicated with her head, "In the cupboard."

Mike opened the bathroom cabinet and took out the box with a red cross and began to minister to her damaged hand. He tried again to reason with her, "Please, Skye, let me help you. I know a really good counsellor… If we can get you through this you can work toward getting permission to see your children again."

She shook her head, "They cost a bundle and I can't afford it."

"If you want to see your kids you'll need proof of a sound state of mind… It will make a difference. I promise you. Let's talk about this." His voice, in an attempt to soothe her became softer. "Think about what I've said."

Mike tenderly stroked Skye's face and they locked eyes.

Tara was feeling agitated and depressed. Being cooped up like this and under surveillance twenty-four seven was grating on her nerves. She nervously paced the room before she sat and stared blankly into space. Her right knee seemed to have a life of its own as it constantly jiggled as if in time to some heavy rock song.

Tara tried to snap out of her anxious state and jumped up. She picked up a framed photograph of her and Steve at a friend's wedding and lovingly traced her finger around Steve's face before replacing it.

Tara couldn't understand what had suddenly made her so nervous. It was as if she was being forced to walk a tightrope blind folded without any circus training. She felt helpless and she didn't like the feeling. It was not like her to act as if she was some sort of shrinking violet. "That has to change!" Feeling stronger she spoke aloud, "I will **not** be a victim. I refuse to be cowed by some perverted psycho." Somehow, saying the words out loud and forcibly, instantly made her feel better.

Across town Mike slurped the last of his morning cup of tea and glanced at the clock. He knew he had to make a move or he'd be late for work. He hurriedly donned his coat, grabbed his briefcase, phone and car keys. He stopped momentarily as he deposited his mobile in his pocket. There was something else in there. He pulled out a wad of paper and a photograph, wondering why on earth he had picked them up. He then reasoned that it was an example of evidence of Skye's behaviour, which he knew was totally aberrant. He studied Tara's photo and the paper printout a moment before shrugging and tossing the items onto his table. He looked at the clock again and with a mild expletive ran to the door and out from his apartment.

13

TILLY MEWED AND GAZED UP at her mistress.

Tara, with no one else present, addressed her cat, "It's no good. I can't stay here. I've had enough. I refuse to be housebound. It's like waiting for something to happen." She looked at her cat, "It's all right for you, Tilly. You don't have anything to worry about. You can come and go as you please."

Tilly watched Tara's face and blinked her eyes as if she understood before she yawned and settled down to sleep. Tara swore in frustration and dashed to the stairs, which she ran up two at a time.

Once in her bedroom she sorted through her exercise gear and selected a comfortable T shirt. She pulled on her sweat pants and matching jacket, scraped back her hair into a ponytail and used a scrunchy to tie it back. Next, she chose a pair of comfortable running shoes and laced them up before diving out of the bedroom and down the stairs.

Tara rummaged in a drawer for her head phones and iPod, which she clipped to her belt. She looked out of the window. The day was bright and sunny so she snatched up her sunglasses and began her warm up regime in the kitchen.

Tilly disturbed by all the activity jumped off the settee and wrapped herself around Tara's legs. "Oh, no you don't. Come on you, out! Get some fresh air. I need to clear my head and you need some exercise." Tara scooped up Tilly and opened the front door and set her down. "Now scoot!"

Tilly was reluctant to scamper off and dived around the back and into the garden. Tara shook her head in dismay. She seemed to know that once she left the house Tilly would be back in through the cat flap. She closed the front door firmly behind her and began to jog down the front path.

A patrol car was passing just as she turned into the road. Officer Shay Connor stopped and wound down his window, "Mrs Lomas, we don't advise you to leave the house."

Tara swore softly under her breath but smiled and crossed to the vehicle. "I'm just going for a short run. I'm going crazy stuck inside. It's a bright sunny day. Nothing's going to happen."

"All the same, I have my orders. It's better to be safe."

Tara could feel her hackles rising, "You can't stop me. I'm not under arrest."

"Then, I'll have to come with you."

Tara was now determined to get her way and exclaimed, "Do what you like." She pulled on her head-phones and turned up the volume and began to jog lightly down the street. The police car cruised alongside her.

Neither noticed a dark Vauxhall Astra that had pulled into the road and parked in the shade across the street from the Lomas house. The driver wasn't clearly visible behind the tinted windscreen. The driver's hands had put on a pair of surgical gloves. The rubber was snapped to make a satisfying sound and a lengthy sigh escaped the driver's lips.

Tara relished the freedom to run and entered the local park. She drank in the fresh air and sprinted off on the path that twisted around the lake. Officer Connor watched her and followed on foot at a discreet distance. Tara inhaled deeply, she felt brighter, better and alive again. She put in an extra spurt and passed other runners. Once she reached the dark clump of trees she stopped, turned and wisely ran back the way she had come and soon met officer Connor. "See, I told you it would be okay." Without waiting for a reply. She sprinted down the bank, in through a small gate and back onto the street.

Shay Connor hurried after her and got back in his car. He continued to cruise alongside Tara as she jogged back home. He parked up outside her house and settled down to watch and wait.

Tara swept into the house and leaned forward breathing hard. She was out of puff and struggled to get her breathing back on an even keel. "Phew, I need to get out again and soon. I'm out of practice." Tara tossed her keys on the stand in the hallway and walked into the living room. She was just about to switch on some music when there was a thud upstairs. Tara froze and listened. She called out, "Hello? Who's there? Steve is that you?"

There was no answer. Tara listened intensely. She held her breath afraid to move. There was a tinkling crash as if something had been dropped on the bathroom floor. The sound galvanised her into action. She gulped and raced into the kitchen. Tara tugged open the cutlery drawer. Her hand was shaking as she studied the array of knives in the compartment and she selected a particularly sharp, long bladed carving knife. Tara grasped the knife and held it in front of her. She cautiously moved back into the living room.

Tara tiptoed to the foot of the stairs. They seemed to stretch up farther than she logically knew they did. Tara called out again. "Hello? Anyone there?" There was nothing. The air was thick with tension and Tara filled with rage at the intrusion. All of her angst multiplied and mounted. Her hand gripped the handle of the blade so hard that her knuckles showed white. Her fury spurred her on and she slowly began to mount the stairs holding the knife in front of her. She hissed, "Damn you, whoever you are. You'll not get the better of me!"

Tara edged her way carefully up the stairs wincing as one creaked. It unnerved her further and her anxiety grew in the way she handled the carver. Her mouth was set in a grim hard line. Her face was a study of pain and anger. It seemed an eternity before she reached the landing. She inched toward the bathroom door and placed her hand on the knob. Tara took a deep breath and yanked the door open. Tilly flew out with a loud meow, brushed past her legs and raced down the stairs.

Tara let out an involuntary scream as the cat rushed past. She picked up a small trinket box that had fallen from the window sill by the toilet onto the floor. The bathroom window was wide open and the curtain stirred in the breeze.

Tara murmured to herself, "So, that's how you got in."

Still shaking, Tara closed the window firmly. She looked around the bathroom and pulled back the shower curtain… nothing. Feeling slightly better she left the bathroom and closed the door. Her breathing became more even and she made her way back down stairs. But she puzzled about the open window as she was certain that all of the windows in the house had been secured. "If Tilly had entered through the cat flap she couldn't have got into the bathroom through a closed door. She must have come in from outside," she reasoned.

Tara looked down at the knife in her hand. "Best get you back to the kitchen drawer," she said and walked into the kitchen where Tilly began dancing around her feet, rubbing against her emitting her pretty, multi-toned mew that said she was hungry. "All right, all right I know." Tara went to pick up Tilly's bowl by the back door but it wasn't there. Tara's eyes searched around the floor. "Where's your dish, Tilly?" The cat continued to press for food. Tara couldn't see it and then gave a gasp of surprise as she spotted it on the counter top by the bread bin. "What's it doing there? I must be going mad." Tara picked it up and crossed to the vegetable rack expecting to see the pack of dried cat food on the top tier. That wasn't there, either. "Where's Daddy put your kitty chow? Hmmm!"

Tara opened the pantry door and saw the bag of Iams inside on the floor. "I am definitely not myself today." She retrieved it and filled the cat's bowl before placing it on the floor. Immediately, Tilly padded over to feed. Tara sighed, "Think I need a coffee." She picked up the electric kettle, filled it up and switched it on. The mundane action was somehow comforting and although feeling somewhat better her heart was still racing. She opened the cupboard unit next to the sink for the coffee but couldn't see it. Tara frowned and hunted through the cupboard discovering it on the top shelf hidden behind the sugar. "I must be losing it!" She made herself a cup of coffee and returned to the sitting room.

Tara relaxed and gratefully sipped her coffee until something else caught her attention. The photograph of her and Steve that she had examined earlier was no longer on the desk but now sat on the coffee table in front of her. Puzzled, Tara picked it up and replaced it in its original position. "Am I going mad?"

James and Tommy had argued violently about what to do regarding Mr Ley and the kiddie porn they had found. Tommy was insistent that they should tell someone in authority whilst James wanted to use it to blackmail the teacher. Tommy tried to reason with him about the damage it could cause. "How would you like it if it was your sister or cousin? Wouldn't you want to kill him? I know I would. I'd want to cut his bits off and shove them down his throat."

"Tommy, if we report him it will all come back on us. How did we get the stick and so on. We'll get ourselves into even more trouble."

"Not if we get the stick into the right hands with an explanatory letter."

James finally succumbed albeit reluctantly to Tommy's argument. "All right. Type your letter."

Tommy set his computer up with a new blank document and typed. 'To whom it may concern'. This flash drive is a copy of one that belongs to the French Teacher, Mr. K. Ley at Alderly High Secondary School. If you open it up you will see hundreds of obscene pictures of naked children, boys and girls and clips of the teacher doing stuff with a little girl and more. He should be stopped. Please do what's right and stop this pervert's behaviour. Tommy then signed it, 'A concerned citizen.'

He sent it to print and got a jiffy bag from his stationery shelf, put the letter inside and held out his hand for the flash drive. James half-heartedly gave him the memory stick, which Tommy inserted and then sealed the pack.

"How you going to get it anywhere? Who are you sending it to?"

"We can't post it. It might get lost or worse be traced back to us. I'll take it to the local cop shop early tomorrow morning. There won't be anyone around then. The small duty office closes at night so it should be safe."

"What about CCTV? You should wear a hoodie and put a scarf over your face. Or you could leave it on the Head's desk."

"That's too dangerous. Someone is more likely to see me. Good idea about the hoodie. I'll see to it; leave it with me."

James wasn't happy about the decision but recognised the need to stop the teacher in his gross behaviour. He had made up his own mind that he would do something else to appease the yearning void inside him and decided that it would be something bad, really bad.

The following morning the sun was shining brightly and benignly. It was very early morning and few people were out and about. It was all good as James Treeves made his way to school. He had left a note for his mum telling her he'd gone in early to finish his homework as he'd left his text book at school. She would believe that as he had done something like that before. James Treeves was an expert prankster and had invented many practical jokes but now, things were different and James had another trick up his sleeve, a particularly nasty, disgusting one. He had to work out when and how he could do it. In his bag he had an empty ice cream tub. This was one wind up he couldn't let anyone know about, not even Tommy. He had arrived exceptionally early and crept in not wanting any other early birds to spot him. No one had seen him on his way to school and no one had seen him arrive. Good... So far, so good.

Once inside the entrance he nipped into the boys' toilets and locked himself in a closet. He removed the empty ice cream carton and unzipped his trousers. He sat on the toilet seat and held the container underneath him and pushed hard. Satisfied he had emptied his bowels sufficiently he wiped his bottom and sealed the receptacle. He secreted the vessel in his bag and with a smug look on his face exited the stall and washed his hands. He checked his watch. It had just turned six-thirty. Good, no one was around or would be around yet.

He cautiously made his way through the maze of school corridors toward Tara's classroom and slipped inside. Once there, he opened the teacher's desk, moved and deposited the contents of the ice cream tub and shut the drawer. He then rid himself of the carton, dropping it in a litter bin.

Treeves slunk out of the building and made his way to a breakfast café in the town and with a smug look on his face ordered himself a full English fry up. He knew this would really freak out Mrs Lomas and he wondered what else he could do to punish her.

14

ANOTHER THREE WEEKS PASSED UNEVENTFULLY and Tara was feeling slightly safer. She tried to bury the fluttering of insecurity that rose every now and again at a creak or some other sound that was the house just settling down for the night. At first, she had been like a nervous kitten that jumped at every sound or shadow that passed the window. But solitude and confinement was taking its toll. Tara was getting more bored every day. She could only dust and clean the house so many times in twenty-four hours. She hated housework anyway. Tara had done all her marking, planned all her lessons for weeks and had managed to read numerous books. She twisted her hair and examined it for split ends almost going cross eyed in the process. She found one or two that she bit off and then she examined the hair and pulled it apart from the split. "You'll have no hair left," she told herself. "Or at the very least you'll need a trip to the hairdresser."

Tara stepped to the window and peered out. The cop car was there, parked right outside. "God knows what the neighbours think," she said. She half thought about inviting the policeman in for a cup of tea but decided against it thinking about the gossip it would generate. As she stood there watching and reasoning with herself another car drew up outside and parked behind the police vehicle.

Tara's face creased into a smile as she saw Lucy step out from the car and begin to walk down the drive. A policeman approached her straight away and stopped her. Tara's face furrowed in a frown as she watched the interchange between them. He appeared to be asking her questions. She handed her bag across to the young copper who searched it and passed it back. Lucy dug in her handbag for her wallet and took out her driving licence, which the young man examined and returned. Lucy was then allowed to walk up the drive and knock at the door, which Tara flew to and opened to admit her.

Tara gave her friend a huge hug, "Oh, how I have missed you," she exclaimed.

"And me, you. Break times are not the same and Rona has a surfeit of her shortbread biscuits that you like so much. In fact, here…" Lucy scrabbled in her bag and took out a bag of homemade shortbread. "Rona sent these for you. Everyone sends their love and hopes you'll be back in school, soon. The kids are missing their favourite English teacher and not happy with the different supply teachers they have had to deal with since the beginning of your absence … Although they're more settled now, with the new substitute. Here." She reached in her bag again, "From your tutor group." Lucy handed Tara a card signed by all the pupils in her form, which said, 'Come back soon. We all miss you.'

Tara was quite touched by the card and set it on the counter top. "That's made my day. How lovely of them all." She picked it up again and scrutinised the signatures, "Even Raymond Campbell has signed. I didn't think even liked me."

"You've got that wrong. After all you've done to help him he's the one who organised the card. They all like you. Especially after experiencing Jean Galbraith. She just yelled at them all the time. It made them realise what a gem they have in you."

Tara beamed. "Coffee? We can have a couple of Rona's biscuits to go with it."

"Ideal." Lucy looked around Tara's stylish furnishings. "This is nice," she said appreciatively.

"You've seen it before."

"No, you've added some new touches. I love the cushions. Say, doesn't it make you feel like a celebrity?" Tara looked questioningly. "All the police guards?"

"Ha! Prisoner more like. Now I know what it feels like to be under house arrest."

"Pretty cute officer to be under arrest with?" said Lucy cheekily.

"Really? Can't say I've noticed…"

"I bet!" said Lucy laughing. "Well, he could put his shoes underneath my bed anytime. He's quite a dish."

"Oh, you mean Shay, Officer Connor."

"First name terms…." said Lucy impishly.

Tara laughed as she carried the tray of coffee things and cafetiere to the table. They sat and she began pouring the coffee. "Sugar?" She passed the bowl and spoon to Lucy. "I haven't got sweeteners."

"Don't worry. I've got my own." Lucy foraged in her bag. Took out her Canderel and dispensed one.

"So, where are all the goodies you promised me?"

"Rona's shortbread isn't enough for you?"

"That will be gone in one sitting."

"Fear not. I haven't forgotten. All in good time. Chocolate and candy bars will be delivered in due course. First give me the skinny…"

"Nothing to tell," said Tara. "Been pretty quiet lately. Hopefully, that's a good sign."

"Maybe it's over."

"Maybe it is. I'm just really worried about my year tens and elevens. They've got GCSE's coming up and my year nines have SATS with Shakespeare."

"No problem. The police contacted the head about everything and so she's got an English Specialist in. Started a couple of weeks ago. She's following your scheme of work. So, you have no need to worry."

Tara breathed a sigh of relief, "I can't wait to come back."

"There was one incident… not very nice. I felt quite sorry for Mrs Galbraith."

"Why? What happened?"

"The first day you were absent Jean Galbraith was sent to cover your tutor group and first two lessons. She complained about an awful pong and when she went to take the register, her red pen had run out so she opened your desk drawer to find another and put her hand in it."

"In what?"

"Someone had defecated in your drawer."

"What?"

"She stuck her hand right in it. The class went hysterical, she went nuts. The whole class was kept in detention until someone confessed. No one did. They all swore it wasn't them."

"Then that was meant for me…" Tara went quiet. "Maybe all these horrible things are something to do with school? No wonder Jean yelled at them all the time."

"The Head was called in. She's now got someone trawling through all the CCTV footage from around the school on the day before and the day it happened. They'll find whoever did it. Anyway, enough of that. Let's try and demolish Rona's biscuits."

The two friends chattered on with Lucy keeping Tara up to date with all the gossip. Tara laughed and smiled more than she had in weeks and said so.

"What are friends for?" said Lucy giving her friend another hug.

They continued in a much lighter and happier vein until Lucy saw the time, "Oh, my God! Look at the time. I have to dash… got a hot date."

"What? And you haven't said a word? I want to know all the details and you have to tell me all about it."

"No time now. Tomorrow, I promise… I'll ring."

"Okay, but don't forget. I need to know."

Lucy laughed and said, "Promise, promise, promise."

Tara unable to help herself giggled and saw her friend out." She waved Lucy off and went back inside. "Lucy… a hot date… wonder what he's called?"

The following morning was overcast and dull. Tara rose and stretched. It was after nine. Steve had already left for an emergency meeting with his boss and clients. He had left a note of love for her on his pillow and tiptoed out. Tara showered and dressed quickly. She was exhausted from everything that had been happening. She supposed she was lucky that she hadn't had a complete breakdown such had been the horror of events so far. She was praying all would be well for Steve and had a hundred other thoughts rambling through the trellis of her mind, but she had a nervous excitement in her tummy for Lucy. She decided she couldn't wait for Lucy's call; she had to ring her.

Tara dialled her friend's number and waited drumming her fingers impatiently on the kitchen counter top. A sleepy voice answered eventually, "Hello?"

"Lucy, it's me. Sounds like I've woken you. Sorry, but I just had to know … how was last night?"

Lucy yawned through some of her words and apologised, "Don't know really. It was weird."

"Weird? In what way?"

"It's hard to say. I mean, he is drop dead gorgeous such penetrating steel blue eyes. Looks wise, he is out of the ball park, really handsome…"

"I'm sensing a 'but' here."

"There was just something. I can't quite put my finger on it. It's like he wasn't completely comfortable with me."

"Didn't you talk?"

"Oh, yes… probably too much. God, he's had rotten luck with women. All his relationships seem to have gone tits up. So, it got me thinking was it him or was it them?"

"In my experience, not everyone who has a bad time of it is responsible."

"No, but he did have a strange sense of humour and a morbid curiosity in crazy things."

"Crazy things?"

"Yes, like addicted to the crime channels on TV and the workings of the criminal mind. He talked for ages about David Koresh."

"Who?"

"A religious cult leader at Wako, Texas. Even told me about a podcast I should listen to… as I said, peculiar. In fact, to interact with him I told him about you."

"What?"

"Oh, I mentioned no names, but just talked about your stalker situation and stuff that had happened to you. He was really interested. Said he'd love us to go out as a foursome so he could meet you. Like I said, strange."

"Are you seeing him again?"

"Not sure. I shall give it a while. He's calling me next week. By then I'll have made up my mind."

"What's his name?"

"Michael something or other. Can't remember his surname..."

"Pity… you could have checked him out on social media."

"Maybe." Lucy yawned again. "Sorry, Tara. It was a really late one last night but I tell you something, he was a hell of a kisser. Lips like velvet. Could almost forgive his weirdness for that."

"Where did you meet him?"

"Some scruffy bar where deadbeats and artists hang out."

"Doesn't sound too exciting?"

"He said he went there for the beer."

"Okay, I'll let you get back to sleep. Sorry to disturb you."

"No probs. I'll tell you more when I know more. Cheers."

They ended the call and Tara looked thoughtful. This guy didn't sound like Lucy's usual type but then, if he could kiss like that...."

Tara laughed it off and went to make herself some breakfast, feed Tilly and the rest of the troops.

One evening later that week, Tara and Steve sat with Officers Connor and Dixon. Steve's expression was serious, as if he couldn't believe what he was hearing, "You're pulling the surveillance? Is that wise?"

"We'll still keep the officer on patrol. Just for the time being," said Cheryl Dixon.

Officer Connor added, "That should keep anyone at bay if they're watching. But no permanent watch outside the house."

"What about my job?" asked Tara.

"I don't see any reason why you can't go back," said Shay Connor.

Tara beamed in delight, "Brilliant!"

Officer Dixon warned, "But, if anything happens, the least little thing; any suspicions about anything; call me. You've got my direct line."

"Don't worry, we will," said Steve.

"One last thing," said Officer Dixon. "Do you know anyone called Jan Bernard?"

Tara shook her head, "No. Steve?"

"Not that I'm aware. Why?"

"Brunette, pretty, in her thirties. Very much like you," said Cheryl Dixon.

Tara probed, "Is that who you think is doing this?"

"No, no," said Officer Connor, a little too quickly.

"Well, who is she?" asked Tara.

The two officers exchanged a look before Officer Dixon answered, "She was targeted, like you."

"What do you mean, was?" asked Steve.

"We're not at liberty to discuss the individual details in an ongoing case but it appears there are some similarities."

"What similarities?" pressed Steve.

Officer Connor looked at his colleague, who nodded. "Mainly in the age and physical appearance of Miss Bernard and Mrs Lomas. But, that could be just a coincidence."

"I don't believe in coincidences," said Tara her face furrowed in a frown.

"Then is it wise to let my wife go back to work and to pull the policeman off watch? It doesn't sound sensible to me."

Cheryl Dixon added, "We are suitably convinced that we are dealing with two different people. If our investigation turns up anything, anything at all, which links Mrs Lomas to the Bernard case then believe me we will be right back."

"So, you really think this is over?" asked Tara.

"We are satisfied that whoever it is that has been terrorising you has simply got tired and moved on to someone else. Sadly, there are a number of sick people out there who get their kicks from making someone else's life a misery. It's a power thing, all about control. Once they see that you have had to alter your daily routine, they feel in charge. But, as we have said, if anything happens to concern you, please let us know."

"Don't worry, we will," said Steve vehemently.

Later that night, Steve was clearing away the dinner dishes, while Tara was on the phone to Lucy. "Isn't that great? I can come back. It's been far too long. I just hope my year nines haven't been slacking!"

"When exactly is that?" asked Lucy.

"I've called the head. I'll be back tomorrow. They won't know what's hit them." She laughed aloud, "I can't believe I'll be free. Free at last."

"You won't feel like that after revision week," said Lucy.

"Maybe not. But anything's better than this confinement."

"You make it sound like you're pregnant," said Lucy with a giggle.

"Not yet… In time." They continued chatting while Steve stacked the dishwasher, added a tablet and set it going. He gestured to Tara to wind up the conversation by twirling his finger in a circle. Tara got the message, nodded, and mouthed at him, "In a minute…"

"I think that calls for a glass of wine," he said more to himself than Tara. He went to the cupboard and opened it expecting to see the glasses. They were not there. "Where's she put them now?" he muttered. He searched through the cupboards and found them eventually. He took a bottle of Shiraz from the wine rack, opened it and poured two glasses before calling out, "Next time you start rearranging the kitchen, let me know."

Tara waved her hand at Steve to shut him up. "Got to go. Steve's chattering on about something… nothing important I expect. Get him to stack the dishwasher and it's a major event. See you tomorrow. Bye." She replaced the receiver with a big smile on her face.

Steve stood holding out a glass of wine for Tara, "It's great to see you looking so happy and smiling," he said. "I have so missed that. It's just wonderful that you are much more relaxed."

"It's because I really feel that it's over. We can start to live again."

There was a liveliness in Tara's step as she headed for the staffroom at morning break. She joined the coffee queue and everyone greeted her with smiles and pleasantries. The staff were pleased to welcome her back, especially those who had covered her tutor group sessions and had to deal with problem student Raymond Campbell, as Mrs Galbraith told her.

Tara kept her mouth shut, she didn't regard Raymond as a problem anymore but believed he was someone with bags of character who just needed careful handling. So, she smiled sweetly and said nothing. She was also keen to find out how Raymond had got on with his meals and the arranged help for his mother.

"I expect we'll learn that it was him that did that awful thing in your desk."

Tara felt compelled to speak, "I can't believe that. That's the action of some maladjusted, twisted person. Raymond isn't that."

Jean Galbraith snorted in derision, "We'll see."

Lucy came and joined the line. She beamed at her friend, "Looks like you timed it just right."

"What?"

"Coming back to school on Friday just in time for the weekend."

"I only hope it's permanent."

"Why wouldn't it be?"

"I don't know, a feeling… Oh, take no notice of me. I'm just being silly. If I was in danger they would have kept me under guard, wouldn't they?"

"True. But I think to make you feel absolutely top notch that…."

"What?"

Lucy paused before announcing, "You need a make-over, a new start. New hair, new clothes, new you. Then you'll feel better."

"That's not a bad idea."

"Of course not. I am rather brilliant, aren't I?"

The two friends finally reached the front of the line, collected their coffee and some of Rona's home cooked treats and retired to their usual seats to chat.

"It's great not having to look over my shoulder all the time."

"Still, you mustn't get too complacent. It's just as well to be careful."

"I know. You're right. It's just so liberating being allowed out without some copper tailing me."

"But he is a very nice copper," teased Lucy.

"Enough of that… it's your helpful suggestions that got me in this mess," said Tara with a laugh. "What about the new boyfriend?"

Lucy made a cutting gesture at her throat. "I think the less said about that the better. Let's say, he's on the back burner. I wasn't rude. I just said I needed more time to think. He hasn't rung since, thank goodness."

Early the next morning Tara had risen early. The sun was poking its fingers through the curtains and into the room. It had prodded her awake. Unable to lie still she had showered, breakfasted and was feeling good.

Steve had not surfaced. Exhausted from everything that had happened over the last few months he had elected to sleep in.

Tara had raided the periodicals rack and selected a number with pictures of the latest fashions, makeup trends and hairstyles. She had flicked through a few while munching her toast but decided she needed a bigger canvas and so grabbed the pile and retreated to the bedroom, where she had more space and Tilly couldn't keep walking over them all or scattering them all over the place.

Magazines lay strewn on the bedroom floor open at pictures of models sporting different hairstyles. Tara had stretched out on the carpet and was examining them all. She was imagining her face superimposed on the pictures in front of her trying to decide if they would suit her or not. She glanced across at the bed where Steve was scarcely visible huddled under the duvet. "Steve…?"

"Not now. Let me sleep, please." He turned over and buried his head in the pillow.

Tara shrugged and continued to pore over the photos. She scrambled up and sat on the stool in front of her dressing table and continued to study herself in the mirror. She pulled at her hair, fiddling with it, changing the parting and piling it on top of her head. She even tucked and pinned it under to see what she would look like with shorter hair. She did not look particularly pleased with any of her attempts to change her appearance.

Tara murmured, "New wardrobe, change of style…" She went to the fitted wardrobes and pulled open the door. What she saw inside, shocked her as it almost tumbled out. "Oh my God!"

Tara left the wardrobe door swinging and ran to the bed, shaking Steve.

"Wha….? What is it?"

"Steve, where did that come from?"

"What?" he sat up and rubbed his eyes. He followed her pointed finger and saw a pump action shotgun leaning against the side of the closet. "Oh, that. I bought it the other day for personal protection. You never know when we might need it."

"I hope not. I hate the things. Is it loaded?"

"It is. If someone attacked us we wouldn't have time to load it or reload if we missed the target. This is safer."

"Don't you need a licence?"

"Got one. It's in the bedside drawer."

"What did you say it was for?"

"Killing vermin and for sport. Now let me sleep, please."

Tara opened the bedside drawer and saw the shotgun licence. She picked it up and read it, "It says here it must be kept in a secure steel cabinet under lock and key that will be inspected."

"And it will be, but not at the moment. Once we are sure you are safe. Look if you're unhappy about it I'll hide it in the spare room under the bed."

"Do that. And don't forget. I don't want that thing staring at me every time I change my clothes."

"Okay, okay."

Tara didn't look convinced but warily replaced it, then hunted through the rest of the contents, "Steve? Where's my phone book? It was in the bedside drawer."

"Where you last left it." He yawned, loudly as if to make a point, "I haven't touched it." Tara moved to the other side of the bed and rummaged in that drawer right near Steve's head. He groaned loudly, "What now?"

"I need to phone the hairdresser; we have a new start, things are good and I need a new look."

"There's nothing wrong with the way you look. I love you just the way you are. Now, let me sleep."

"You're sweet. I just feel like a change." Tara closed the drawer. Steve turned over, pummelled his pillow and lay face down in an attempt to block out Tara who had now crossed to her dressing table and opened the top drawer. Her address book was there lying on top of her underwear. "Well, I didn't put it there. Must have been you on one of your tidying up sprees."

Tara hunted through her book to find a number. She picked up the phone by Steve's side of the bed who rolled over and groaned. Tara dialled. "Hi. I'd like to make an appointment with Sarah-Lou please for a cut and style ... Today, if possible ... Great, eleven o'clock?" There was a crackling on the line. "That's fine... Yes ... Tara Lomas." As she replaced the receiver she put the address book in the drawer by the phone and picked up a bottle of aspirin standing next to it. "Didn't know you had a headache, sweetheart."

Resigned that he was not going to get more sleep he sighed and poked his head out from under the duvet. "I haven't."

"Then why the aspirin?"

"I didn't put them there."

"Do you know, we've either got a ghost or we need to get you to the doctor."

"Why?"

"Got an early case of Alzheimer's on our hands."

Huh?"

"You. Moving stuff around and forgetting you've done it."

Steve still groggy from needing sleep looked totally confused and plonked his head back down and closed his eyes. Ending all further conversation. "I'm too tired to argue. Please, just leave me in peace."

Tara dropped a kiss on his forehead, "Okay, you win. I'll leave you be. Sleep tight." Tara smiled fondly as she looked at him with his eyes closed. He was now breathing deeply, so she tiptoed out of the bedroom.

She was actually feeling quite excited about braving a new style and maybe even a new colour.

Tara chatted happily to Sarah-Lou, her hairdresser, who listened in amazement at the tale she had to tell. "Good grief, Tara. That's awful. You must have been so scared."

"It was terrifying. I've never experienced anything like it in my life. But, it's over now. I can breathe again and sleep easier."

Tara admired her new cut and style in the mirror. Sarah-Lou took the mirror and showed her how it looked from the back. "What do you think?"

"It's terrific, I really love it and the highlights. I hope Steve will, too."

"How could he resist?" said Sarah-Lou cheekily. "You look gorgeous."

"Thanks." She took off her gown and brushed herself down. "Gosh, is all that hair mine?" She looked at the tresses of dark hair on the floor that the junior was sweeping up. "There's enough there to make a wig, if I change my mind."

Tara paid at the desk and Sarah-Lou helped her on with her coat. Tara pressed a five pound note into Sarah-Lou's hand. "Thanks. It looks great. I feel like a new woman." Tara took a final look at her new bob in the mirror and left hardly able to keep a smile off her face.

Up the road from the hairdressers a dark car with tinted windows was parked. It had been there some time. The driver became alert when Tara emerged from the hairdressers. At first, the person had to look twice and almost didn't recognise Tara and wouldn't have done if it hadn't been for the beige military style raincoat that she was wearing.

Tara crossed to her car parked across the street. There was a jauntiness in her stride. She liked the way her hair felt and how it bounced when she walked. She paused at the driver's door to remove her car keys from her bag when a vehicle appeared from nowhere. The roaring engine was revving hard and the vehicle drove straight at Tara. Initially, she froze in horror but at the very last minute she jumped out of the way and across the bonnet of her car. The other vehicle smashed into the driver's door shuttling Tara over the bonnet and onto the pavement before it raced off into the town. Stunned, Tara burst into tears and heaved herself up from the ground. Her shoes were scuffed, her tights torn. She looked at her knees, which were bleeding and she hobbled back to the hair salon.

Tara tumbled in through the door and crumpled to the floor in a heap. The receptionist and other hair stylists clustered around wondering what on earth had happened. Tara was shaking uncontrollably. Her skirt had ripped, her hands were grazed. She smothered her sobs and struggled to keep her voice even. "Please, call the police. Someone just tried to run me over."

The receptionist grabbed the phone to dial nine, nine, nine. But Tara stopped her, "No wait…" she fumbled in her bag for Cheryl Dixon's card. "Ring this number, it's the officer in charge of my case."

Sarah-Lou helped Tara to her feet and settled her in a free chair. "I'll get you some water." The stylists rallied around while shocked customers looked on. There was much whispering and shaking of heads. Pretty soon, police sirens from more than one car were heard in the distance and the hairdressers got back to work leaving the receptionist and Sarah-Lou ministering to Tara.

Sarah-Lou was bathing her knees and removing pieces of grit embedded in her wounds when the shop bell jangled and officers Dixon and Connor entered the shop. The two coppers exchanged a worried look and Cheryl Dixon urged Shay Connor to question the customers and staff, while she attended to Tara whose face was now drained of colour. Tara was trembling as if she had some sort of ague and was freezing cold. She whispered, "Please call my husband."

Cheryl spoke soothingly to her, "We will. We need to get a few details first. Can you tell me exactly what happened?"

Tara launched into an explanation of what she could remember ending with, "It came out of nowhere. It was dark blue… maybe black. I don't know. It all happened so fast."

"Did you see who was driving?"

Tara shook her head, "No, it had tinted a windscreen, I think. I could have been killed." It was as if the realisation had suddenly hit her. "I'm lucky to be alive," she gasped.

Cheryl Dixon turned to Sarah-Lou, "Did you see anything?"

Sarah-Lou apologised, "Sorry, I was in the back, between clients. I just heard a car engine roaring and tyres screeching. I came out to see what had happened and the next thing I knew, Tara came running in. Sorry, I can't be of any more help."

Cheryl looked at the receptionist, "How about you?"

"No, sorry. I heard the noise outside and then Mrs Lomas coming in…."

Officer Dixon flipped shut her notebook and glanced around for her colleague who it appeared had learned nothing more when another policeman, Brandon Rowe, walked into the salon. Cheryl turned to him, "We need to get Mrs. Lomas home. Is her car drivable?"

"It should be. I've given it a cursory look over. There's no real damage to the front, except for part of the bumper. But, the driver's door is badly dented. The wing mirror's smashed."

Cheryl helped Tara to her feet. "Do you feel up to driving?"

Tara's initial fear was now being replaced by anger and she nodded stoically, "I can drive. I refuse to let this beat me."

The police ushered Tara from the salon and they walked her to the car. Officer Dixon visibly winced when she saw the driver's door covered in scratches and dark blue paint. "You were right, it was a dark car. We'll get some of these paint flakes to the lab and see if they can be identified." She nodded to Shay, "Call Forensics."

Shay took his mobile phone to call the station while Tara tried to open her door but it was so badly stoved in that it wouldn't budge.

Tara walked around to the passenger side and entered that way, clambering across to the driver's seat. Her colour had returned and she had stopped shaking. Her fury at being targeted was growing. Officer Dixon tapped on the passenger window, which Tara opened.

"Why don't you let me drive? It might be better after the shock you've had. Normally we'd have it towed but it looks like you'll need a new door. Officer Rowe doesn't think the damage is too severe. I'm sure your husband will be able to get the door open and then he can organise the repair."

Tara shrugged. She was past arguing, "Whatever. I've had enough." She slid back across the front seats and stepped out allowing Officer Dixon to climb across.

Once behind the wheel, Tara manoeuvred herself into the passenger seat and passed Cheryl the car keys. The car started first time and Cheryl set off, followed by Officers Rowe and Connor.

Conversation was snappy and to the point as the policewoman drove the car toward Tara's house. The first few blocks passed uneventfully until they arrived at a crossroads complete with a set of traffic lights in the process of changing from amber to red. Officer Dixon applied the brakes but to her horror nothing happened. She continued to pump the brakes. Still there was nothing. She felt forced to increase her speed to beat the lights and narrowly avoided a collision with a car coming across from the left. Fortunately, the roads were not too busy. She steered sharply and weaved from side to side and shifted into a lower gear. The car slowed down and she was able to stop by brushing up against the curb, applying the handbrake and switching off the engine. She sighed in relief, "That could have been very nasty."

Tara sat in silence, horrified by what had just happened.

The police car driven by Officer Rowe followed with lights and siren on, after seeing the vehicle weaving as if Cheryl was drunk. He drew up behind them and stopped.

Tara was finally galvanised into action and exited the car. Cheryl popped the hood and scrambled after her. Tara leaned against a garden wall with her arms folded. Her face looked pinched with worry. She finally, spoke as Cheryl was lifting the bonnet and peering inside. "It was fine on the way to the hairdressers. Nothing wrong with the brakes at all," she said in a small tight voice.

Officer Rowe peered in at the engine with Cheryl. "Check the brake fluid."

Cheryl bent over and examined it. "It's definitely the brake fluid. There isn't any."

Tara interrupted, "But Steve took it in for a service last week, as I wasn't using it. They did an oil change and topped off all the fluids…" A questioning look passed between the two officers. "What? What aren't you telling me?"

Cheryl chose to ignore the comment and led Tara to the police car and opened the rear passenger door for her. "We'll talk further when we get you home. I don't want to jump to any conclusions." Tara had to be satisfied with that and slipped into the rear seat. "I'll just lock your car." She closed the back door firmly.

Cheryl walked back to Tara's motor, as Officer Rowe closed the bonnet. She spoke in low tones to her colleague, "Seems a little too similar to the Jan Bernard case for my liking. Remember how she was harassed? It started right before she was murdered. Her car had been tampered with as well."

"I wonder what Tara's hubby has been up to lately? Do you think another woman may be involved?" asked Officer Rowe.

"It doesn't seem likely, but you never know. Don't they say, 'Hell hath no fury like a woman scorned'? We should check it out."

They secured Tara's car and moved back thoughtfully. No one spoke on the journey home. Each person was lost in their own thoughts. They soon turned into the treelined avenue where Tara lived. The sun shone down benignly and there was little cloud. The scent of freshly cut grass was in the air but Tara didn't notice any of this. She was just keen to get inside and away from twitching curtains and nosey neighbours.

Tara couldn't get the key in the lock quickly enough. Her hand was shaking and twice she dropped her keys. Officer Rowe took them from her and opened the door. Tara fled inside.

She flopped onto the sofa and tossed her bag onto the coffee table where there was a note from Steve. 'I've just popped out for a paper and brunch. I'll be back in a couple of hours. Looking forward to seeing the new you. Love S. xx'

Tara tossed down the note before she rose and announced, "I'm exhausted. Mind if I take a nap until Steve gets here? Help yourself to anything in the kitchen."

Cheryl nodded kindly, "Go ahead. I'll make a coffee. I need one after that escapade. Do you fancy one, Brandon?"

"Sure."

Tara forced a smile and plodded up the stairs to her room.

As Cheryl went to enter the kitchen there was a terrified scream from upstairs. Coffee forgotten the two officers looked at each other in alarm and sprinted up the stairs to Tara's bedroom.

Tara looked as if she was broken. She stood there shivering and swallowing hard. Cheryl put an arm around her to comfort her. Scrawled on the mirror in lipstick was one word, BITCH. Her makeup that sat on the dressing table had been swept to the floor as if in temper.

Officer Rowe took charge, "You can't stay here. We need to get you to a safe house."

"Yes," added Cheryl. "Pack a few things. I'm sure it won't be for long."

"What about Steve?"

"It's best if you go alone. Let us do our job."

Tara was in no fit state to argue. She opened her closet to get a weekend case but gasped in horror as she saw most of her clothes had been shredded and slashed to ribbons. She could also see the shotgun had been removed.

"I don't believe this." Tara sounded defeated. She sat on the bed and stared dully into space.

"Don't worry, Mrs Lomas. I'll sort something out." Cheryl opened the case and sorted through the few items that had escaped the malicious damage.

"I'll check downstairs," said Officer Rowe quietly.

He carefully looked in each room upstairs before he ran down and entered the kitchen. He stared in disbelief at the kitchen window, which was wide open. He immediately got on the phone, "Hello... we need a Forensic team at the Lomas house, pronto.... Yes... We need to catch the perp before we have another murder on our hands.... Great!"

As he pocketed his phone he stiffened. The hairs on the back of his neck began to stand up, chills ran down his spine, as he heard a strange noise from outside. Very slowly he turned back toward the window and jumped when Tilly startled him by leaping in through the open window. "Cat! You nearly gave me a heart attack," he murmured. Tilly gave a loud complaining mew before trotting up the stairs.

Officer Rowe was now calmer from his scare but more than relieved when he heard a van pull up outside. He admitted the Forensic team of four and watched them examine the point of entry without getting in the way. They scoured the rooms downstairs before preparing to examine the bedroom.

Tara emerged from her room carrying her bag. She took in the personnel examining her property. Her face was drained of colour. She looked both frightened and angry. Cheryl tried to ease Tara's fears. "You're safe now."

"I don't feel it," muttered Tara. "What about Steve?"

"We've not managed to contact your husband yet. His mobile's off. We will call him again once we reach the station."

Two male CSI's brushed past her and mounted the stairs as Tara left with the police. She turned to Cheryl, "I don't think I can do this."

Cheryl smiled and tried to reason with her, "Of course you can. It's not Steve that's in danger. It's you. Whoever destroyed your clothes didn't touch Steve's, did they?"

Tara shook her head, "No." They reached the police car outside and Cheryl opened the door for her and put her case in the back.

"No. Someone is out to make your life a misery. We need to get you away from the situation. We have to find out who's doing this. You have no ideas, do you?" Cheryl got in and started the engine. Tara stared in front of her, a blank expression on her face. "Mrs Lomas?"

"What? No, well... maybe..." And she began to recount a number of events that had happened to her at school. She then decided it was time to mention the social media network, Friend Finder, which she hadn't done before.

15

THE CLOCK CHIMED OUT THE hour as Steve walked in through the front door. He entered the living room on the sixth stroke. His shoulders were hunched and he looked a picture of abject misery.

Tilly ran to him and rubbed herself around his legs and purred in delight. He bent down to fuss her, "You missing mummy, too?" The cat appeared to understand and let out a loud meow.

Steve pulled off his jacket and slung it on the sofa. He plodded to the fish tank, his sombre mood was apparent in every step. He sprinkled some flakes in the top for them to feed on, and then added some pellets for the others. He watched the baby sturgeon swimming and diving and murmured, "If only you could speak. You'd tell us a thing or two."

Tilly mewed again. Steve picked her up and nuzzled her, took her to the settee and sat. He cuddled the cat, which gave him some comfort. Tilly wriggled out of his arms and ran to her dish. "All right, all right. Let's get you fed." His movements were still dulled, his manner subdued, he was distraught and not in control of anything. He wasn't hungry. He felt totally lost. "I need a drink, but I'll see to you first," he said to the cat and went into the kitchen to feed her, before going to the fridge and taking out a bottle of chilled Pinot Grigio. "Easy drinking and light," he said to Tilly who was watching him with an inscrutable expression on her face. He filled a glass and took the bottle and his drink to the couch and plonked himself down. He switched on the TV and flicked through the channels before switching it off again and sat and drank.

The night dragged on. Steve sat there and attempted again to watch some television. A film was playing. Steve hadn't a clue what it was about. The noise was just background chatter to make him feel less alone. The clock chimed again and broke him out of his trance. He stretched and yawned deciding it was time for bed. He switched everything off and trundled up the stairs to sleep.

When he got into bed, he buried his nose into Tara's pillow to drink in her fragrance then flopped onto his back and stared at the ceiling. He found it hard to sleep without her and spent the next couple of hours staring at the clock. He tossed and turned and examined the time again. It was now five minutes past two. He felt as if he'd been awake forever. He pummelled his pillow, turned on his side, firmly closed his eyes but still struggled to get to sleep.

Outside a figure in shapeless clothes wearing a hoodie tentatively approached the house. The road was examined for any activity. All was still. The street lamps cast a ruddy hue, which pooled on the pavement and intermingled with the light of the full moon when it escaped the bubble wrap of clouds.

The night marauder checked the time. It was three forty-nine. There was scarcely a breeze and the night was warm. The Lomas house and the houses adjacent to it were in darkness.

Surgically gloved hands wielded a baseball bat that was slapped into one hand as if getting ready for action. The stalker stepped stealthily like a panther hunting its prey and crossed the road to the Lomas house. As soon as one foot was set on the path the light blazed on, lighting everything up like a stage show.

There was a hiss of fury. The figure wielded the bat and smashed the security light, which shattered. Attention was then turned to the video camera with its red blinking light, which was also brutally disabled. More assured now the figure crept to the front door, key in hand and entered.

Upstairs Steve had finally fallen into a longed for, deep sleep. The sound of breaking glass infiltrated his dream. He stirred slightly but soon settled down again.

The covert figure moved furtively around the living room and kitchen before quietly slinking up the stairs. One step creaked and the sound seemed deafening in the dark. The person stopped, afraid to breathe, but no one was alerted and the figure continued up the stairs to the bedroom and entered. The person stared at the bed and saw Steve sleeping alone and silently cursed.

The bedside clock now read four fifteen. Steve was now truly asleep and breathing deeply. In the dim light the figure moved around the bedroom. The person was clearly familiar with the layout and contents of the room.

Something was scrawled on the wall opposite the bed. Steve stirred and turned over. The intruder froze and looked back at the bed where Steve continued to sleep. The trespasser let a soft sigh escape and silently tiptoed out of the room.

Time passed.

The clock ticked onto five fifteen. The morning light was spilling through the gap in the curtains when the smoke alarm went off downstairs. The irritating bleep penetrated Steve's head and he began to wake. He rose groggily. His brain was still fogged from sleep. He shook his head as the piercing noise became louder. It was then he saw the words scrawled on the wall. "THE BITCH WILL DIE!"

Wide awake now, Steve dashed from the bedroom as smoke drifted up the stairs. The noise from the alarm was unbearable as it screamed in his head. It was coming from the kitchen. Steve ran inside and could see and smell the acrid smoke rising from a frying pan on the stove. The burner was on full blast. He was sickened when he saw the pan was full of dead fish that had been removed from the tank. He turned off the gas and stumbled about to reset the smoke alarm. He opened the back door to clear the smoke from the kitchen and let out a horrified cry of sorrow, "Oh no!" There on the back porch step lay Tilly. She was injured and unconscious. He tenderly picked up the little cat and carried her inside settling her on the settee.

Steve frantically grabbed his mobile phone that was charging on the kitchen counter. He rummaged through the drawer for the phone book and called the vet. "My cat... she's been attacked and is scarcely breathing... No, I can't bring her in I have to call the police.... Yes... Animal ambulance?... Great."

He ended the call, snatched up his wallet and pulled out a business card and dialled. His voice was shaky but filled with urgency as his call was answered. He tried to contain his sobs as he spoke, "Yes, I need to speak with Officer Dixon, now..."

Officers Dixon and Rowe questioned Steve while the Forensic team scoured the house for more clues. Cheryl was trying to placate Steve and reason with him. He was not only upset but enraged at the evil deeds that had violated his home.

"We don't think it's safe for you to stay in the house."

"It's outrageous. What if Tara had been here? She could have been murdered. What am I going to tell her about Tilly? It will break her heart. What sick bastard would do this? Forcing me out of my own home." His eyes had filled with tears.

"That's what we're trying to find out. You really shouldn't stay here."

Steve appeared to think more rationally and proposed, "I suppose I could stay with Tara, at least we'd be together. Or I could go to her dad's, mine are away."

Cheryl Dixon shot a look of concern at Officer Rowe and replied hesitantly, "Er ... No.... ah... we feel that's not in your or Tara's best interest right now. Do you have another place? Someone else you could stay with?"

Steve thought for a moment, "Mum and Dad are out of town at my sister's... I suppose my friend, Paul from work could put me up...."

"Why don't you give him a call?" suggested Officer Rowe.

"Yes, it will give Forensics time to go through the house properly and we can get things cleared up," added Cheryl.

"Cleared up?" questioned Steve.

"Till we get a handle on this... figure out if someone's after Mrs Lomas, or you, or both of you," explained Brandon Rowe.

"If, whoever it is, was after me they could have killed me quite easily. They had plenty of opportunity." Steve's distress was growing stronger. "Why should I be forced out of my own home?"

"We can't order you, but we'd prefer it if you did and also..." Cheryl paused, "It's better that you have no contact with your wife for the moment, Mr Lomas. It's for your own good," she stressed.

"But Tara will want to know about the fish and Tilly...." He trailed off as he slumped into a kitchen chair. "I won't know about Tilly until the vet calls back."

"There's no need to upset her even more. Things are already difficult enough."

"I suppose..."

"The officer on patrol will stay in case the perpetrator comes back."

Officers Rowe and Dixon exchanged another of their looks, which screamed suspicion. This time Steve caught it, "Surely, you don't think I had anything to do with this? You can't believe I'd want to hurt my own wife and Tilly or the fish?" There was an uncomfortable silence. "You do! You think I had something to do with it. I don't believe this..." he dropped his head into his hands and sobbed.

Cheryl composed herself and put on a conciliatory tone, "Mr Lomas, we don't think anything. We have to look at every possibility and we are keen to eliminate you from our enquiries and get to the truth. You have to trust us. Now please, ring your friend."

Back at school rumours had been flying. Gossip grew wings amongst the students who relished in the fact that the school's biggest bully had been hauled into the head's office to be carpeted before Miss Stevens. Few pupils liked him and most avoided him. As far as they were concerned James Treeves would get what he deserved.

James Treeves stood before the headmistress and was looking suitably cowed. "This is the last straw. It was a disgusting act and this vendetta you have against Mrs Lomas must stop."

"It wasn't me, I've told you," protested James.

"Don't lie! We have clear footage of you on CCTV entering the school first thing in the morning. You have been picked up at various points, entering the boys' lavatories and emerging with a container of sorts. You have been filmed going into Mrs Lomas' classroom, tossing the vessel into a litter bin and sneaking out of the building and all before the start of school. You are herewith suspended. I shall be contacting your parents immediately. You … just get out of my sight and wait in the Time Out Room. There you will write letters of apology to Mrs Galbraith and Mrs Lomas. Do you understand?"

"Yes, Miss."

"Now, go."

James Treeves shuffled out of the office with his head bowed. Once in the corridor he perked up and put on a brazen front of bravado. His one friend Tommy was outside. "What happened?"

"Nothing much. Got suspended that's all."

"What will your folks say?"

"They won't care and I don't either. I'll be back before you know it and I'll find a way of getting my own back."

"James, give it up!"

"Only failures give up," snapped James.

"Then, we're over. I can't get involved in any of this or back you up. It's wrong and it's just not worth it."

James shrugged, "Easy come, easy go. Do what you like. You're nothing to me." James strode off toward the Time Out Room.

Tommy Porter shook his head sadly, he knew that was no way for James to treat a friend. Tommy felt he didn't know James as well as he thought. He watched his mate walk away and take a swipe at the notice board on the wall. James kicked the Time Out Room door open with his foot.

Tommy was just about to walk away when he saw two men approaching the school foyer from down the corridor. Tommy's eyes narrowed as they breezed up to the reception window and spoke to Mrs Graff, the school secretary. Tommy could overhear what was being said and listened hard. His mouth dropped open.

"Detective Sergeant Denton and Detective Constable Palmer. We called earlier. We have an appointment to see the headmistress."

"Ah, yes. Come through, won't you?" She opened the office door and admitted them before knocking on the Head's door, who called, "Enter."

Tommy cursed silently, as he couldn't hear anymore, but he was convinced they had come about Mr. Ley. He would have to keep his eyes and ears open.

In the headmistress's study, Miss Stevens indicated the policemen should sit, which they did. "Would you like tea or coffee?"

"No, thank you. We will be brief." Miss Stevens acquiesced with a nod of her head. "We have come into possession of some extremely disturbing information about a member of your staff."

Miss Stevens became alert and sat forward in her seat. "Go on."

"We have file of photographs that suggest this person is involved in child pornography."

Miss Stevens' face registered extreme distaste and shock, "Surely not?"

"There were images of this person involved in an unsavoury, lewd act with a very young child." The lead detective, sergeant Denton removed a photograph from his pocket. It was a close up of Ken Ley's face in the throes of ecstasy. He passed the picture to Miss Stevens. "Do you recognise this person?"

Miss Stevens studied it and gasped. "Why, yes. That's one of my language teachers, Ken Ley."

"Thank you. That confirms it. I will need his home address and details to get a search warrant."

"But, how can this be? All my staff are vetted very carefully."

"If he hasn't committed any crime and no suspicions have been raised before then it wouldn't show up."

"What do I do, now? I mean, are my pupils safe?"

"I believe so. The children depicted are all primary school age. I must insist on your absolute discretion. We don't want to alert him. I just need his personal details."

Miss Stevens nodded, picked up the phone and pressed the button for her secretary. "Julia, can you bring me the staff personnel files, please."

"All of them?"

Miss Stevens looked at the detectives for assurance, "Hold on." She put her hand over the receiver. "I can't single him out, can I?"

Sergeant Denton answered with a shake of his head. "We only need contact details."

Miss Stevens continued, "Um, just the staff contact sheets, please."

"Very well."

Miss Stevens replaced the receiver. There was an uncomfortable silence until the study door opened and Julia Graff entered with a sheaf of papers. "Thank you, Julia." She waited until the secretary had left and passed the papers across to the police.

Sergeant Denton leafed through them until he spotted Ken Ley's details. He removed the paper, "Is it possible to have this copied?"

"Of course." Miss Stevens walked to the photocopier in her room. She copied the selected sheet and passed it to the detective, who examined it and folded it up and placed it in his pocket.

"Thank you, Miss Stevens." The detectives rose and moved to the door.

"Wait!" There was authority in the head's voice and the men stopped and turned. "Is there anything more I should know? Do I need to make provision for losing a teacher?"

Sergeant Denton hesitated. "For the moment, do nothing. Carry on as normal. Do not treat him any differently. We have to get a warrant and find out if there is any substance to these allegations or if it is some clever photoshop work and mischief making. We will be in touch. In the meantime, you will have time to prepare, just in case."

Miss Stevens nodded, "Of course." She shook the detectives' hands and they left her office. Miss Stevens took her seat again with a worried look on her face. She sighed heavily, picked up her pen and resumed what she was doing before the interruption.

Tara sat in the living room of a police safe house in a suburban neighbourhood. She was trying to read a book. Her foot tapped in an agitated fashion and she seemed distracted. Tara was yearning for the outdoors and her eyes kept being drawn to the big bay window and the scene outside. The day looked fresh and inviting. It was a perfect day for running, not too hot with a slight breeze and some cloud cover. Eventually, she tossed down her book. "It's no good. I can't concentrate. I must have read the same sentence sixteen times. I still don't know what it said. I need to go for a run to clear my head. My limbs are seizing up."

Officer Dixon was preparing a report in between gazing out of the window. "I can understand that. You've been through a lot and it isn't exactly exciting sitting here twiddling your thumbs. You must be fed up."

"It's ridiculous. I'm going mad cooped up here. My muscles are jumping. I need to jog and burn off this energy. Not only that I'm bored stiff. If I just had my laptop… or even some school work to do…"

"Watch some TV."

"I'm bored with that, too. Repeats and commercials drive me crazy."

"We can go for a run if you like?"

"In these shoes?" Tara indicated her high heels. "I can't even *walk* that far in these. They are purely car to restaurant and restaurant to car shoes."

Cheryl laughed, "You have a point."

"All my running gear's at home otherwise I would. I need to get outside, now. Do I have to stay here?"

"You don't have to do anything. We advise you to stay put. It's for your own good."

"So, I could leave if I wanted to?"

"You're not under arrest."

"Well, it feels like it."

Cheryl had finished her reports and was now involved in her book, it was a real page turner, a suspenseful political thriller called, 'The Electra Conspiracy' while Tara flicked mindlessly through the TV channels looking for something … anything to watch. She eventually gave up and tossed down the remote control with a sigh. She stood up, "I'm taking a nap." Cheryl looked up to nod her assent and returned to her novel, which she was clearly finding gripping.

Tara removed her shoes and carried them as she walked to a downstairs bedroom door and went inside. She closed the door quietly behind her and paused before she moved to the window and opened it slowly and carefully. She glanced back at the door praying that no one had heard the slide of the sash. She waited a moment longer, put on her coat, popped her mobile into her pocket and collected her bag. Still carrying her shoes, she slipped out of the window and into the back garden. She hopped on one foot as she struggled to replace her shoes and tiptoed to the side of the house where she could check the front. There was a cop car sitting on the road outside with a police guard. Tara retraced her steps and scurried through the back garden, over the lawn and finally, climbed over the locked back gate, where there were a couple of conveniently placed dustbins, which led to an alley. The alley led to a road, which Tara walked down steadily. She turned another corner into a different road. She was feeling like a naughty schoolgirl who had disobeyed her teachers. It actually gave her something of a kick. The feeling of fluttering of excitement within her was far better than the churning fear she had experienced before.

Tara hurried down the street until she reached a busy thoroughfare. She was in an unfamiliar part of town. She looked around wildly and spotted a department store with a taxi rank outside, where there was a cab waiting. She dashed across the road waving at the driver and slipped in the back. She gave the cabbie her address and sighed as she leaned back in the seat.

Tara removed her phone and switched it on. It bleeped immediately with a succession of text messages, all were abusive. She ignored them and hit her contacts button, which she scrolled through until she found Lucy.

"Lucy? Hi…"

"Thought you were grounded? No contact and all that…"

"I've been going stir crazy. I can tell you… So, I've jumped ship. Just going to get my running gear, Nikes and few other things from the house and then slip back. No one will know. I can run with Officer Dixon then."

"Tara, is this wise? What if this sicko is watching your house?" Lucy's voice was filled with concern.

"There's a duty policeman on patrol. I'll have to dodge him. It'll be fine."

"Well, I think it's dumb."

"Too late now. I'm not giving this whack job the satisfaction of frightening me, anymore. Catch you later." Tara ended the call and put the phone back in her pocket.

As the cab approached the end of her road Tara leaned forward in her seat. "Stop here, please. Can I take a card? I will need someone to take me back."

"I can wait if you like, lovey?"

"No, it's okay. I don't know how long I'll be. How much do I owe you?"

Tara paid the driver and scrambled out of the back. She stepped back into someone's front garden where she was partially hidden but could still view the road. She saw the cop car cruise past and murmured, "Right, Tara. You've got five minutes."

Lucy was sitting at her desk in an empty classroom studying her mobile phone. Her expression was thoughtful as she put it in her jacket pocket. She gathered her books together to go home but paused and took out her phone again.

Lucy was troubled and obviously undecided about what to do. She chewed the side of her cheek nervously and came to a decision. She dialled a number, "Hello? Police?"

Tara took a deep breath, removed her shoes again and sprinted down the road wincing when she stepped on a loose bit of grit. "Get a grip, Tara. Don't stop now." She ploughed on down the street, hurtled down the path and fumbled with the front door, searching around her with her eyes for anything sinister. She dived inside and leaned against the door.

She checked the time, fled to the utility and grabbed a holdall. From there she dashed to the hall closet, grabbed her Nikes, an undamaged sweat top and joggers from the floor and stuffed them in her sports bag.

As an afterthought, she nabbed her briefcase, added more paperwork to her loaded holdall and threw in a copy of The Tempest. Tara picked up her laptop and placed it in the bag. She scanned the room and spotted the fish tank with its goldfish missing and no baby sturgeon. Tara frowned and shivered.

Outside in the back garden a cat began to mew. "Tilly!" Tara exclaimed. She set down her things and went to the kitchen. The mewing was louder now. Tara opened the kitchen door expecting to see Tilly come running in with her tail straight in the air but she didn't. The meows were noisier now and seemed to be coming from the garden shed.

Tara crossed the grass to the hut, undid the combination padlock, opened the door and stepped inside making soothing noises, "Okay, Tilly. It's all right. Mummy's home. Where are you, baby?"

On the workbench was an old fashioned tape deck playing the sound of the cat. Tara looked aghast and spun around to see the shed door slammed and locked behind her. She ran to the door and hammered on it, "Who is this? Let me out, now!"

There was a swooshing sound and some sort of liquid was poured around the door and the exterior of the shed. Tara sniffed, "Oh my God, petrol!"

Tara was horrified to hear the whoosh as the gasoline was ignited and everything went up in smoke. Panicked Tara searched around the workshop. She picked up a chisel and plane. She smashed the chisel into the lock. It gave a little but the flames began to lick up around the shed window, crackling and snicking, as it devoured the seasoned wood. She feverishly hammered at the lock, "Damn you! Break!" She bashed at the lock more urgently, which splintered a little more.

Smoke was seeping under the door and pluming up. Tara tried to hold her breath but couldn't and she coughed. Her eyes began to water. There was a sickening crack as the glass in the window fractured. Tara looked up in horror at the rupturing glass that threatened to implode. Finding inhuman strength from somewhere she gave the lock another almighty whack with the plane. The lock finally gave way. She forced her way through the growing inferno and ran coughing to the back door where she collapsed on the step at the precise moment that the glass from the shed window blew out.

Tara scrabbled for her phone and dialled nine, nine, nine. She barely managed to blurt out her words as her throat burned with the acrid smoke she had inhaled. Tara started to shake with shock at what had just occurred. She realised how stupid she had been as Lucy's words had come back to haunt her, 'I think it's dumb.' Tears began to stream down her face. She recognised that she had almost lost her life again. As she pondered this thought sirens could be heard approaching her neighbourhood.

Firefighters arrived and rushed the hose around to the back. They had to prevent the burning shed from igniting the spreading branches of the leafy oak tree hanging over the fence. The wind was fanning the flames. It wouldn't take much to set fire to the creosoted fence and leap onto the house next door.

Tara was reprimanding herself as she sat in the patrol car, door open, her feet on the pavement and head in her hands. She looked up and watched the activity as a few neighbours came out to watch the action. An ambulance was next to arrive. The paramedics dashed out to examine Tara who was now trembling in shock. They placed a clip-like device called a probe on her middle finger to measure how much oxygen was in her blood. One signalled to the other, "It's low. Fetch oxygen." A tank was brought and mask placed over Tara's face. "Three deep breaths, then breathe normally. You're one very lucky lady." A silver foil emergency blanket was wrapped around her to keep her warm.

Tara certainly didn't feel lucky and she groaned inwardly as Officer Dixon arrived on the scene with Officers Connor and Rowe. They stood on the pavement watching Tara's treatment, talking quietly amongst themselves.

Eventually, Cheryl walked across to Tara and said sternly, "That was a pretty stupid thing to do."

Tara removed the mask from her mouth, "I'm sorry… I just thought …"

"That's just it. You didn't think. Thoughts like that can get you killed. We can't risk you being anywhere near here. Whoever it is means business."

"We could go back to the safe house."

"No, we can't. I've just had my ear chewed off about that."

"I'm sorry."

"So, you say. Is there anyone else you can stay with?"

Tara scrunched her nose up as she thought, "No, I don't…" then, blurted out, "Yes, my friend Lucy. She's got a spare bedroom. I'm sure she won't mind." Tara replaced the oxygen mask. And took some more deep breaths.

"Do it. We'll have a look alike in here, posing as you. It may draw the perpetrator out or it may not. But at least you'll be safe. Here, use my phone to call her. Don't use your own in case it is somehow monitored or tracked. We need to be extra vigilant. We will also have someone watch over your friend Lucy's place. Now, call her." Cheryl handed over her mobile phone.

Tara moved the mask again, "I'll have to check my contact list I don't know the number off-hand."

Cheryl nodded and allowed Tara to access her phone book. "I suggest we get you a 'Pay as You Go' handset until we've caught your stalker. I'll get Shay to transfer your contact list for you. Only use it when absolutely necessary. It will be mainly for you to receive calls from us regarding the investigation."

"What about Steve?"

"For the moment there is to be no contact. It's just safer this way in case his phone is tracked, too."

Cheryl turned to the Paramedic in attendance, "Does she need to go to hospital?"

The Medic shook his head, "No, there isn't any lasting damage. She isn't burnt. Just a little hoarse from the smoke inhalation. Her oxygen levels are almost back to normal, her BP is within the normal range now. She'll be fine." He turned to Tara, "Sit here for a few minutes more…"

The firemen had succeeded in getting control of the blaze, which was almost out. The shed had been almost totally destroyed and the fence was just smouldering. They played their hoses on it a while longer until there was nothing to worry about. The fire officer was examining the garden shed and had concurred that it was arson by person or persons unknown.

As Tara sat there waiting to be given the all clear she was much more subdued and repentant. The paramedic nodded at her and she removed her mask. She kept the emergency blanket around her and the ambulance went on its way. Tara attracted Cheryl's attention, "Tell me, please, what happened to the fish and Tilly?"

Officer Dixon's tone was sympathetic, "I'm afraid your fish are gone. The perp found it amusing to try and fry them all up. You nearly had a kitchen fire. The smoke alarm alerted Mr Lomas."

"Oh, no. Not my little baby sturgeon?"

"All of them I'm afraid."

Tara hardly dared ask the next question, "And Tilly?"

"Tilly is at the veterinary hospital in recovery. She survived a vicious attack, but quick thinking by your husband got an animal ambulance out that placed her into emergency treatment at the vets."

Tara shook her head in despair, "Poor Tilly. It's so unfair. Will she be all right?"

"It's my understanding your cat will make a full recovery. It will take a little time, that's all."

Tara nodded in understanding. She said, sadly, "This vendetta against me and those I love … Why? Why is it happening?"

"That's what we need to find out. Now, call your friend."

16

NOW THAT FORENSICS HAD FINISHED examining the Lomas home WPC Donna Carter was house sitting. She had been there a week and yet nothing out of the ordinary had happened; no silent or threatening calls no intrusions into the house and the female officer was beginning to believe it was all a waste of time. The Tara look alike had tried to act and move like Tara after meeting her even down to performing early morning stretches and working out to a fitness DVD.

She reported into the police station with her twice daily call and spoke to her boss, "Either the perp has made me and knows I'm not Tara or has just given up because of the heavy police presence. Drawing the stalker out just doesn't seem to be working."

Instructions came directly from the Superintendent, "We will just give it one more night. Tomorrow morning you can pack up and go home and then I believe you are due some leave. Take it, get rested and we will see you back in a week."

"Yes, Sir. Thank you, Sir."

Donna replaced the handset and looked around the comfortable house that had been her home for a week and murmured, "I need to get myself something like this and get out of that poky flat. In time, Donna, in time."

Donna packed up her few items of clothing and placed them in her car parked in the garage before returning inside. She hadn't fully drawn the curtains and could be seen inside doing her usual workout.

Outside in the shrubbery of the opposite property stood an individual watching. There was an escape of breath in the form of a hiss as the person watched Donna going through her exercise routine. The words from the marauder were barely discernible in the evening air. "So, Bitch, you're back. Well, so am I."

Ken Ley sat at home waiting for the kitchen timer to go off. The table was laid with flowers and candles and the delicious aroma of his Marks and Spencer's meal wafted out from the kitchen. Wine was chilling in the fridge. He was expecting Valerie.

Ken congratulated himself on how well things were progressing. His relationship with the school cleaner was developing really well. In turn, his connection with Daisy was getting stronger, too. He felt aroused as he thought of her sweet innocence and pretty little face with those huge eyes.

He sighed contentedly. Tonight, would be the acid test. He would see how far Valerie would be prepared to embrace him. Then and only then could he court her properly and in turn, Daisy. He took out his phone and scrolled through some of the pictures he had taken of her. He particularly liked the photos of when they all went swimming together at an outdoor lido. He patted his jacket and felt his flash drive secure in his pocket. His lips curled lasciviously convinced he would be adding some more very intimate pictures to his collection.

His doorbell rang. Ken jumped up to admit Valerie. She came in smiling happily. He took her coat, "You managed to get a sitter, then?"

"Yes, I called in a favour from my friend."

"I wouldn't have worried if you had to bring Daisy. I have a place set for her, anyway. But, I must admit it's nice to have you all to myself," he gushed.

Valerie laughed and said, "I must confess, you have played this very well."

"What do you mean?" said Ken, a note of alarm entering his voice.

"Courting the mother through the daughter. Very clever. I am most impressed that you have taken me on board with a child. It's so refreshing."

Ken relaxed, "As far as I'm concerned, mother and daughter come as one. Daisy is a delightful child."

"That's what I mean. Most men run a mile when they know I have a child. It doesn't fit in with their scheme of things." They walked into the sitting room. "Something smells good," said Valerie appreciatively.

Ken tried to laugh it off, "I'm no culinary expert. I'm afraid I was so afraid of messing up I was forced to rely on good old M & S. You can't go wrong with that."

Valerie was ushered to a seat. He removed his jacket and hung it on a chair before sitting next to her. He tilted her chin and kissed her tenderly on the lips. Valerie relinquished herself in his arms. Ken stood up quickly, "Better take it slowly or we won't get to eat," he joked. "Now, a glass of wine I think. What would you like?"

"What have you got?"

"You mean, apart from me?" Ken was rewarded with a girlish giggle and continued, "I have Prosecco, and Soave chilled. If you prefer red I have a smooth little Shiraz, Hardy's Bin 161. Or there's a beer...." He trailed off, "My God, you are beautiful."

Valerie blushed and looked down shyly, "I scrub up well, don't I?"

"More than well."

"Then let's toast our friendship with a glass of Soave,"

"Done," said Ken and went into the kitchen for glasses and wine just as his timer went off. "He called out, "Sit up. It won't be long."

Ken returned with the wine and glasses and poured them each one. He raised his glass and chinked hers, "To us," and then he added, "And Daisy."

Valerie repeated the toast and drank. "And now, milady, dinner will be served in a jiffy." Ken disappeared into the kitchen. He emerged moments later with two paellas "As you can see, I have added extra prawns, fish and mussels."

"I love Paella."

"I know. That's why I bought this meal!" He deposited the plates, "Now eat up!"

They settled into their dinner. The atmosphere was relaxed and happy. Ken poured some more wine. They chinked glasses again. "What about dessert?" asked Ken.

Valerie rose and went to the settee, "I think dessert can wait a little while, don't you?" she said provocatively.

Ken followed and settled next to her when the doorbell rang. "Who on earth can that be?" he said in irritation. "Sorry, Valerie. I'll get rid of them as soon as I can."

Ken went to the front door and opened it only to be led back inside by a uniformed copper. A number of police and detectives entered. "What's the meaning of this intrusion?" remonstrated Ken.

Sergeant Denton waved a piece of paper at him. "We have a warrant to search this house. You are Ken Ley, are you not?'

"Yes.... A warrant? Whatever for?"

"If you don't mind. We will undertake the search first." A policeman stood in front of the couple ensuring they didn't move.

"I'm so sorry, Valerie. I have no idea what this is about. It's all some horrible mistake."

The police seemed to be everywhere, in his study, upstairs, hunting through his bureau. One policeman emerged with a laptop and removed it to a vehicle outside. Similarly, his desk top PC was also unplugged and taken to a waiting car.

Valerie rose, "Perhaps, I should go?" she said fearfully.

Ken looked anxiously about him, "I don't see why you should. I'm sure there has been some error. They must have the wrong house or something."

"All the same. It seems to have killed the mood."

She stood up, a policeman came across, "I'm afraid I can't let you leave without taking your details..."

Valerie gave her full name, address and phone number and allowed herself to be patted down and her bag and coat pockets searched before she was allowed to leave. "I'll call you later," she said to Ken.

The police were in the living room, opening drawers and rifling through them. They took Ken's mobile phone and one copper began searching Ken's jacket pockets. He shouted, "Now, hold on... you have no right..."

Sergeant Denton said calmly, "We have every right and a warrant to prove it."

The policeman investigating Ken's coat called, "Serge!" He held up the memory stick with the red cap."

Ken began to bluster and fuss, "That's my exam test papers. You can't take that. I need it for work."

"Do you now?" said Denton. "Constable, bring me the police laptop and let's see exactly what is on here."

"Sir."

The constable went outside and returned with a police computer and fired it up. They inserted the flash drive and downloaded the contents. Ken went white and his hands began to shake.

Denton scrutinised the seemingly innocent pictures that became lewd and obscene as he scrolled down. He turned to the copper, "Cuff him and read him his rights."

"You are under arrest on suspicion of child pornography. You do not have to say anything, but it may harm your defence if you do not mention when questioned something, which you later rely on in court. Anything you do say may be given in evidence." Ken Ley blustered and fussed as he was led away shouting that he'd been framed and it was a set up.

Sergeant Denton followed them outside leaving his officers to continue searching the house. Valerie was standing on the kerb waiting for a cab that she'd ordered. Denton crossed to her. "Are you all right for getting home?"

She nodded, "I think so. I've called a cab."

Denton continued, "Have you by any chance got children?"

"Er, yes. A little girl, Daisy."

"And how old is Daisy?"

"She's eight. Why do you ask?"

Denton pursed his lips, "I can't say too much, but I think you've had a lucky escape. We will be in touch."

Valerie's complexion became ashen; just then her cab drew up. With trembling hands, she opened the car door and got inside, gave her address to the cabbie and the vehicle moved away.

Tara was well settled into Lucy's apartment, having been there a week. Lucy had been late home from school and they had finally sat down to eat after ordering a Chinese takeaway and opening a bottle of wine to share.

"Tell me again about all the events, all that you can remember."

"You've heard it before."

"But not all of it and not in detail. I am trying to formulate a plan."

"Oh, what?"

"Just tell me from the beginning."

This time, Tara was feeling more relaxed as she recounted events. She finished describing the fire, took a mouthful of her stir fry and wagged her fork at Lucy, "I have never been so scared in all my life. I honestly thought I was going to die."

"This is madness. You can't go on like this. If only we could work out who it is."

"Fat chance of that. The police are stumped."

"Let's eat first and then I have an idea."

The two friends chatted happily through the rest of their meal and Tara caught up with all the school news. She even managed to forget her situation and laughed at a huge faux pas made by the head when she asked for volunteers to clear out her back passage. "You should have seen the students' faces. They didn't dare snigger. There was a lot of coughing and spluttering. They couldn't even look at each other. Even the staff were shuffling their feet and looking down."

"Sounds hysterical. Wish I could have seen it."

Lucy swallowed her last mouthful of noodles and soy sauce dribbled down her chin. She mopped it away and took a swig of wine. "Right, let me clear this lot away and you sit tight."

"Wait, let me help."

"You can pour us another glass of wine."

"I haven't finished the first!"

"I'll hang on for you; just get the bottle, while I put this lot in the bin."

"You're not keeping the remains for another meal?"

"Why? Do you like the congealed mess it becomes? I don't."

"Then, bin it. I just thought the noodles and rice would be worth saving. You can freeze it for another time. Mind if I pick the rest of the cashews out of this dish?" asked Tara pointing at the remnants of a chicken and cashew dish.

"Be my guest," said Lucy with a wave of her hand. "Maybe I will freeze the rice and noodles... better let them cool first." She swept the other items into the trash can and scurried to a drawer to get a notepad and pen. She plonked herself back in her seat, "Right, when did it start?"

"You mean for us to work out who it is?"

"Well, if the police are stymied they clearly need our help. Now think. We want to put everything down, all the incidents and likely suspects."

"Okay."

"Tell me everything, no matter how small, from the stuff at school and everything else."

Lucy scribbled notes on a pad as Tara recounted all the incidents she could recall. "It all seems to come down to when I started on Friend Finder."

"Don't forget the school tricks. Do you feel they are separate events?"

Tara scrunched up her face. "I think so. Except for the flowers and rat. I think that came from somewhere else."

Lucy looked thoughtful. "Friend Finder? Hard to believe that something that's so much fun could turn into something so sinister," said Lucy.

"There was the Craig's list killer in America."

"Before my time."

"What I mean is, if it happened there it could happen here. That's supposed to be a fun site for selling unwanted items like on Gum Tree or eBay."

"You had a suspicion about Lee Powell, didn't you?"

"Not really. He seemed so nice. He was massively shocked when he looked at my page. I believe his reaction was genuine."

"Didn't you tell the police?"

Tara gasped with the realisation, "Oh my God, no. I meant to, but things just kept happening and I haven't mentioned it."

"Tara, you must tell them what you know. They'll interview him and if it's all above board, he'll soon be eliminated from their enquiries."

"Or, we could go online and message this Lee Powell, confront him. If he's got nothing to hide…. And if we can find out where he lives I may just do a little following myself."

"Tara! You can't!"

"Watch me." Tara rose and picked up Lucy's telephone directory. She began scrolling through the numerous people called Powell in the book. I know he lives around here." Tara found a number of entries under L. Powell. She looked at the area codes for each number and dismissed them all except for one. "This is it. It's got to be."

Lucy peered at the address, "That's only about five miles away."

"It has to be right. Come on, let's go."

"Tara, are you sure about this?"

"Faint heart never won fair lady."

"What's that supposed to mean?"

"I don't know; seemed the right thing to say. Get your keys. We're going sleuthing!"

"You make us sound like Rizzoli and Isles."

"But not as glamorous, more Rosemary and Thyme."

"Speak for yourself. I'll have you know I'm gorgeous," said Lucy.

Tara looked regretfully at the bottle of wine, "Stick it in the fridge. Are you safe to drive?"

"I've had one glass, haven't touched the second. I'll be fine. I'll put it with the wine to keep chilled. Come on, let's go. I'll set the Sat Nav." They left the lights on and switched on the TV. "People will think we're home. No need to advertise the fact that we're out." Lucy picked up her keys and jacket and the two left the house, checking first that it was safe and that they weren't observed. They scuttled to Lucy's car and set the Sat Nav.

The shadows of night caressed the car on the quiet suburban cul-de-sac where Lee Powell lived, protecting it from residents' eyes. It didn't look out of place as there were a number of vehicles lining the road and they had managed to get a spot directly opposite his house.

They slunk down in their seats, so they couldn't easily be seen and watched. The curtains of Lee's front room were open and Lee was visible working away on his computer. So engrossed was he in what he was doing, chewing his pencil, scribbling notes on a pad, stuffing the pencil behind his ears and tapping on his computer keys that he was oblivious to the eyes that watched.

Lucy yawned loudly and sat up stretching her arms. "Ouch! I've got cramp in my leg." She bent over and vigorously rubbed her right calf. "I need to get out and stamp my feet and walk a bit."

"You can't!" exclaimed Tara. He may see us."

"So? He doesn't know who I am."

"No, but he would recognise me."

Lucy glanced at her watch, "We've been here three hours and nothing. The man's a geek. He doesn't even get up to pee. Tap, tap, dib, dab. Nothing."

"He doesn't look dangerous... more like he belongs on a surfboard."

"He looks rather nice but we mustn't be fooled...Remember, the documentary we watched on Ted Bundy? He was handsome and charming. He didn't look like a psychopathic killer. Heck, women fell for him all the time."

"You may be right. Let's get back and go with your idea and interrupt him. Disturb his night."

17

LUCY AND TARA DROVE BACK to Lucy's and parked. They scurried inside like two conspirators planning a robbery. Lucy booted up her PC, while Tara retrieved the wine from the fridge. "Gimme, gimme!" exclaimed Lucy. This is just what I need," she said holding out her hand and wriggling her fingers.

Tara laughed as she said, "You look like a demented puppet master, stretching your fingers like that!" and passed her the glass. Lucy turned back to the screen and clicked on the Friend Finder icon and did a search for Lee Powell. "You can do it through my page. Then your messages will get through."

"Good idea. Log us in and then I'll take over."

Tara sat in Lucy's vacated seat and pulled up her page. Fortunately, there were no more abusive messages; her blocking tactics had worked. She pulled up her private message box and typed in the recipient, Lee Powell. She sent a message, "Can we talk?"

Sitting at his PC Lee Powell wiped his brow and murmured, "I need a break and a cup of coffee to keep me awake." He was just about to rise from his chair when his laptop pinged with information in the top right hand corner of his screen that he had a personal message from Tara Lomas.

Curiosity got the better of him and he clicked on the message and opened up a dialogue box between him and Tara. He typed, "Yes, of course. How are you?"

Tara typed back, "Things are not good. I am being persecuted by some vicious stalker and have almost lost my life. I'm quite emotional at the moment so I am going to pass you across to my friend Lucy. She will talk for me. She types quicker than me."

"O…Kay…" There was uncertainty in the tone of the typing.

"Hello, Lee. I'm Lucy, Tara's friend. Do you know anything about this vendetta on Tara?"

"No, I only saw the messages, for the first time, after Tara contacted me."

"You know, she's been threatened and terrorised in her own home and nearly lost her life twice?"

"No… This has nothing to do with me, I swear. I am truly shocked."

"So, if it isn't you….?

"I'll say it again, I'll do a lie detector test or anything. It is not me."

"Then, who could it be? This whole thing seems to have started after she joined Friend Finder."

"I don't understand how a simple online friendship could escalate into something like this."

"We don't know, either but it has."

A thought suddenly occurred to Tara, "Ask him if he knows Jan Bernard."

"Who?" asked Lucy.

"Just type it." Lucy did as she was asked.

The reply was immediate, "Jan? Why? Do you know her?"

"It seems that you do," typed Lucy.

"We were friends, good friends. We used to work together until…"

"Until she was murdered."

"Yes…"

Lucy waited for Lee to continue but he didn't; so Lucy resumed her typing. "Did you know that she was harassed like Tara before she died?"

"I know, I heard … I can only think…"

"What?"

"My ex-wife, Skye. I've told Tara about her."

"What about her?"

"She works in telecommunications."

Lucy stopped typing and looked at Tara, "That's it! It's got to be. She would have the means to trace your numbers, where you live… it all fits."

Lee continued, "Tara, you have to tell the police. Skye is unhinged. Oh my God, it all makes sense. Call them now and tell them. They can come and see me or contact me. I can tell you where she is. If it is her, there must be evidence on her computer."

"Sounds like you are the key to this. Can you tell me where she lives and works?"

"Sure." Lee typed out Skye's address, her work place and her phone numbers.

"Thanks. Okay, signing off now. Bye." Lucy closed the dialogue box. "It has to be her. She would be able to get your new number and your mobile number, where you live and work ... I bet she sent you the rat at school."

"What are we waiting for?"

"Call your cop friend."

Ken Ley had been let out on bail and was on his way into school. He was not relishing facing other members of staff. He wondered how much they knew, if anything. He believed rumours had been flying about, rumours he was hoping to quash. He turned into the staff car park, picked up his briefcase and hurried in through the main entrance. The school secretary, Mrs Graff spotted him and called out, "Mr Ley? Mr Ley?" The teacher stopped and turned questioningly. "Miss Stevens would like to see you in her office." Mrs Graff forced a half smile.

Ken Ley tried to interpret the secretary's manner and beamed back a little too broadly. "Of course, Mrs Graff. What time?"

"She asked to see you as soon as you arrived. You can go in now," said Mrs Graff who attempted another smile but the smile didn't reach her eyes. Ken's heart was pounding as he nodded his head.

He walked into the office and crossed to the head's door and knocked. "Enter!" Ken took a deep breath and went inside. Miss Stevens peered up at him over her spectacles and rose. "Mr Ley, please take a seat." She indicated the chair on the opposite side of the desk. Ken Ley sat on the edge of the seat leaning forward. He tried to put on his most benign, innocent expression.

"Miss Stevens, I can assure you that there has been a grave error..."

She cut him off, "Really? And what error would that be?"

He blushed and blustered, "I am being accused of some heinous crime of which I am totally innocent."

"Are you? And what crime would that be?" Ken Ley stopped and swallowed. He had the good grace to look down. "Abominable stuff. I've been fitted up, some student wanting to do me down has faked some pictures of me in compromising situations."

"Really? I was assured by the police that the photographs were genuine."

"They can't be. They must have been photo-shopped."

"Never-the-less, Mr Ley, I simply cannot take any risks. Parents would have me pilloried if a sniff of this got out. Innocent or not, I have no option but to suspend you until all investigations are completed."

"But…"

"No buts. You are to leave the premises immediately. Mr Ley, my hands are tied. I hope for your sake and ours that it proves to be a cruel trick. You have to appreciate that I have to take precautions to protect the school's name."

Ken Ley nodded his head, turned on his heel and left. Miss Stevens watched him move out through the door. She sighed sadly and murmured, "Alas, Mr Ley I believe you are guilty as charged."

Ken Ley skulked out of the office not bothering to say goodbye to Mrs Graff or anyone else. He wondered how on earth someone had copied his flash drive and then a name burst from his lips, "Tara Lomas." Vindictively, he wondered how he could wreak his revenge on the English teacher.

Lucy had left for work, her words of advice rang around Tara's head, "Lock all the doors and windows. Don't go out. Keep safe." Tara laughed at her little addendum as she went out through the door, "Oh, and prepare me a feast for when I get back."

Tara had made a full report on the phone to Cheryl Dixon who had promised to call her back on her unregistered mobile. This was one number the perpetrator wouldn't have and was safe to use.

Tara was still in her dressing gown. She wandered into the kitchen to make herself a coffee when the phone in her pocket began to buzz. "Hello?"

"Cheryl here. I just want to verify a few things before I give the full report to the other officers."

"Yes?"

"Firstly, I am curious as to why you didn't give us Lee Powell's name from the start? It would have saved us an awful lot of hassle."

"To begin with, I didn't connect him to the calls or anything else. It just didn't seem likely. After all, he only knew my name from Friend Finder, no personal details and it seemed doubtful, but never-the-less, a coincidence. When Steve and I discussed it, we were going to tell you but then so many things happened it just went out of our heads. Stupid really."

"Yes, it was. If we had known this from the start we could have done something about it immediately." Cheryl Dixon's tone was full of displeasure.

"Sorry," said Tara sheepishly. "What happens now?"

"Firstly, I have to give my full report to the Super and a copy to the other officers working this case and then we will examine the evidence. At the moment it's just supposition. We need hard proof. We have to persuade the powers that be that we can bring this woman in for questioning and conduct a search of her work premises and home address. I will keep you posted."

"Thanks, Cheryl."

"Don't thank me, yet. We have to get the permissions first. I'll be in touch."

She ended the call. Tara sighed and remonstrated with herself, "How could I have been so stupid?"

At Tara's house, Donna Carter had just finished breakfast. She cleared away the breakfast things and packed the remaining food items from the fridge into a cool box. She checked the house making sure everything was locked up tightly. Donna entered the spare room, pulling back the bed linen that needed changing before going downstairs, through the garage to her car. She opened the garage door and drove out onto the drive before getting out and closing it manually after leaving the zapper on the shelf by the entrance to the house. The door slid down and automatically locked.

Donna got back in her car. The patrolman had been pulled off watch and she began to drive away. Donna didn't see the dark vehicle with tinted windows move out into the road behind her and follow her on her journey.

The pursuing car was careful, believing it was Tara in the other car. The journey twisted and turned taking both vehicles to the other side of town. Donna was looking forward to a shower in her own place and a night in her own bed. She would do her washing and pack a few items and go to visit her mother who was always nagging her to come and see her. Donna was carried away on her own thoughts as she drove into a dusty side street and entered the grounds of a block of flats. She parked in a space around the back. The other vehicle followed.

Donna grabbed her case and locked her car. She hummed a Kylie Minogue song as she walked in through the entrance to the lift. She pressed the button when a young man came running down the stairs. He called to her, "Lift's out of order again. You'll have to take the stairs."

"Oh, great!" grumbled Donna as she moved to the stairs and began to walk up them.

A hooded figure appeared at the end of the passage way and hurried to the stairwell and looked up, watching carefully where Donna was headed and followed at a discrete distance. Donna lugged her valise up the steps and turned left into the third floor corridor. She was then able to pull the case on its wheels, which was easier going and stopped outside one door. She fished in her bag for her keys. "Why are they always in the bottom of my bag?" she groaned.

Donna opened the door and ventured inside her flat, dragging her case inside. She left it inside by the front door and walked into her sitting room and veered off to her shower room. She turned on the water to give it time to warm up and strolled into her bedroom, stripping off her shirt. She divested herself of her clothes and took a big bath towel from the linen cupboard and wrapped it around her, before retreating back into the bathroom.

Tara's stalker had followed Donna watching which flat she had entered believing it was yet another safe house for the teacher and grinned. "You won't escape me this time, bitch! No way."

The assailant checked along the corridor on both sides and moved toward the door of number thirty-eight. From the jacket pocket a small flat card-like device was removed that was used to slide between the lock and door jamb. On the second attempt the door clicked open and the intruder was inside. The door closed softly and the person stealthily crept to where the sound of running water could be heard. A large blade with a serrated edge was moved from the other pocket and wielded in the hand of the perpetrator.

Donna was singing now at the top of her voice as she lathered her hair in the steaming hot shower. She didn't hear someone entering her flat or the bathroom, she didn't hear the squeak of the shower door as it opened. In a frenzied attack the assailant leapt onto the back of the naked, vulnerable police officer and quickly drew the blade across her throat. Blood fountained out and mingled with the shower spray. Blood ran in rivulets down Donna's body pooling at her feet.

She had no time to struggle or scream but the sound of a frothing gurgle filled the small space and the coppery smell of arterial blood filled the air. Donna's body slumped to the floor as her limbs twitched involuntarily in her final death throes. Surgically gloved hands turned off the shower spray and the figure stooped down and twisted the policewoman's head around and into view, almost wresting it from her neck. In spite of the agonised expression on

Donna's face the killer could now see that it wasn't Tara and a snarl of fury erupted with a cry of "Nooooooo!"

In the next flat, ninety year old Betty Sumner was buttering a fruit scone to go with her cup of tea when she heard a strange burbling noise followed by a deep bellowing cry that seemed ripped from someone's belly. Betty stopped and listened, her mouth dropped open. She put her ear to the wall and heard the sound of next door's shower and then silence. She shrugged, "Water must have been too cold," said Betty aloud and laughed.

Betty returned to buttering her scone when she heard another crash like someone wrecking something or pulling furniture over. Then a door slammed. Betty crossed to her front window and looked out but could see nothing. She opened her front door and peered outside to see a figure disappearing around the corridor to the stairwell.

Cheryl Dixon finished photocopying her report. One she left on the Superintendent's desk and another she slapped in front of Officer Brandon Rowe. He looked up from his computer screen and raised an eyebrow quizzically, "What's this?"

"The call we had from Mrs Lomas. It's all explained in here. Check it out."

Brandon picked up the sheaf of papers and began to scan read. He studied one section closely and gave a long low whistle, "This Skye Powell ... She works at Bartmer Telecommunications, which explains a lot."

"Easy enough for her to get unlisted numbers and contact information. Goddamn she can find out loads of personal details," said Cheryl.

"Any priors?"

"Restraining orders preventing her from contacting her ex and her kids."

Officer Rowe's eyebrow went up again, "Why?"

"She tried to knife them... all of them."

Officer Rowe rose and grabbed his jacket. "Connor still on patrol?"

"As far as I know."

"Then let's get going." Brandon led the way out of the office.

Cheryl Dixon and Brandon Rowe ran up the steps of the large building that was Bartmer telecommunications. They proceeded through the revolving doors into the lobby and marched across to the Reception Desk. The middle aged security man looked up expectantly. "Yes? Can I help you?"

The coppers showed their identification, "Which floor is Bartmer Telecommunications Personnel Office on, please?"

The Security man scratched his head. "I believe it's on 6th along with Accounts. If you check the board by the lifts it will confirm the room number." He smiled affably.

"Thanks." Cheryl and Brandon crossed to the elevators, checked the information board and pressed the call button. Doors opened immediately as there was one waiting on the ground floor. They travelled up and stepped out into a clinical looking corridor. "What was the number?" asked Brandon.

"Six-one-four, if I remember rightly," said Cheryl. "It'll be marked Personnel, anyway."

Brandon pointed at the notice on the wall stating even numbers to the right and odd numbers to the left. "Right," said Brandon. "This way." He gestured with his hand and they stepped out purposefully to find Personnel. They knocked and entered.

In the outer office was a secretary busy filing. She turned in surprise. "Yes?"

"Police. We need to speak to the Personnel Manager on a matter of utmost urgency."

"Of course." The young woman picked up the phone on her desk, "Mrs Stanton, the police are here to see you. They said it's urgent." She listened to the reply, replaced the receiver and turned to them, "Mrs Stanton will see you now." They nodded their thanks and entered the plush office with large windows and expansive views over the city.

An attractive woman with her blue grey hair swept up in a French pleat looked up from her desk, "Hello. How can I help you?" The name plate on her desk read, Mrs Joyce Stanton Head of Personnel. They flashed their police badges and introduced themselves. Mrs Stanton indicated that they each pull up a seat. She was horrified by what they had to impart.

Cheryl Dixon concluded, "So, you see it's imperative that we don't alert Skye Powell that we are investigating her but we need to do a search on her work computer and station. The only way she could possibly have gained personal information about someone is through your company. We need proof of that."

Mrs Stanton sighed and looked thoughtful, "I see…. Well, Officers you are in luck. Skye is currently on annual leave for two weeks. So, she isn't in the building. She's not back for another week ... Do you have a warrant?" The last question was asked almost casually.

"We can get one. It's no problem but with something as serious as this when a woman's life is in danger, we need to act quickly."

"Of course, I appreciate that. Let me make a call."

Mrs Stanton picked up the phone, "Bernice, can you put me through to Stuart Riley, please?" She waited until the call was connected and explained the situation to the CEO of the company. "I see. Yes, of course." She disconnected the call and used the internal phone to dial the Accounts Department Head, Marie Yately. "Marie? Joyce Stanton here. I have two police officers who will be along to your department in a few minutes. You are to give them complete co-operation on Mr Riley's instructions... Yes ... They wish to examine Skye Powell's work station and search her desk... No, nowhere else... Thank you."

She replaced the handset and turned to the officers who had exchanged a look of satisfaction. "That's all been cleared. I had to get permission from the top, you understand? When you leave my office, turn right and walk straight to the bottom of this corridor. There is a large open plan office and a meeting room together with Marie's office, which is off the main one. She will help you all she can."

"Thank you, Mrs Stanton. You have been most helpful," said Cheryl as they left. Brandon nodded politely and smiled.

They left Personnel with purpose in their stride, "That was easier than I thought," said Brandon.

"Well, the company has nothing to hide. Why wouldn't they help us?" They had reached the end of the corridor. "This is it," Cheryl looked up at the name in bold typeface, Accounts. "Gosh it's massive," she added as they walked through the swing doors. The place was filled with people all working on computers and manning phones. It was a hive of activity. They spotted Marie Yately at her office window who beckoned them across and inside. They closed the door.

Brandon explained their reasons for being there. "I can't stress enough how important it is that no one knows why we are here. It is vital that no one alerts Mrs Powell."

"That can be easily explained. You are not in uniform. No one is aware of who you are. I will take you to her work station, move her relief co-worker and you can examine her desk and computer. If anyone asks I can always explain it away as a software problem that needs fixing. Follow me."

Marie led them into the busy office where there was a constant buzz of chatter. Aubrey looked up curiously as he saw his boss lead two people to Skye's desk. "Ah, Gillian. Can you take a break for ten minutes. I need to get this PC checked over."

"Certainly Ms Yately." The temp moved to the coffee station and staff room.

Aubrey looked across and watched curiously. "Anything I can do to help?" he asked hoping to elicit some information.

"No, it's all right. Thank you. There's a glitch with the programme sending out account overdue letters from this computer. I have already had six complaints this morning." She nodded brightly at Aubrey who returned to his own work. "I'll leave you to it. If you need anything else, you know where to find me." Marie moved away and began her patrol of the floor checking in with some of her workers while Brandon got to work on the PC.

Cheryl went through Skye's desk carefully. There was nothing there to suggest anything untoward. No personal details or printouts of anything except work related material. Cheryl sighed and turned to Brandon who had logged onto Skye's computer. He examined a number of desk top files that all appeared legitimate and shook his head. He swore under his breath, "There doesn't seem to be anything here"

"Try her search history, the whole lot."

Brandon accessed the list of sites and searches and trawled through them. His eyes gleamed as he spotted one entry with the name Tara Lomas and pulled it up on screen. It was a search for a new landline number with Tara's full name and address.

"Bingo! Found one."

Cheryl peered over his shoulder and grinned. "Keep going. See what else is there."

Brandon continued to search further back and gave a low whistle, "Got another here."

"Where?" Brandon highlighted it. "My God, Jan Bernard! We'll have to take the whole unit. It needs one of our techies to look for all the deleted files. I'll see Miss Yately."

Brandon continued his search while Cheryl approached the department head. "Er... Miss Yately?"

Miss Yately stopped conversing with a young girl with pink hair and a nose ring. "Yes?"

"We have found two correctable problems but there are a number of other irregularities. Do you have a replacement computer for this station, as we will have to remove this one to work on at the office?"

Marie nodded, "Yes, we have spares for just such a purpose. Take it away. I'll just copy her files onto a memory stick to upload on her replacement one."

Marie took a flash drive and inserted it into the PC and once she was satisfied that everything had downloaded onto the stick, she removed it and said, "All yours."

"Thanks." Brandon shut it down and unplugged it.

"I'll get a replacement here, right away."

Brandon picked up the PC and passed the keyboard to Cheryl, before turning to Marie. "We'll get it back to you as soon as possible."

Marie nodded, "I'll see you out."

As they left the busy hub, Aubrey turned to the person at the next desk, "Is it just me or was there something odd about that? I certainly don't remember Skye's computer playing up. The temp hadn't noticed anything."

"Marie did say that it was a glitch in sending out letters. I doubt we would notice something like that. All the complaints came through to Marie."

"There is that, I suppose," said Aubrey who shrugged and returned to his work.

The two officers left Bartmer feeling confident that when the computer was checked thoroughly it would reveal all of Skye Powell's browsing history. "We need to get Mr and Mrs Lomas back together and update them on our latest findings. Organise a car to collect them from their respective lodgings and bring them to the station," said Cheryl.

"I'm sure they'll be delighted to see each other," affirmed Brandon.

"Yes, and I believe their cat is due to come home soon, too. It will be a real family reunion."

Cheryl and Brandon walked back to their car and safely stowed the computer in the back together with its attachments. Cheryl took out her mobile while Brandon slipped into the driver's seat and used his phone to arrange cars for Mr and Mrs Lomas. He gave the dispatcher the details and started the engine while Cheryl called Steve Lomas on his direct line.

"Mr Lomas? ... A car will be along shortly to pick you up to bring you to the station and then take you home. We have a break in the case... Yes, your wife will be there, too... Great" Cheryl curtailed the call and rang Tara on her unregistered mobile. "Hi, it's me, Cheryl, Officer Dixon.... Yes.... Looks like your suspicions were correct. We're sending a car for you and Mr Lomas.... We'll bring you up to speed at the station.... Yes, see you then. Bye." She turned to Brandon, "Car organised? All done?"

"Done," he affirmed.

"Great. Now let's get this P.C. to our guys and see what else they can pull up."

Tara and Steve held tightly to each other's hands in Interview Room Three as they listened to Cheryl Dixon's report. A young police constable knocked and entered carrying a tray of coffee, which he placed on the desk and left.

"From what you've said so far, surely you have enough to detain her?" said Steve.

"She's been careful and deleted her search history but we did find one entry relating to Mrs Lomas."

"Tara, please. We know each other well enough, now."

Cheryl nodded, "Tara... Interestingly, we also found an earlier search entry regarding Jan Bernard." Steve and Tara looked at each other as Cheryl continued. "Skye Powell had just been given two weeks off so we were able to access her place of work."

Brandon Rowe chipped in, "Her computer has been removed for further examination. We will have it thoroughly scrutinised and should get back all her deleted files and search history. There's bound to be more evidence in there."

"How did you explain taking her work computer away?"

"Easily, her manager reported a fault. Her relief co-worker was given another PC to work from. It has been taken away to be repaired or so she thinks. Skye is unaware that we have her machine. She thinks it's with techies within the company."

"Could this other co-worker be under suspicion, too?" asked Tara.

"No, the search history dates don't tally with the co-worker's duty hours."

"Do you really think it's her? This Skye Powell? I mean, a woman doing all this to another woman..."

"Yes, after speaking with her husband, we feel it is highly likely but we need more evidence. A computer search is not necessarily a sign of either physical attacks or cyber abuse and bullying."

They sat quietly a moment digesting this information and sipped their coffees. Tara was looking increasingly thoughtful. It was clear some sort of plan was forming in her mind. She spoke slowly, "What if.... What if you use me to draw her out?"

Steve objected instantly, "Tara, no!"

Tara ignored him and Cheryl pressed her, "Go on."

"I want this to be over. We can't have investigations that drag on for months. I want my life…" she corrected herself, "Our life back. I want to be free from fear. Let's do it. Your look alike clearly didn't work. It has to be me."

Cheryl looked at Brandon who chipped in, "It would help us out and speed things up. That is, if it is this Skye person."

"I'll be the bait."

"That's not quite how I would put it but, yes," said Brandon.

Again, Steve protested, "No, you've been through enough."

Tara turned to her husband and insisted, "Steve, it's my decision… let's do it. What do we have to do?"

"Firstly, you need to get back in your own house," said Cheryl.

"Thank goodness for that," interjected Tara.

Brandon Rowe continued, "You will have to change all the locks, including the garage and door from the garage to the house."

"I can deal with that," said Steve. "I'm due some time off. Work will understand. I can get that all fixed today."

"Good. Officer Shay Connor will continue to patrol the area as before. We don't want to make it too easy. She needs to think she can out-fox us."

"This is all very well but …"

"Steve, please." Tara quieted her husband with her words and then spoke to the officers, "What do I have to do?"

Cheryl continued, "Try to act as normally as possible."

"Like we did before all this happened?"

"Yes, the same routines, usual activities. We want her to think you're more relaxed about everything, after all, nothing has happened for a while. Like you said, she probably made your look-a-like and knew it wasn't you so she didn't strike. Do you think you can act like everything is okay?"

"I can do that. Anyway, it will be good to get home." Tara smiled reassuringly at Steve who continued to look doubtful.

"There will see be the fall back of the police patrol, duties shared between us and Officer Connor," said Brandon Rowe. "Now, are you completely sure you want to do this?"

Tara nodded vigorously, "Absolutely. Bring it on."

18

TARA SAID A TENDER GOODBYE to Steve who left the station with a police locksmith. Cheryl turned to Tara, "Okay, we'll swing by your friend's place and pick up your stuff. Leave a note for her that you're going home and then we'll move onto the vets to collect, Tilly."

The first look of concern crossed Tara's face, "Will Tilly be safe?"

"I'm sure she will. Cats are very resilient and they do have nine lives."

"Maybe," and for the first time Tara sounded uncertain.

"Only if you want to, you can keep her in for a few days. Don't let her roam at night. Lock the cat flap. If she stays close to you she should be safe. But it's up to you."

"I suppose," said Tara wistfully. "All the same, I would never forgive myself if anything happened to her. But, I would love to see her. I have so missed her."

"Then let's get going. First stop, your friend, Lucy's place." They left the station together and Cheryl took her to the police car park where she picked up an unmarked police vehicle, a smart silver BMW.

As they travelled to Lucy's address they chatted freely. It was as if arriving at this monumental decision had given Tara new purpose and enthusiasm. "I still find it hard to believe that a woman would act in this way," said Tara.

"Don't be fooled. Women can be just as cruel as men and often worse as they are definitely more devious than the male of the species."

"I thought it just happened in films, like Fatal Attraction."

"Don't think I know that one." said Cheryl.

"It's an old movie with Michael Douglas and Glenn Close, really scary. You should watch it. It's a classic. I think it was made in the late eighties. Still gives me the creeps. I reckon this Skye lifted her antics straight out of that screenplay. Right down to the bunny boiling."

"Bunny boiling?"

"Yes, the psycho boiled their pet rabbit."

"Bit like frying your fish and Tilly."

"Yes. How could anyone do that?"

"I don't know. There are some crazy people in the world." Cheryl pulled up outside Lucy's. "Okay, in you go. Get your stuff and write that note, I'll wait here." Tara nodded and got out of the car. She ran down the path and into her friend's home. After about ten minutes she emerged again with a small bag and got back in the car. "Right, next stop the vets."

They set off for the local Veterinary Surgery in Channing Lane. It didn't take long and conversation was limited as Tara worried about her feline friend and her safety. Cheryl was more circumspect and respectful knowing how much the little cat meant to Tara. They parked and went into the vets together and approached reception.

"I've come to collect Tilly, Tilly Lomas."

"Ah, yes."

"How is she?" asked Tara anxiously. "Will I be able to take her home?"

"It's been a long haul, but thanks to your husband she got to us in time. An hour or two later and it would have been a different story." The receptionist left her station and went through to the back.

"You'll have a hefty bill," said Cheryl.

"We have pet insurance but whatever it cost we would pay it. She is so worth it."

"I know. These fur balls get right into our hearts, don't they?"

A few minutes later the receptionist returned with the vet who had treated Tilly. "Ah, Mrs Lomas." Tara rose and went to meet David Caulfield. "Tilly has had a very bad scare, she is no longer as trusting with people. It has made her quite timid, but I am sure she will be fine with you." Tara nodded in understanding. "The pet insurance has covered most of the bill. There are just two night's lodging to take care of, but in view of the circumstances we have discounted her keep by ten percent."

"Thank you."

"If you'd like to settle up with Marian," he indicated the receptionist. "I'll get Tilly."

Tara walked back to the counter and paid the bill. She looked jittery as if she was nervous at seeing Tilly and began to pace in the area. Cheryl patted a seat, "Come and sit down. You won't make it any better by pacing. You need to be calm for your cat. Animals have a way of sensing these things."

Tara nodded and sat down but soon leapt back to her feet when the vet emerged with a subdued very quiet Tilly in her pet carrier. "Tilly!"

At the sound of her mistresses voice the little cat let out a strident mew, which echoed around the surgery. Tara's eyes filled with tears as she saw her well-loved cat with a shaved patch on her leg and the lampshade collar on her neck.

"You should be able to remove that collar when you get in. If she starts worrying her healing injuries with her tongue put it on again. But I think she should be okay."

"Thanks, Mr Caulfield. I will." Tara poked her fingers though the bars and Tilly began to purr in a frenzy of delight.

"You see, she's feeling better already," said the vet.

"Time to get you home," said Tara and she swept out of the practice with Cheryl Dixon back to the car.

As they travelled to the family home Tilly mewed plaintively in the back and batted at the bars of the pet carrier; she clearly didn't like travelling in the vehicle. Tara talked soothingly to Tilly, reassuring her and comforting her beloved pet. She was screwed right around in her seat, which was very awkward but wanted to make sure Tilly felt loved and safe. She was glad when they arrived at the house, "I'll need a good massage after this, Tilly… I've got a crick in my neck and back!"

Tilly mewed.

They pulled up just as the police locksmith was leaving. Tara scrambled out lifting the pet carrier and ran down the drive, while Tilly complained. Steve flung open the door and hugged Tara to him. Tara exclaimed, "Anyone would think you hadn't seen me for months."

"It feels like it," said Steve. "I never want to let you go ever again." Tilly mewed. "Tilly," said Steve in delight. "Let her out."

"Let's get inside first."

Cheryl retrieved Tara's bag and they all went inside. The door clicked shut behind them and Tara said, "Make sure all the doors and windows are closed and the cat flap then I'll let her out."

"There's not even a chink where a whiff of air can get through," said Steve. "Let the beast free… Drum roll please…" Steve patted his hands on the back of the settee and made a rattling sound in his throat while Tara unpinned the carrier door. Tilly peeped out cautiously and tentatively put out a paw. She finally stepped out and shook herself trying to remove her lampshade collar.

"The vet said I can take this off now," said Tara and she fiddled with the item and removed it. Tilly stretched immediately, glad to be free from her encumbrance. She pushed her head into Tara's hand and begged to be petted. Tara put out her arms and Tilly jumped straight into them purring loudly. Even Cheryl was touched and she put out her hand to stroke the cat. Steve crowded around as well and Tilly gloried in all the attention, before jumping down and running into the kitchen with her tail straight up in the air and mewing. She stretched up and patted the door where her food was kept. "She's well and truly home all right," laughed Tara.

Steve opened the door and picked up Tilly's bag of Iams when Tara stopped him, "Wait!"

He stopped, "What's the matter?"

"Nothing, I hope. But think about all the things that have been done here, what if that mad woman has tampered with her food? After all she did try to kill her."

Steve opened the bag and checked the contents, "My God, you're right! Look!" Officer Dixon and Tara peered inside and could see something glistening like diamonds.

"Broken glass," breathed Tara on a sigh. "We could have hurt her even more. What a bastard."

"At least we have a new bag here. I'll open that."

"I'll take the other. It's evidence," said Cheryl.

The mood became very subdued making Tara even more determined, "We have to catch this woman. Tell me again what I need to do."

At the police station Ken Ley had been thoroughly grilled by Sergeant Denton. "You have no explanation except to say the pictures were fabricated and yet our lab categorically states that these photos are genuine."

"No comment."

"You may well keep replying 'no comment' but the evidence is irrefutable."

Sergeant Denton smacked his hand on the table. "You people make me sick." He turned to the uniformed copper in attendance. "Take him away."

Ken Ley rose and the policeman led him to the door. Sergeant Denton stopped him but Ken Ley didn't turn around. "Mr Ley! I will find that little girl you violated so brutally even if it takes me a lifetime."

Ken Ley was ushered into the corridor. Coming from the other direction was Valerie Linley and her daughter, Daisy. Ken Ley spotted her and hung his head, not wishing to engage with her.

Valerie's face suffused in anger as she saw her erstwhile beau. She pushed Daisy protectively behind her and screamed at him, "You bastard. Courting me to get at my daughter. I hope you rot in hell." She addressed the policeman, "Leave him with me for five minutes and I guarantee you he won't be interfering with anyone else, ever again."

Wisely, the copper said nothing and continued to march the prisoner down the corridor.

Ken shouted back, "Don't believe it, Valerie. It's all a mistake."

Valerie flew down the corridor after him and began pummelling his back. The policeman had to restrain her. She stumbled to the floor in a flood of tears and began to sob.

Sergeant Denton came out from the Interview room and rushed to her side, yelling, "Get him out of here, NOW!" he spoke softly to the distressed woman. "It's all right. He's not going to hurt anyone, anymore." He helped her to her feet and led her back to her little girl who was now looking very frightened. "Step this way." He accompanied her to the Interview Room, where a female detective was waiting to take Daisy to a safe environment to play and talk.

Once they were seated Sergeant Denton asked, "How well did you know Ken Ley?"

"Not very well at all. We had only just started seeing each other."

"Was he ever left alone with your daughter?"

"No, we were always together. He used to read to her, when I prepared dinner, I was in and out all the time. I know nothing happened."

"Then you were lucky. His behaviour all points to him attempting to groom you and your daughter. Ms Linley, we have reason to believe that Ken Ley was part of a very large nationwide group. Anything you can tell us, however small, will be of significant help to us."

Valerie shook her head, "I can't think of anything, Unless…"

"What?"

"I did notice that he had two mobile phones. I thought it odd. He said one was for work and the other was personal."

Sergeant Denton raised his eyebrow. He closed the interview and stood up. "I won't be long. Any idea where he kept this other phone?"

"He always had it on his person except when he didn't want to be interrupted and then he would lock it in a drawer in his study."

"Thank you. You have been most helpful. Wait here." Sergeant Denton left the room and went into the main office. He crossed to his constable, "Did the search of Ley's home turn up another phone?"

"No, just the one."

Get back there and do another search. Look for anywhere he could have secreted it. It has to be somewhere."

"Serge."

Denton returned to the Interview Room and spoke again to Valerie Linley. "That's it for now, Ms Linley. You are free to go. I'll take you to Daisy."

He led Valerie through the maze of corridors to a playroom where the female psychologist and WPC sat with Daisy playing a game and tapped on the window. They looked up and Denton signalled to them. They stopped what they were doing and Daisy skipped out to join them. The WPC led the pair out of the police station. Denton spoke to the Psychologist, Karen Barker, "Anything?"

"I believe the child is fine although she did say something…"

"What?"

"She said that when she sat on his lap to listen to the story there was a hard bump that stuck in her so she moved to the side of him."

"Did she by damn?"

"When Daisy mentioned it, he said it was his mobile phone in his pocket. He took a cell from his jacket, not trouser pocket, and placed it in bowl of rose petals on the dresser and covered them over. She mentioned that there was still a funny lump in his trousers and he said it was his fountain pen."

"Some fountain pen!"

"Apparently, he returned to his seat and continued with the story and that's when her mother came in. He made a joke of having too many odds and ends in his pocket, and went up to change."

"I see."

Denton got on the phone immediately to his constable, "Bill? Look for a bowl with rose petals or pot pourri or something like that on the dresser. There may be a phone in there."

"Right, Serge."

"Get back to me if you find it and bag it as evidence." Denton ended the call.

He didn't have long to wait before his constable rang him back. "Got it, Serge. You were right. It was hidden right underneath all the flower petals."

"Great! Get it back here pronto. Let's see what's on it."

Denton waited anxiously for the return of his constable who arrived back at the station in a flurry of excitement. They disappeared inside Denton's office and after donning gloves looked at the smart phone in their hand. Denton tried to open it. It was locked.

"It's fingerprint touch or a six number password."

"Fingerprint is out. We can't show our hand to him yet. What about the number? When's Ley's birthday?" Denton picked up Ley's file, "5th September 1981. So, try 05-09-81" His constable tried the number but it just shimmied on the screen as incorrect. Denton thought again, "Okay, what about 09-1981?" The numbers were pressed again and once more the password dots vibrated as incorrect. "05-1981." Again, the password registered as wrong. Denton was becoming more frustrated, "591981. Bingo!" he was rewarded with the phone unlocking. "So many people use birthdates as passwords, too easy really."

The usual apps appeared on the screen together with a file marked photo-play, another for Kids Stuff and a chat room called Tweenies. Denton scratched his head, "Kids Stuff? Isn't that a social media site for five to ten year olds?"

The constable shook his head, "I have no idea."

"And Tweenies, what's that? Some sort of chat room for kids?" Denton clicked on the icon and went straight into a chat room for eight-year-olds. There were some saved conversations, which the detective pulled up. He was horrified by what he read. "I can't believe this…. There is enough evidence here to put Mr Ley away for a very long time. It would be good if we could find this little girl in his photos. But somehow, I feel that will be an almost impossible task. We don't know when this was taken or in which part of the country. We need to get some sort of history on our French teacher and then we may have a better idea. But, for now, we have enough to charge him and ensure he is not released on bail. He needs to be kept on remand …Good work."

"Thank you, Sir."

"See if you can marry up the little girl in the picture with any of the other photos. We just want head and shoulders and we can go public with trying to find her. She is bound to need counselling."

"Sir."

"And check out who belongs to these phone numbers. I feel sure Mr. Ley belongs to a bigger network of paedophiles. If we can reel some of them in we may do their dirty association a great deal of damage."

"Yes, Sir."

Cheryl Dixon sat at her desk, her head in her hands. She had just received the tragic news about Donna Carter. She turned to Shay Connor, "I can't believe it. How did it come about? Who found her?"

"When she didn't return to work as expected and no one had heard from her I rang her home number. There was nothing just the answer phone, so I tried her mobile. Still nothing. I can't explain it. I just had one of those odd feelings in my gut. So, I went to the Inspector. He ordered me to get around to her flat immediately, which I did." Shay stopped and his eyes filled up.

Cheryl prompted him, "Go on."

"When I got to the flats I parked around the back I could see her car there. So, she should have been in." Shay swallowed the sob in his voice. "I rang the bell and knocked hard. I peered through the letter box and could see mail had piled up behind the door. There was the most awful smell, fetid like rancid meat or dead animals. The lady from the flat next door came out to see me and she said she hadn't seen Donna for over a week…" Shay stopped again as he tried to control the quaver in his voice. He swallowed hard, "Cheryl it was awful. I had to break the door down, the smell was really ripe then. Her coat, case and keys were just there as she left them. I could see the bathroom door was ajar and oh God, Cheryl. She was just lying there naked and caked in her own blood. Why? Why would someone do this. It's sick… totally sick."

"Do you think it's our killer?"

"I don't know. Forensics are over there now. Uniform are doing door to door to see if anyone saw or heard anything."

"Are you okay?" asked Cheryl.

"I was as sick as a pig. I couldn't help it."

"You two were close?"

"I suppose you could say that. I was on the point of asking her out."

"Oh, Shay, I'm so sorry!" Cheryl was visibly moved. She stood up and opened her arms, which he fell into sobbing. "We'll get the swine who did this. If it is this Skye Powell, she's killed before and she's made a number of attempts on Tara's life. If it's someone else… we *will* get them. That I promise you."

Shay pulled back and wiped his eyes. "Sorry, I…"

"You don't need to apologise. Come on, we need to get into our positions near the Lomas' house."

19

Tara sat up in bed. It was early, really early and the sun was just beginning to rise. "It's no good. I've had a lousy night's sleep. I'm going to get up. Don't want to waste the day. Looks like it's going to be good."

Steve poked his nose out from the duvet and yawned, "Wait. I haven't had my morning cuddle." Steve rolled toward her and placed a protective arm around her middle and kissed the back of her neck, "Oh, how I have missed this."

"Not only you, me, too."

"Do you have to get up now?"

"Yes, come on sleepy head. I'll get up, dress and feed Tilly. I feel like poached eggs on toast this morning. What do you say?"

Steve groaned and relinquished his hold on her. She swung her legs out of bed and pulled on her wrap before disappearing downstairs. Steve called out, "Come back! Come back. Don't leave me." But his cries fell on deaf ears. Resigned to not getting his own way, Steve rose and went for a quick shower.

Downstairs, Tara was staring at the empty fish tank looking lost and forlorn and there and then she determined that they would have their fish back again and she would get another baby sturgeon or maybe even two so they could have babies. That is if anyone knew how to sex a fish. Tara certainly didn't have a clue. She shrugged, filled the kettle and switched it on before busying herself with preparing breakfast.

Tilly interrupted her kaleidoscope of thoughts with a plaintive multi-toned mew indicating she was hungry. Tara spoke soothingly to her beloved cat and at the sound of Tara's kind notes in her voice she leapt straight up into the arms of her mistress and rubbed her face into Tara's chin.

"Oh, Tilly, I have missed you, too. Come on, let's get you fed with some safe kitty kibble." Tara filled Tilly's bowl and the cat munched contentedly whilst purring at the same time. "Don't know how you do that, Tilly. I've never heard you do it before."

Tara set the table and poured some orange juice while boiling up some water for the eggs. Steve came down and put his arms around her waist and kissed her. "What's cooking?"

"Nothing fancy, some toast and a couple of eggs. Why don't you make the tea, coffee or chocolate or whatever you prefer?"

"Ooh choices... not used to that! What do you want?"

"I'll go with coffee, thanks."

They got through breakfast with light inconsequential chatter and Steve volunteered to clear away the dishes after pouring himself another coffee. Tara dashed upstairs and came back down in her running gear. She tied her hair back and began limbering up with some stretches.

Steve took a swig of coffee and watched her. "You don't have to do this, you know?"

"What? Warm up?"

"You know what I mean."

"I know."

"Then why do it? Why put yourself in danger?"

"Because..."

"Because what?"

"Because I don't want to spend the rest of my life looking over my shoulder and feeling unsafe. Besides, it'll be okay. The police are watching."

"I still don't like it. Surely, the cops have enough on this woman? You don't need to risk your life."

"Steve, we need it to be over. Then we can get on with our lives."

Tara blew him a kiss and jogged to the door. She opened it. And ran out into the bright morning air.

It was a perfect day for running. The sun peeped out from a bank of cloud every now and then casting shadows on the ground. It was cooler than expected and a gentle breeze ruffled her fringe. Tara glanced about her and forced herself to focus and practise her breathing. She sucked in her cheeks and blew out slowly in time with every third step.

Tara ran to the end of the road, crossed over and opened the gate to the park. She ran along the path that took her around the lake. She recognised but didn't acknowledge a police officer sitting on a park bench perusing a newspaper and another female officer with a friend feeding the ducks and geese. All this served to make Tara feel secure. She knew she had to re-establish her routine.

As she nearly competed her circuit around the lake she overtook some runners, two of whom she'd seen before, which she acknowledged with a wave and a cheery, "Good morning." The puffing racers waved back with a smile. Tara reached a clump of trees, turned and jogged back the way she had come. She slowed deliberately and stopped to fix her running shoes and tightened her laces.

She took a huge intake of breath and ran back the way she had come. She was aware of Shay Connor in an unmarked car parked in the road pretending to be on the phone. He waited until she reached the end of the road before moving off. Her safety net was there but wasn't obvious.

She soon reached her house and tumbled inside panting with her exertions. Steve had made a fresh pot of coffee, "Want one?"

"Nah! I need a cold drink after that run." Tara moved to the kitchen and let the cold tap run for a bit before filling her glass. She walked back to the sitting room and gulped it down. "See, you didn't have to worry. I spotted some plain clothes coppers. They were watching me very carefully. It was fine and now I just have to keep it up."

"I still don't like it," muttered Steve.

"It will be fine," reassured Tara and plonked herself on the settee. "I'll just drink this and then I will go and shower. Eau de Jogger's sweat is not very attractive." Tara bounded up the stairs while Steve watched her. His look of love was replaced by one of concern.

The next few days continued in the same vein. Tara was pleased that her routine had been established. She enjoyed her runs and now that the school had broken up for the summer holidays she was feeling more relaxed. Steve had decided to return to work. His boss was anxious to have him back and with a number of outstanding contracts to close, he was needed. They had been understanding about the situation but work was work, Steve had said.

On the morning he left as she was preparing for her run, he caught her by the wrist and held her hard, crushing her to him. "I don't really want to leave you, you know that don't you?"

"I know."

"Remember, if anything happens we have that gun."

"Gosh, I'd forgotten about that."

"It was taped under the bed in the spare bedroom that's why I don't think the police ever found it, but I have taken off the tape and it is now easy to reach if you need it."

Tara shivered, "I hope to goodness I won't. I hate firearms of any description. I don't even know how to use them."

"This one is loaded and the safety catch is off. All you need to do is aim it and pull the trigger. It's bound to do some damage."

"Don't say that. It's frightening."

"It's just a precaution."

"Do the police know?"

"No, no one's mentioned it. So, let's keep it that way."

"Okay," Tara sounded unconvinced.

"Remember, it's for emergency use only. If someone broke in or threatened us. Keep quiet about it for now. We are entitled to protect ourselves."

Tara was about to argue but thought better of it and gave Steve a half smile. He held her close and kissed her again. "I suppose," she agreed. "It can't do any harm."

"That's my girl." With that he left the house through the garage and set off in his car. Tara observed him through the window and saw him drive away from the house.

A movement caught her eye in the shrubbery opposite. Tara froze. Was this Skye Powell? She stared hard but heaved a sigh of relief when a man moved out from the bushes. He seemed to study her house and looked interested in her watching from the window. He pulled a piece of paper and a map from his pocket and examined it before scratching his head and moving off down the road. Tara gave herself a talking to, "You'll be seeing boggarts and bogeymen everywhere if you're not careful. Now get moving. The routine must not be broken."

Tara ruffled Tilly who was asleep in her basket. The kitty opened one eye and settled back down to sleep. Tara opened the front door and jogged down the path. It was another good day for a run.

Skye Powell sat in her car and watched, as soon as Tara left the house she stepped out of the vehicle and hurried across the road toward Tara's home. She fished in her bag for a key. Much to her annoyance the key didn't fit and she rattled the door in anger. Tilly woke at the noise and padded to the door. She sniffed at the threshold, laid back her ears and hissed before scooting upstairs to the safety of Tara and Steve's bedroom and dived under the bed.

Skye scurried back to her vehicle and drove through the streets to the main entrance of the recreational area where Tara took her daily exercise. She parked on the kerbside and, keeping a wary eye out for any observers, strolled inside and selected a bench close to the lake path and trees and waited.

Skye counted the number of runners she saw and people relaxing on the grass or on a seat, reading or on the phone or just enjoying the sunshine. No one appeared interested in her. Skye timed Tara's run, where she paused to fix a trailing lace that seemed to have a habit of coming undone. As soon as Tara turned to run back the other way Skye rose and returned to her car. She made some jottings in a small notebook, slung it on the passenger seat, started her car and drove out of the suburban street at speed.

Officers Dixon, Rowe and Connor sat with a cup of coffee in hand and explained to Tara the next step in their plan; "Tomorrow you will be wired up for your morning run."

Tara laughed through her words, "What are you going to do? Electrocute me? Might make me run faster."

Cheryl smiled, "We're just going to try it out now so you know what it feels like. You're going to have to run with it, not attract attention to it so, you'll need to be comfortable. It is just a foretaste of what to expect so it feels entirely natural."

"Okay," Tara sounded a little apprehensive.

"It's nothing to worry about I assure you. And you'll have to wear something loose to run in not a tight fitting Tee Shirt. We don't want to give the game away."

"That's easy enough. I alternate between proper sportswear and baggy tops, since most of my clothes and running gear were shredded. I'll just go and get the duds I'll wear tomorrow."

Tara scooted up the stairs and went into her room. She tossed off her tunic top and trousers and donned her running gear. This consisted of a loose baggy top with short sleeves and a pair of cotton elastane shorts. Tara ran back down and came back into the living room. "Is this okay?"

"Perfect. Officer Rowe will you do the honours?"

Tara removed her top revealing her sports bra and lean midriff. Brandon averted his eyes and concentrated on the job in hand. He fixed and taped the microphone to the front of her bra directed up toward her mouth. The wires were taped to her stomach and a small receiver attached to her waist band. Brandon switched the unit on and Tara slipped her top back on.

"Okay, now can you move all right in this?" asked Brandon.

Tara attempted some stretches, she stooped down as if fixing her lace and then ran on the spot before jogging around the room. "It pulls a little on the tape by my waist," said Tara.

"I can adjust that." He lifted her top and moved the tape higher up her midriff. "Try that."

Tara repeated the exercises and nodded, "That works fine."

"Right, let me put in my earpiece. I'll go into our kitchen. You pretend you're on a run and talk to me."

Tara went through her movements again and spoke softly, "Can you hear me? Am I coming through?" And just for good measure she began to sing a song. Brandon returned to them and nodded, "All working well. Are you sure it's comfortable?"

"It is. Roll on tomorrow. Gosh, I'm getting quite nervous about this."

"There's no need to be. You won't be alone. There'll be plenty of us to keep an eye out for you."

Tara accepted this and took off her top again for the equipment to be removed. Brandon marked the position of everything with a black marker. "Don't shower tonight and leave your morning ablutions until after your run."

"Will do, I'm squeaky clean anyway."

Brandon packed everything away. "We'll be over earlier tomorrow to get you set up. We want to do it before she comes back to watch you. Now, we'll be off. Get a good night's rest. I don't know how many times we'll have to do this."

"Let's hope it's not too many," chipped in Steve. "We want this over and done with as much as you."

20

THE MORNING ALARM STUTTERED INTO life as Tara lay there with her eyes wide open. She had awoken early and watched the clock go around from three-forty-five. No matter how she tried she could not get back to sleep. She had gotten up once in the early hours to go to the loo and no matter how firmly she closed her eyes or how still she lay sleep just would not come.

Steve on the other hand hadn't stirred. Tara had rolled him off his back twice as he lay there snoring like a porker. Nothing, it seemed, would disturb his night's rest. However, the strident alarm finally assailed his senses and he slapped it off and buried his head back in the pillow.

"How you can sleep so soundly is beyond me," said Tara. "I haven't slept a wink. My mind has been racing. I didn't believe I could think so much. I must have wriggled and twisted in the bed like an eel. I'll be surprised if any of those pen marks have stayed on."

Steve suddenly sat bolt upright in bed taking all the covers with him. "My God, I'd forgotten. The police will be here to wire you up."

"You make it sound like I'm going to the electric chair."

"Could well be, for all I know; walking into the jaws of death. I'm frightened and I don't mind admitting it," said Steve.

"How come after a night like I've had I want to go to sleep now? Always sleep comes just when I am about to get up."

"If you want to sleep, sleep. I can always call them and say you've changed your mind."

"No!" she said more forcefully than she intended. "I'm doing it and that's that. I better move, splash my face with cold water, wake myself up." Tara sidled out of bed and went into the bathroom. She was soon out again and slipped into her running gear. "Come on sleepy head. You want breakfast before they descend on us, don't you?"

Steve grumbled and stepped out, "Okay, okay. I'm out... I'm out." He went into the en suite for a shower. Once he began singing, Tara winced and fled downstairs. She put the coffee on and fed Tilly who was finally getting used to being back home. Tara laid the table and set out the milk, butter, jam and cereal boxes and placed some slices of bread in the toaster ready to pop down. She felt nervous, apprehensive but felt a faint tingling of excitement, too. Her heart had begun to race and she took several deep breaths.

Tara poured herself a cup of coffee and sat at the table, "Steve..." she called out. "Breakfast."

Steve emerged from the bedroom, washed and dressed but still yawning and made his way downstairs. He looked at the table set before him and muttered, "My, we should have more breaks away from each other if this is what happens. I feel spoiled."

Steve sat down and watched Tara pour him a cup of coffee. He picked up the cereal box and filled his bowl as Tara popped down the toast. They sat in silence as they contemplated the morning ahead.

Tara stood in the living room being wired again by Brandon Rowe. Tara glanced across at Steve who looked extremely concerned. "It'll be all right."

Brandon believing Tara was speaking to him said. "Yes, it will. Don't worry. We will be around at all times and watching. If you get alarmed, feel uneasy over anything, anything at all, just say so and we'll be there. Got it?"

"I think so."

"You've been setting a regular pattern now and we know she's been out and watching you."

"Really? That gives me the creeps."

Cheryl Dixon added, "You're safe. Remember that. You're doing good."

Tara continued, "Do you think she'll strike? We've been trying to draw her out for nearly a month now..."

"We need her to make a move. We believe she's close to acting. That and what we found on her computer will seal it," said Cheryl.

"What did you find?" asked Tara.

"Well, we found the two entries we told you about. The techies have been working on restoring the deleted files. They are almost there."

Steve had been listening and following the conversation looking from one to the other. "If Tara is running, I don't care what you say, I'm going to be there, too."

Cheryl Dixon exchanged a look with Brandon Rowe, "We don't advise that, Sir."

"To hell with what you think. She's my wife and you can't stop me." Steve was adamant.

"Okay, we have quite a large team involved in this. I dare say we can find a place for you, somewhere. But you must be inconspicuous, not noticeable."

"He could go in the ice cream van with Shay," said Brandon.

"He'll need a white coat. Ever sold ice cream, Steve?"

"I'll learn," said Steve smiling grimly.

"Or he could walk with me?" said Brandon. "Two friends out for a stroll?"

"I'll go with that," affirmed Steve.

"But you could be recognised. Remember she knows you," said Cheryl.

"Different clothes, a bit of a disguise. It'll be a doddle," said Steve.

"Hmm... I'm not so sure," said Cheryl. She took in Steve's determined expression and caved in. "All right. I'll see what I can do. I'll call it in." Cheryl picked up her phone and dialled. She spoke quietly and paced around the sitting room. She ended the call and turned, "Okay, a delivery van will arrive in the next thirty minutes. It will look like a white goods delivery. Let them in and Emily Caldwell will sort Steve out." The others looked puzzled. Cheryl laughed and waved a hand over her face like a magician and said mysteriously, "All will be revealed."

True to her word a large delivery van drove into the drive some thirty minutes later and a driver got out and opened up the back. He hopped inside and using the hydraulic lift came down with a trolley carrying a large cardboard box. He wheeled it expertly to the front door and rang the bell. Tara answered and admitted him. The box was opened and Emily Caldwell stepped out with her case of tricks and some clothing items. She beamed at them all, "Well, this is a first for me. You'll have me jumping out of cakes next."

The delivery man made his escape, left the house and drove away.

After some brief introductions Steve was pushed forward. Emily appraised him, "By the time I've finished with you your own mother won't recognise you."

Cheryl explained, Emily works mainly with our witness protection programme. She helps people to change their appearance, their mannerisms, so they are not easily recognisable.

"How long have I got?" asked Emily.

"No more than half an hour. Can you do it in that time?"

"I can do something... Right, let's get started." Emily went with Steve into the kitchen and sat him in a chair and started work while Cheryl continued to brief the others.

"I have six officers lined up in the park, as well as Steve. I will be parked in the street by the gate, someone else will be watching your house. You will be the only one leaving by the front door. We will go out from the back down the alley behind your house and into the street. We will be in radio contact with you all the time. If you need us just call out."

Tara nodded her understanding. She blew out between her lips and took several deep breaths. She was feeling her nerves now and jiggled about unable to keep still. "I need to get this over with. Is Steve ready yet?"

As she spoke, Steve emerged from the kitchen looking totally different. He had a hairpiece on, making his hair longer, his nose had been altered to make it pudgier and was now sporting a small beard. He wore a loose, button free jacket with an open necked shirt.

Tara looked at him in amazement, "Wow, what have you done with my husband?"

Steve grinned and added, "Aren't you glad you married me?"

"Yes, but not looking like that."

"Now, don't get pernickety... What you see is what you get," said Steve with a smile.

"Okay, team. Let's get this show on the road. Tara are you ready?"

Tara gave her husband a huge hug and then left through the front door. The others scrambled to the back. Emily just muttered, "I'll wait here."

"Help yourself to coffee," called Steve.

Tara, complete with wire, jogged along the road as was her usual routine. She reached the side gate to the park and ran up the grass bank and into the lake area. Knowing that there were undercover police around Tara tried to spot them without being obvious. She knew they would be strategically placed.

A runner in her twenties wearing earphones passed by and Tara looked sideways at her. She didn't think it was anyone she had seen before. As she ran on she passed a woman in her forties walking her dog who acknowledged her with a nod. The dog was quite large and Tara wondered if it was a police dog. A fisherman in his thirties sat by the lake. He turned his head slightly as she ran past. Tara continued on her morning jog.

She stopped to retie her shoe laces and glanced around her but could see nothing untoward. "Can't see anything suspicious," she murmured to whoever was listening. It was then she noticed Steve walking along the path at a discreet distance with Officer Rowe. They were chatting as they walked. If she hadn't seen him before she left the house she certainly wouldn't have recognised him.

Tara was feeling more relaxed now. She approached the clump of trees on the path where she usually turned to run back the way she had come. Tara spoke again into her mic, "Everything clear, so far. All's well."

Tara dipped out of sight and view of the officers, as someone stepped out hurriedly from behind the trees wearing a hoodie, and started to jog toward Tara. The person speeded up and pulled a knife into view, a large blade with a serrated edge that glinted evilly in the sunlight.

Tara's words came out in a rush as she spoke into the mic, "Oh my God! She's here and she's got a knife!"

It seemed like Skye had reached Tara in a flash and she pounced on her like a cat after its prey. Tara was prepared and more than up for a fight, albeit a fight for her life. It was clear that Skye was unprepared for the strength of Tara's resistance.

The police listening in were aghast at the sounds coming from the two women and urged their colleagues to intervene. Tara kicked out and let out a terrified scream. She managed to dodge the blade as Skye struck out at Tara's face but met with air instead. The officers and Steve heard Tara's cries and raced to her aid.

Skye had now fallen upon Tara, in a maniacal frenzy, trying to stab her but Tara had grasped Skye's hand and was forcing her away. Skye's face was a mask of fury. She shrieked abuse dementedly, "You're nothing but a whore. I'll make you suffer, make you pay for stealing my husband. Bitch!"

Officer Rowe reached the scuffling women and just managed to haul Skye off Tara. Skye's knife slashed through the air just missing Tara's face as Brandon Rowe apprehended and restrained the psychotic woman. Tara rolled over gulping for air and Steve tumbled down on his knees next to her and took her in his arms.

Steve cradled her murmuring softly in between kisses, "Baby, Tara, nothing is going to hurt you ever again. And I'm going to be around much more to make sure of that. I promise."

Tara looked up at him with a steely determination in her eyes and smiled. Relief took over and she began to shake uncontrollably as Officer Dixon ran up. "It's over, Mrs Lomas. It's over."

Sirens could be heard in the distance as Brandon Rowe put handcuffs on Skye to lead her away. She pulled back from the officer and spat over her shoulder. "This isn't over. Not yet."

Officer Rowe hissed in her ear, "Oh, but it is. For you, it is." He hustled her to a waiting police car.

By now, a crowd of people had gathered, who had watched the unfolding drama in awe. Steve helped Tara to her feet, "Come on, let's get you home."

"Is it really over, Steve?"

"It most certainly is."

"Then can I have my husband back, please," she whispered. Steve laughed and held her tight as they made their way back through the park.

21

TARA AND STEVE FINALLY RETURNED to their house followed by Officer Dixon, where Emily Caulfield sat and waited. Emily set to removing Steve's disguise and his extra hair. "I quite liked the hair. You should grow it," said Tara.

"Don't think work would like it. It makes me look like a surfer or hippie."

"Well, we could always learn to surf or join the peace movement or maybe a commune," said Tara with a laugh.

"I don't think so," said Steve. "Ouch!" he exclaimed as the hair piece was removed.

"Sorry," said Emily. "Although, I agree with your wife. Longer hair really does suit you."

Cheryl Dixon said, "We'll have to take your statements. I can send someone round later if you like, save you coming into the station and then I'll transport Emily back."

"Can't we do it now?" asked Tara.

"Well, we can. If you're sure you're up to it?"

"I'd rather get it over and done with."

"Well, okay. Perhaps we could have another coffee while we work," said Cheryl with a wink.

"Putting the kettle on now," said Steve.

"You know," said Cheryl. "You have been one brave lady. There are not many who could have done what you did today."

"I don't feel brave. I never want to go through anything like that again."

"And I don't expect you ever will," said Cheryl with a smile. "You can finally relax."

An hour passed and after two or three coffees each, Cheryl and Emily left the Lomas' house. Steve and Tara hugged each other as Tilly came and wound herself around their legs.

"Yes, okay, feeding time," said Tara. "You know, I think we should get a companion for Tilly to keep her company during the day."

"What do you have in mind? A Rottweiler? It will probably eat her although it would be a great alarm system against any future intruders."

"No, not a dog. I don't think Tilly would stand for that."

As if she understood, Tilly yawned in disdain and proceeded to wash herself before running to the kitchen with her tail puffed out straight in the air.

"I think you're right. I don't think she's too impressed with that idea."

"No, another cat. It might stop her wandering off. It could be good for her," said Tara.

"Would that be fair on her? After all she is used to our undivided attention."

"It would keep her eyes off the fish."

"You're forgetting we haven't got any."

"I haven't forgotten. We'll replace them and the baby sturgeon."

"When?"

"Soon. What about another cat?"

"I'll think about it," said Steve ending the discussion.

Tilly mewed loudly and sat looking at her empty dish. "Okay, you win," said Tara. "Chow time." She took the dried cat food and poured it in her bowl, "What do you say, Tilly. Would you like a little friend to play with?" Tilly looked up and mewed. "There, you see. She would."

Steve shrugged and smiled, "Right now, if you wanted Father Christmas to come and live with us. I think I'd agree. Let's sleep on it and be rational. Remember it will be double the vet bills, double the food, double the cattery fees…"

"Double the love, double the purring and one each for us to cuddle. Don't be such a grouch. Anyway, I think she would like a friend," said Tara petulantly with her lips in a pout.

Steve just caught hold of her and whispered, "Come here," and he kissed her tenderly before picking her up in his arms and carrying her upstairs. "I'm going to show you just how much I care."

Tara snuggled happily into his arms and whispered, "And I you. I love you,

Steve." Tilly followed them curiously up the stairs and mewed in complaint when Steve kicked their bedroom door shut.

The next night, Tara was cooking dinner. Her 'my favourites' playlist was playing and she sang along with the old hits and melodies that held special memories. She stirred the pot on the stove and sampled a taste "Mmm! That is good," she murmured in approval before she took a big sip of wine from her special glass that was engraved with two hearts saying 'Steve and Tara forever'. "I am such a sentimentalist."

She smacked her lips in distaste and studied her wine glass before sniffing its contents, "This just doesn't taste right to me. I must be coming down with something." She poured herself a cool glass of water and drank deeply. "That's better. Ha!" she laughed. "Fancy me preferring water to wine."

She took two plates from the cupboard and popped them into the oven to warm. "I am so glad everything is back in its rightful place and in order." A sweet smile of satisfaction settled on her face she was determined that nothing would ever faze her again. Tara moved into the dining area of the living room and admired her handiwork. She danced around the table as she checked the place settings and teased a napkin that had flopped over in its glass. She bent over across the table and straightened the cutlery congratulating herself. "Girl, have you so done a good job! ... Why am I talking to myself? Because there's no one better to talk to," she answered her own question. Her stomach rumbled. "I am definitely not feeling quite right. But nothing is going to spoil this evening."

Still singing, she went to the sideboard drawer and took out a bag of rose petals and strew some on the table for the finishing touches. Tara was humming so happily she didn't hear the stealthy footsteps approaching her. Two hands reached out behind her and were placed over her eyes. She laughed delightedly and turned to meet Steve's embrace. They kissed. Once they came up for air, Steve asked, "Are you up for a surprise?"

"I'm always up for a surprise." Steve looked at her quizzically. "What, what is it?" she asked in concern.

"Go into the garage and look on the back seat of my car."

"Why?"

"Just do it." Tara batted Steve playfully on his nose and bit her lip. "I just love it when you do that," he whispered.

She wiped her hands on her apron, opened the side door that led to the garage and made her way out to Steve's car. A slight noise at the back of the garage startled her. Her head snapped around and she laughed nervously. "What are you like, Tara Lomas?" She reprimanded herself before she opened the car door.

She squealed in delight when she saw a polyethylene box with a perforated lid, inside which swam a number of small fish, fantails, goldfish and two baby sturgeon. Next to it was another box and something inside it was scratching.

Tara peeked inside the other box and was overcome with sheer pleasure when she saw the cutest, most adorable fluffy little grey kitten. "Aw, bless you. You are so cute, so ... darling." Tara picked up both boxes and closed the car door.

Something scuttled behind her and Tara caught a glimpse of a bird trapped inside the garage. Tara laid the boxes down on Steve's work bench and flicked the switch that opened the garage door. It rolled up painfully slowly and Tara tried to shoo the bird out, which was now terrified and flew up into the beams of the roof. "Pesky bird. Shoo! Fly away!" The bird did nothing but hopped along the girder. "I'm going inside. Now, you take yourself out. Fly away home!"

Tara picked up the boxes and went back inside. She carried the boxes to the coffee table, "You didn't say it was a double surprise."

"I didn't want to spoil it!"

"Can you get these little beauties in the tank, while I see to the newest member of our family?"

Steve busied himself with filling the fish tank that he had already cleaned and prepared. He placed the new arrivals inside. The baby sturgeon played in the bubbles from the oxygenator and examined every corner of their new home. "I think they like it," he said.

"What's not to like?" replied Tara as she cuddled the fluffy bundle with oohs of happiness. "Oh, Steve she's beautiful."

"What are you going to call her?"

"Smoky, no... Misty. Definitely Misty."

"Then, Misty it is. If you look in the hall closet, you'll find all Misty's needs." Tilly came up to her mistress curiously and put her paws up to Tara. "Look Tilly, this is your new friend. You be kind and gentle now." Tilly gazed at the newcomer and mewed. "Look, she likes her."

"Well, that's a relief. I really didn't want a spitting cat fight."

"Oh, Steve you have thought of everything. I'll settle them both down. Can you close the garage door?"

"Why?"

"A bird was trapped. It should have gone by now."

Steve finished feeding the fish and went out to the garage. Tara set Misty down and Tilly ran to the kitten and sniffed her all over. Tara smiled, "See, I knew you'd be friends." She walked to the hall closet and took out the kitty items Steve had bought. Misty and Tilly followed Tara inquisitively and tailed her to the kitchen where Tara set out the two cat beds side by side. She laid out the feeding mats and put down the new bowls for Misty next to Tilly's. She watched as Tilly stepped into her bed and Misty climbed in with her and snuggled up. Tara clapped her hands in delight and beamed when the older cat began washing and grooming the little kitten. "Purrrfect," she laughed, "Get it!" The cats took no notice of her and Tara strolled back into the living room. She picked up her glass of water and took a sip before sighing contentedly and sitting on the settee to wait for Steve.

In the garage Steve listened for sounds of the bird. There were none. He took a cursory glance around the garage to satisfy himself that the bird had indeed gone. He flicked the switch that engaged the motor that brought the garage door down and went to return inside the house. There was another faint sound behind him and a shadowy indistinct shape was fleetingly seen in the back of Tara's car. Steve stopped and turned but saw nothing. Convinced it was his imagination Steve shrugged and whistled as he disappeared back inside the house, where Tara was emerging from the kitchen carrying a hot casserole pot, which she set on a trivet on the table.

Tara retreated back to the kitchen to get the warmed plates and laid them down on the place mats. Steve replenished his wine glass and turned to Tara, "Not drinking?"

"I've just got a bit of a dicky tum and it doesn't taste quite right to me."

"It tastes just fine. Your loss," teased Steve.

Tara wrapped her arms around his neck. He crushed her to him in a loving embrace. They kissed gently at first, it was a kiss that became more urgent and passionate.

Steve laughed, "I feel so free." He threw Tara over his shoulder in a fireman's lift and moved to the stairs with Tara who squealed with laughter.

"What about dinner?"

"Dinner can wait. Suddenly, I'm not hungry except for you. And I've got something to tell you...."

"What? Tell me."

"No, you have to wait until I have you at my mercy." He laughed again and continued up the stairs with Tara.

Misty sat up in her bed and went to investigate her litter tray and began to scratch as Tilly sat up, laid back her ears and hissed.

Steve threw Tara onto the bed. She kicked off her shoes as Steve fell on top of her showering her with kisses. Tara stopped him and wriggled out from underneath him. "Are you feeling okay?" he asked.

Tara just nodded as she started to take off her dress and Steve removed his shirt. They couldn't get them off quickly enough. Entwined in each other's arms their breathing became more laboured. Tara flipped over and straddled him. She stopped and placed her hand up as a sign to wait. He watched longingly as she removed her slip.

In the corner of her eye she caught a glint of something reflected in the dressing table mirror. She turned to look and saw a masked intruder wielding a knife. She screamed and scrambled off Steve. The figure dived on the bed and tried to stab Steve. Tara shrieked, "Noooo!" She jumped and put herself between the blade and Steve. The blade sliced into her side and she clutched the wound where the blood pumped out. She stood there stunned and doubled over.

The intruder stopped momentarily, shocked at having stabbed Tara. Suddenly alert he fled from the bedroom chased by Steve. The attacker rushed down the stairs. Steve leapt after him and dived at his legs. They tumbled down the last few steps and grappled on the floor. Steve attempted to wrestle the knife from him, but filled with an inhuman strength the knife wielding maniac began to overpower Steve.

The struggle continued and the masked man, with his eyes filled with hate, rolled on top of Steve and pinned him down. He raised the wicked knife triumphantly ready to plunge into Steve's heart.

Just as the knife began its descent, accompanied by a grunting cry a shot rang out. The masked man fell forward onto Steve who was able to avoid the blade which had now slipped from the man's grasp. Steve pushed the man's body off him in disgust and stared up at his wife.

Tara stood on the stairs. She clutched the bloody injury in her side as she let the smoking rifle fall.

Breathing heavily Steve crawled to the man and ripped off his mask revealing Mike Piercey, Lee Powell's friend. He looked baffled as he was sure neither of them knew this man. Steve then rushed to the stairs to catch Tara as she fell in a dead faint. He carried the unconscious Tara to the settee and laid her down carefully and dialled nine, nine, nine.

Police swarmed all over the house as paramedics bagged Mike's body and removed it. Tara was placed on a stretcher and her vitals taken before they took her to a waiting ambulance. Steve stood in a daze, as tears coursed down his cheeks. Officer Dixon watched him sympathetically.

Steve ran his fingers through his hair, "I don't understand. Who was that man?"

"A friend of Lee Powell called Mike Piercey, who had got involved with Skye. He's got a history of unpredictable behaviour. Under interrogation Skye put us onto him. Her obsession with Tara became his. We weren't sure if she was telling the truth. Now we know she was," said Cheryl Dixon ruefully.

"And you didn't warn us? You promised us it was over."

"And, so we thought. We didn't know ourselves about this character until earlier today. I was on my way here to warn you when you rang."

"I can't deal with this now. I must see my wife." Steve ran outside after the medics and insisted, "Let me through. It's my wife, please."

The paramedic allowed him to climb into the back of the ambulance with Tara. Her face was white and her breathing shallow. He held on tightly to her hand, "Don't die, please don't die. I can't live without you and we have so much to live for." Steve bowed his head in silent prayer as the sirens blared and lights blazed as the vehicle raced through the night traffic for the hospital.

The ambulance drove into A & E. The doors flew open and Steve jumped out. Two orderlies hurried out of the doors to help the paramedics usher in the injured and unconscious Tara on a stretcher. Steve watched anxiously as she was whisked away for emergency surgery.

Steve anxiously paced the corridor outside ICU while he waited, his own bruises and abrasions completely forgotten. He muttered more prayers under his breath before finally sinking into a seat with his head in his hands. Cheryl Dixon came running in and sat next to him, "Any news?"

Steve shook his head, "Not yet."

"She'll be okay. Tara is a fighter, you'll see."

"You don't understand, she put herself between the knife and me. She saved my life."

"You can't beat yourself up over this. It's not your fault."

"Then who as hell's fault is it? I should be in there, not Tara."

A serious faced doctor came out through the doors and approached Steve.

"How is she?"

"We've managed to stop the bleeding."

"Can I see her?"

The doctor nodded, "You can go in now, but don't tire her out."

Steve glanced at Cheryl who smiled wanly and encouraged him, "You go on in. Say hi to her from me. I'll see you both again." Steve rose much relieved and followed the doctor back into the unit. There was an urgency in his stride as he walked along the corridor to a private room. The doctor pushed open the door for Steve to enter and followed him inside.

Steve took in his wife's ashen look, the profusion of tubes and wires that were attached to monitors and machines, which bleeped intermittently. Steve took her hand and kissed it. The tears from his lashes dropped onto her hand and her eyes fluttered open. "Steve…"

"Hush now, don't talk."

The doctor interrupted them, "She'll be okay. You're lucky the knife hit where it did."

"Lucky?" said Steve perplexed.

"An inch the other way…"

"It doesn't bear thinking about…"

"No, just an inch and the baby would be dead."

"Baby?"

"Yes, didn't you know she was pregnant?"

Steve's eyes filled with tears. Tara squeezed his hand and smiled weakly, and whispered, "You're going to be a father. We're having a baby…"

Steve leaned over and kissed her tenderly. They were both laughing and half crying.

"That's two celebrations, then."

"Two?"

"I've got my promotion."

Tara looked across at the doctor and mouthed, "Thank you."

"I'll leave you to it, "the doctor said with a smile.

"We'll have so much to discuss, baby names, colours to paint the nursery."

"We need to get you both fit and well, first," said Steve.

"Can you call Lucy? Tell her what's happened."

"Of course, she's bound to want to see you and I'll tell the school."

Tara nodded. Her eyelids fluttered, "I'm just so tired."

"That'll be the anaesthetic."

"Don't think I'll have any trouble sleeping tonight," she murmured. "What about Tilly and Misty?"

"All fine. I'll let you rest. You get some sleep and I'll be in later to see you. I have to go and feed the family."

Tara nodded sleepily and closed her eyes gratefully and went to sleep.

Steve arrived home to a mewing Tilly and did his usual routine of feeding them and clearing out Misty's litter tray. "Don't need to keep the cat flap locked now, Tilly. You can let yourself in and out and show Misty the ropes. The sooner we dispense with kitty litter the better as far as I'm concerned," he said to the curious cat. "But mind you look after the little one if you go outside." Tilly blinked as if in agreement. "Now, to phone Lucy."

Steve searched through Tara's address book for Lucy's number, "Ah…. Got it," he put it in his contact list and dialled. He waited for her to answer.

"Oh, hi Steve, you're lucky you caught me. I was on my way out."

"I won't keep you, I just wanted to let you know that Tara's in hospital in ICU."

"Oh my God, no. What happened?" Steve launched into a description of the events as they happened and Lucy listened in shock. "That's awful. I thought you guys were over all that stalker horror. Who the hell was it?"

"No one we knew. Someone who was involved with Skye Powell and was working with her. Apparently, he was a friend of this Lee Powell. Poor sod to have two lunatics in his life."

"What was this perp's name?"

"Mike someone or other," Steve suddenly remembered, "Yes, Mike Piercey." Lucy went quiet on the other end of the phone. "Lucy? Lucy are you there?"

"Yes, yes, I'm here." Her voice sounded strange and tight almost strangled.

"Lucy? Are you, all right?"

"Mike Piercey, you say?"

"Yes, why?"

"God, Steve this is terrible."

"What?"

"Mike Piercey was the name of the weirdo I went out with weeks ago. I told Tara all about him."

"You're joking. She never said."

"Why would she? I was the one who was spooked by him. But he did tap me up for information about Tara after I told him about her stalker. Heck, how could I have been so stupid? I know he was fascinated with her story… now, I see it. He must have been obsessed with her, too."

"Think you'll have to give a statement to the police."

"Sure, anything to help."

22

STEVE SPENT EVERY NIGHT VISITING Tara and praying she would soon recover. He was pleased when seven days later he arrived to discover she was no longer being monitored and wired up to bleeping machines. This time she was propped up on pillows and looking much more like her old self. She had even managed to put on some makeup.

He told her, "Staff nurse tells me, you will soon be allowed other visitors, not just me. That'll be good."

"It will. I'm just so tired still, but I feel I'm getting better. Can you ask Lucy to come and see me?"

"Sure thing. I'll call her later when I get back to do all my chores. In fact, if you don't tell," he nodded at the sign on the wall asking people not to use their cell phones. He took out his mobile, "I'll call her now." Steve scrolled through his phone for her number and hit send.

Lucy soon answered, "Steve! Good to hear from you. How's Tara? The school are really concerned."

"I said I'd let you know… she's being allowed visitors now. I'm coming in again to see her later. I know she'd love to see you."

"Try keeping me away. I'll let school know. I know there are others that would like to visit. What time?"

"I'll pick you up. Shall we say six thirty?"

"I better get my skates on. See you later." Lucy put down the phone.

Just as Steve promised he went to pick up Lucy. She scrambled into his car clutching a bag full of goodies.

"Goodness, what have you bought?"

"Grapes, some of Rona's shortbread, a couple of magazines and a letter from school."

"A letter from school?"

"Yes, from Social Services about Raymond Campbell, one of her students."

"Ah, yes. She's talked about him… bit of a sad case."

"Very. Tara was really getting somewhere with him. I think he feels a bit lost now, her being off and all."

Steve listened as Lucy chattered on and he negotiated the roads to the hospital. He swung in through the entrance and followed the signs to the visitors' car park. "I can see this is going to be a nightmare. Oh, for a police car and lights."

"Why?"

"No problems parking then. Straight to the main entrance and park. Easy."

"I'll have to call on my parking fairy."

"Parking fairy?"

"Yes, I just put the word out to her and hey presto a space will appear just for me."

"Now, that I'd like to see."

"There, there, quickly." Lucy pointed to a car just reversing out of a space. Steve was onto it, drove onward, waited, indicated and slipped into the vacated spot.

"Parking fairy, eh? I must remember that especially while Tara is in here."

They alighted from the car and walked briskly to the hospital foyer where Steve dashed into the hospital shop and bought some flowers before they took the lift to the Intensive Care Unit. They walked along the corridor and pressed the bell. The staff nurse soon came to let them in. They dutifully sanitised their hands and followed her to Tara's room. "We'll be moving Mrs Lomas to the main ward later and then it shouldn't be long before she's home. We've had so many calls about her progress. It's lovely to know that people care about her so much. I expect a number of them will come to see her now she's allowed visitors."

Steve smiled delightedly as he said, "Coming home? That's great news."

"Shall I take those and put them in water for you?" The staff nurse asked Steve, indicating the flowers.

"Yes, thank you." He passed her the bouquet and she disappeared with them.

To their surprise there was someone already in the room. Steve walked in, crossed to Tara and kissed her. He raised his eyebrow quizzically at the young man with the shaggy hair as Lucy exclaimed, "Raymond? Whatever brings you here?"

Raymond Campbell shuffled his feet nervously. "When we heard at school what had happened and Miss was in hospital I wanted to come and see her as soon as it was allowed. I brought her something."

"That's admirable, Raymond. What is it?"

Sheepishly, Raymond opened his art folder and took out an A 3 piece of cartridge paper. He had drawn a pen and ink portrait of Tara, "I wanted to thank her for all she has done for me. She has really helped me to start to turn my life around." He faced Tara and said, "I hope you like it, Miss."

Tara looked at the sketch and gasped. He had really captured the essence of her personality and her smile. "Raymond it's lovely. Thank you." Tara beamed at the boy. "What do you think, Steve?"

"I think it should be framed and have pride of place on our wall. You're very talented, Raymond."

Raymond blushed, "Thank you and thank you, too, Miss," he said to Lucy. "You are the two best teachers in the whole school."

Lucy grinned in pleasure, "And you, Raymond are a delight to teach." Raymond shuffled his feet in embarrassment. "I must say, Raymond," said Lucy. "You are looking a whole lot better."

"It's the extra help we're getting from Social Services, thanks to Mrs Lomas."

"I'm pleased to see you looking so much happier," said Tara. "If you need anything else, give me a call. You have my number."

"Yes, Miss. Thank you, Miss." He looked around at them, "I'd best get back to Mum, now. Don't like to leave her on her own for too long. Bye." He turned to Tara, "Looking forward to seeing you up and about again, soon, Mrs Lomas." With that he shuffled out of the door and along the corridor.

"Well, that was a surprise," said Lucy. "I do believe he's getting more confident."

"That must be what the letter was about," said Steve to Lucy.

"What letter?" asked Tara.

"Oh, gosh I nearly forgot… I bring goodies and a letter for you from Social Services. It's about Raymond."

"Sit down and read it, please;" asked Tara, who turned to Steve. "I could murder a cup of tea."

"Not coffee?"

"Nope, I've gone off coffee. I'm off alcohol, coffee and spicy foods…."

"Are you…?" said Lucy not finishing her sentence.

Tara grinned and nodded, "Yep, I'm up the duff!"

"Wow! Tara! Congratulations. That's excellent news," said Lucy.

Steve interrupted, "I'll go and sort out a cup of tea for you. Do you want anything, Lucy?"

"Ooh, coffee for me please."

He left the two friends chattering excitedly and went in search of the hospital café. He was overjoyed to see Tara looking so much better and brighter. As he walked to the ward entrance he passed a man with long curling fair hair wearing glasses carrying flowers together with another older woman with two young children. Steve smiled at them and walked on.

The woman said to the man, "We'll wait here for you. Good luck." She remained at the nurses' station with the children who sat and played on their v tech innotabs while they waited. The young man strode on toward Tara's room.

The fair haired man knocked tentatively on Tara's door and poked his head in, "Excuse me, Tara Lomas?"

Tara was now propped up on pillows; she studied the man who stood in the doorway. There was a flicker of recognition on her face, "Aren't you…?"

Lucy finished her sentence, "Lee Powell as I live and breathe. It is you, isn't it?"

"I didn't know if I'd be welcome after everything that had happened. I knew my ex-wife was psychotic but had no idea she would go this far and as for Mike… the news that he was involved, too, has knocked me sideways. I just wanted to see that you were okay… after everything…"

"You must be the man who has been ringing to check up on my progress. I wondered who it was."

"Guilty as charged."

"Sorry, this is my friend Lucy. You kind of know each other from online… Tell me, how did you discover what had happened?"

"The police came around as soon as Skye had been arrested. They told me what had happened. Then, I heard about Mike. I found that tough to take, too."

Lucy groaned, "Mike Piercey... major weirdo. I can't believe I went out with him. Mind you once was enough."

"He wasn't always bad. Misguided maybe. I had no idea of the effect Skye would have on him. I am so sorry."

"Who's sorry?" asked Steve appearing in the doorway with a tray of drinks.

Tara looked at Lucy who paused before speaking, "Um... Steve... this is Lee Powell. Lee, Tara's husband Steve."

Lee put his hand out to shake Steve's hand but Steve hesitated; "Lee Powell? The husband of the nutcase who tried to kill you?"

"Ex-husband," corrected Lee.

"No matter. All our troubles began with you."

Tara attempted to calm him, "Steve, it was nothing to do with Lee. I told you. He's as much of a victim as we have been."

"Maybe so. I am just finding this difficult that's all."

"I better go, my mum and children are waiting out there." Lee placed the flowers on Tara's locker. "Um... these are for you. And for what it's worth, I am truly sorry."

"Hold on, Lee," said Lucy. "I'll walk with you. Let's leave these two together. I know they have a lot to talk about." Lucy gave Tara a kiss and Steve a peck on the cheek. "I'll stop by tomorrow. Promise. I'll see you in your new ward." Lucy left with Lee and conversation appeared easy between them.

Tara looked at Steve critically.

"What?" he asked.

"You were bordering on rudeness. It's not that poor man's fault. He seems okay," she said.

Steve sighed, "I know you're right but you can't blame me. It did all start with him. Don't let's fall out. If I see him again, I'll apologise."

Tara smiled at her husband and opened her arms, "I can't be cross with you for long."

Lucy Wheeler accompanied Lee, his mum and the two children out of the ward. "So, these are your two?"

"Yes. This is Amy, Peter and my mum, Dora."

They continued out of the ward and to the lifts. "Going down?" asked Lee.

"Well, I'm not going up," said Lucy with a laugh.

The lift soon filled up with other people on its descent to the ground floor and hospital foyer. Amy and Jack looked enquiringly at Lucy. Eventually Amy piped up, "You've got paint on your jacket."

Lucy peered at her sleeve where Amy was pointing and where everyone in the lift was now looking. "So, I have," said Lucy brightly.

"Why?" came the next question.

"Hush, Amy. Don't be rude," said Lee.

"No, it's fine, honestly." She smiled at Amy and explained, "It's a hazard of the job."

"Why are you a decorator?"

Lucy laughed, "No, I'm an artist and I teach art."

Clearly Amy was impressed, "Ooh, I love drawing and painting. Do you mean you get to do it as a job?"

It was then the elevator came to a halt and people spilled out into the hallway. Lucy, it seemed was quite charmed by Amy and the conversation progressed and continued to the main entrance. The doors slid open to reveal two youths brawling on the ground. One was Raymond Campbell, whose art folder was open and his work strewn over the grass, the other was James Treeves. Lucy waded in to break them up calling them by name. Lee stepped into help her and they finally split the two of them apart.

"Whatever's going on?" asked Lucy.

This time Raymond was not afraid to speak up. "It's him, Miss. Saying horrible things about Mrs Lomas and what he's going to do to her."

"Was he now?" said Lucy sternly.

By now a small crowd had gathered including Lee's mother and the children. Lucy severely reprimanded James Treeves, who merely sneered back at her, "You can't touch me, Miss. I've been suspended and this is out of school. So, why don't you just piss off and mind your own business?"

Lucy was in no mood to be trifled with and said so. "In school or out of school. This behaviour is appalling and I will be making a full report to Miss Stevens. If it were up to me I'd have you expelled."

Lucy was really fired up and James was not going to back down. He squared up to her and gave her a hard shove. Lucy tumbled on the ground, Lee helped her up and intervened, "I think you've said and done enough, young man. I suggest you take yourself off home before you get done for assault." He indicated the crowd of people watching, "There are plenty of witnesses."

James snorted in derision and sloped off muttering something under his breath. Lucy put her arm around Raymond, "Are you okay? We need to get you home. I'll call a cab and take you back first. I'll help you pick up your work." Amy and Jack went to help Raymond gather his paintings and sketches together.

Lee asked, "Don't you have your car?"

"No, not here. I rode in with Steve, Tara's husband."

"Then allow me. We will take both of you home."

"Are you sure? Do you have room?" Lucy asked looking at them all.

Lee's mother Dora spoke up, "Lee has a people carrier so we have plenty of room. Do accept and you can tell us all about yourself. And I'm sure the children would love to look at your student's work."

The children chorused, "Yes, please."

Lucy smiled, "Then, yes, thank you. We will, won't we Raymond?"

They walked together to the hospital car park and Lee's vehicle.

James Treeves stood by the ambulances watching and glowered at them. "So, you want me to leave Mrs Lomas alone? Okay, I will. How about I start on you instead? You'll deserve everything I can throw at you, you evil bitch," he growled. He skulked off and made his way to where the bicycles were parked, unlocked a padlock and cycled off on his mountain bike, singing a song to himself. "Oh yes, Miss Wheeler had better watch out."

In the car, the children were enchanted with Raymond's artwork. "He's really good, Daddy. Really good." Raymond basked in the praise especially when Lucy commended his work and extolled the lad's virtues. Raymond may have had a brush with the school bully but his confidence had been substantially boosted by Lee's family by the time he was dropped off at his house.

"Wait! Raymond." Raymond stopped. "If you need anything, anything at all. Give me a call." Lucy scrawled her number on a pad and tore it off to give the lad before they said goodbye.

Lee turned to Lucy, "Now, where can I take you? Unless, if you don't mind, I'll take Mum and the children back first and then get you home."

"Yes," said Amy enthusiastically. "She can come in for coffee and I can show her my pictures and my room."

"I don't expect Miss Wheeler would be interested," said Lee.

"Oh, yes I would," said Lucy.

"Then why don't you come in and have a little something. I can stay with the children and Lee can take you back afterwards," said Lee's mum.

Lucy grinned broadly, "I think I'd like that… a lot," she said smiling at Lee.

Amy clapped her hands in joy and Jack looked thrilled. "Oh, yes, please, please, Daddy. I want to see Lucy draw. She can teach us."

"Hold fire, both of you," said Lee. "We don't want Lucy overwhelmed."

"I really don't mind," said Lucy. "I'd love to do some drawing with your kids."

"See, Daddy," they chorused.

"Okay, okay, I give in!" said Lee with a giggle. "Well, all right. Let's get inside."

They tumbled out of the vehicle and with a lot of laughter and teasing ran down the path to Lee's house and practically fell in through the front door. Amy grabbed hold of Lucy's hands and thundered up the stairs to show Lucy her room. Close on their heels was Jack also pleading for Lucy to see his bedroom. Lucy went quite happily with both children.

Dora watched the delight on her grandchildren's faces and turned to Lee, "They like her. They like her a lot. She seems really pleasant. I approve."

"Mother, I gave her a lift; nothing more."

"Really? From where I'm standing you seem to have quite a connection."

"I hardly know her."

"Then take your time and get to know her better." Lee blushed. "I'll put the kettle on." Dora walked into the kitchen with a big smile on her face.

Lee watched his mother go and shook his head in bemusement. Amy and Jack came hurtling back down the stairs breathlessly. "Dad! Lucy says my pictures are good and show promise, don't you, Lucy?"

Lucy smiled and nodded. She was caught up in the children's enthusiasm. Jack added, "And she's going to teach me how to draw animals, aren't you, Aunty Lucy?"

Lee grinned. "Aunty Lucy?" Lucy shrugged and smiled impishly.

"Then we better sort out when these beauties can have these lessons," said Lee. "You better sit down." As she did, Amy and Jack bounced down beside her. Lucy was clearly a big hit!

23

JAMES TREEVES HAD CYCLED HOME. His anger had grown out of all proportion. He scrabbled about on the telephone table and dragged out a local telephone directory. He hunted through the 'W' residential entries in the book for Wheeler. His finger ran down the list of names to the 'L's. He scrolled down. There were four. "Well, we will soon find out if Ms Lucy Wheeler is any of these." He scribbled the numbers on a piece of paper.

He masked his number before dialling each number. The first one he rang was answered immediately. A male elderly voice answered, "Hello?"

James said, "Sorry to disturb you is it possible to speak to Lucy, please?"

"No one here of that name, I'm sorry."

"I must have the wrong number. Sorry, to have bothered you." He scribbled that number off the list and went on to the next, which had an answer phone reply, stating that Leonard and Veronica were unable to take their call. It was a woman's voice on the message, which did not belong to Miss Wheeler. It was another strike out.

James went onto the next number, which was answered with a gruff man's voice, "Larry Wheeler." James apologised that he had the wrong number and hung up.

There was just one left. "Fingers crossed," he murmured. "This has to be it!" He dialled and waited, drumming his fingers impatiently. An answer phone kicked in, "Hi, you've reached Lucy Wheeler. I'm not at home right now but leave your name and number with any message and I'll get back to you. Byeee!"

James curtailed the call, "Bingo!" He rubbed his hands in glee. What a great start. Now, he could write down her address and make his plans. His eyes gleamed with a malevolent light. He disappeared up to his room and locked his door.

Later that night Lee drove Lucy home. They had been getting on remarkably well, finding they shared the same sense of humour and taste in music. Lucy clambered out and said goodbye. She started off down the path when Lee plucked up the courage to stop her and called her name, "Lucy! Hold up."

She stopped in the middle of the path, turned and beamed brightly at him. "Yes?"

Lee. Became almost tongue tied and finally blurted out, "I... er ..."

"Yes?"

"I just wondered, but it's probably a stupid idea, I thought... Lucy, would you like to go out one evening? Maybe a drink? Or for dinner? Don't worry if you can't."

"No, I'd love to."

"I'll understand, if you don't..."

"But, I do... I will... I'd love to."

"Really?"

"Really."

Lee laughed nervously, "Well, all right... Um... I'd better get your number then."

"Hang on, I'll just get a pen and paper. Come in for a moment." Lucy fumbled for her keys and went inside. Her phone was ringing as she opened the door. Lucy grabbed the receiver, "Hello?" There was no one on the other end of the line. "Must have answered too late," she mused. "I'll check who called later." She grabbed a notebook and pen and scribbled down her two numbers. She tore off the page and passed it to Lee. "Will you give me yours? I never answer numbers I don't recognise." She added shyly, "And I don't want to miss your calls." Lee beamed at her and jotted his numbers down for her.

"I'll put them in my phone now." Lucy quickly tapped into her contacts list and left the scrap of paper by her home phone. "Done."

Lee stood by shyly, uncertain what to say. Finally, he muttered, "Well, I'd best be off."

Lucy smiled saying, "Er, yes. I'll wait for your call... Thanks for the lift and your help with Raymond."

"My pleasure."

They both stood there looking awkwardly at each other. Lee had a silly grin on his face and Lucy's face ached from beaming so much. "Night."

"Night."

Lucy opened the door and watched Lee walk down the path. He turned to look back at her. They both waved and she waited for him to get in his vehicle and drive away before closing the door and leaning against it. She smiled happily, "Things are looking up."

The phone rang. Lucy picked up, "Hello?" There was no reply, just an odd silence followed by a long rasping sigh that dissolved into a giggle. "Who is this?" demanded Lucy. There was still no answer. Frustrated Lucy slammed down the phone. "Stupid pervert."

The phone rang again.

24

THE DAY LOOKED BLEAK IN spite of the heat and humidity. The smoky clouds enveloped most of the blue sky and it was the last day of school before the half term break. Lucy looked drawn and tired. Her sleep had been disturbed by continuous phone calls through the night. The only saving grace, or so she thought, was that whoever was making the calls wasn't getting much sleep either.

She hadn't yet told Tara as her experience was proving so similar to Tara's and she didn't want to alarm her friend that there was still some creep out there making lives a misery. Anyway, she had better things to look forward to as Lee was taking her out that evening. She promised she would tell him all about it. She needed a sympathetic ear, someone on whom to offload.

So, involved was she with her many and confused thoughts that she didn't spot James Treeves hanging about in the road approaching the school. Lucy drove past the crowds of excited children who knew that half term had arrived and she made her way back.

Tommy Porter emerged from the building with a group of boys. They were laughing and joking together, playing with a football. One of the boys kicked it hard. James stepped out and caught the ball teasing the other lads with it, refusing to give it back until he saw Tommy. He booted it back to the others and hissed at his friend. "Tommy! A word in your shell-like."

Tommy walked across reluctantly, "What do you want, James?"

"Just a few words and a little help."

Coming behind the group was Raymond Campbell in the company of some of the girls; a more confident and neatly dressed Raymond. He was hardly recognisable from the unkempt, meek youth he had been before. He halted when he saw the school bully and advised his friends that he would catch them up. The girls walked on and Raymond slipped behind the two boys, dropping into the shade of a tree on the avenue. He strained to listen to what was being said.

"Tommy boy, I need to call in a favour. Remember you owe me."

Tommy snorted, "I don't owe you anything. You got me into more trouble than I reckoned with…" He studied the expression on his old friend's face and thought better of turning him down flat.

"I need help. I want to break into Miss Wheeler's house, around the back. There's an alley behind her house with a door into her back garden."

"Whatever for?" said Tommy in alarm.

"Best, you don't know. I just want a hand getting in then you can leave me to it."

Tommy frowned. It was not something he wanted to do, but he didn't want James's wrath on him. He decided to prevaricate, "How do you even know where she lives?"

"Oh, I know. I know her phone number, her number on the electoral roll, her birthday and I now have her mobile number, too…." James laughed. "Will you help me?"

Tommy shook his head, "Sorry, mate. I can't get involved. I don't know why you have it in for Miss Wheeler but…"

He stopped there as James caught him by the throat, "You will help me. You will meet me tonight at 9:30 outside the newsagents on Palfrey Lane. If you're not there, you'll regret it. I guarantee it." He let Tommy go and dusted him down. "So, Tommy boy. I'll see you later." With that he swaggered off.

Tommy was left shivering and frightened. Raymond came out from hiding and spoke to him, "You're not going to help him, are you?"

Tommy was startled but managed to say, "What else can I do?"

"We can warn Miss Wheeler."

"He'll know it was me."

"Not if we do it right," said Raymond.

The two boys continued talking on the way home.

Raymond hurried into his house and asked, "Mum, can I use the phone?"

"Of course, then you can make me a cup of tea. I'm gasping."

Raymond picked up the cordless phone, he looked in the phone book and called Tara Lomas and explained what he had found out."

"What?" Tara was shocked. "You must call her, tell her what you know. I'll get in touch with the police."

"Thanks, Mrs Lomas. I'll ring her now." Raymond ended the call and dialled Lucy Wheeler's number.

It rang and rang. He was about to hang up and try her mobile but finally she answered and screamed down the phone, "Leave me alone, will you? Pervert!"

Raymond tried to interrupt, "Miss Wheeler, please, it's me, Raymond."

Lucy stopped, "Raymond? What is it?"

Raymond explained again. Lucy went quiet, "So, it's James Treeves. I should have known."

"I've called Mrs Lomas and she's getting the police. He's trying to drag Tommy Porter into it. He threatened him, too."

"Thanks, Raymond. Thank you. Leave it with me."

"Yes, Miss." Raymond put down the phone and went to make his mum a cup of tea.

Lucy got straight on the phone to Lee. "Lee, those calls I've been having, it seems it's that horrible boy involved in that fight that we broke up." Lucy continued to tell him what she'd learned.

"Well, you won't be alone. I'll get mum to look after the kids and I'll be straight round. Hold tight. I can't believe after everything with Tara... it beggars' belief. Stay safe until I get there."

Lucy felt calmer and much better. Her phone rang again. She picked it up tentatively waiting for a horrible silence and malevolent laughter. It was Tara.

"Lucy? Cheryl Dixon and Shay Connor will be across, as will we, although the police don't want us there, they can't stop us. It must have been him who did all those things to me at school."

Lucy laughed. It will be a bit of a squash. I'll have a houseful."

"Doesn't matter. We will be quiet and lie in wait for the psychotic brat. Cheryl has it all worked out."

Lucy blew out through her teeth. Her stomach was fluttering wildly. She hung up and it rang again, "Oh, what? Hello?"

"Miss Wheeler? Officer Dixon here. I will just explain what will happen tonight. We are taking this threat very seriously, very seriously, indeed."

At eight o'clock Lucy had a houseful. She had made them all coffee and they were receiving their final instructions. Lucy was to try and act normally and do the things she usually did in the evening, as if she was home alone. She was to leave the drapes of the living room and kitchen open; only partially closing them once the light had begun to fade.

Tara, Steve and Lee were to wait in Lucy's upstairs bedroom with the door to the landing open, main lights off with just a small bedside lamp shining and the curtains closed. They were not to get involved. Cheryl cautioned them about their presence but Tara was adamant. Officers Dixon and Connor would wait downstairs in the second reception room.

Lucy was nervous and apprehensive. Although, she knew the boy was going to break in and was prepared for it; it was still scary. "What do you want me to do when he comes in?"

"Try and keep your distance. We need to hear him threaten you or try to menace you otherwise it will be put down as breaking and entering. All he'll get is a slap on the wrist and probation. Something more serious and the judiciary will be forced to send him down to a youth detention centre. He's sixteen now. He needs some type of rehabilitation with anger management. He already has a rap sheet for juvenile offences. Attempted aggravated burglary or similar will get the result we want."

"Can I at least have some sort of weapon at hand."

"That could be construed as provocation, but if it will make you feel any better …" Cheryl glanced across at Shay for support.

"I can't see that a rolling pin on the table could be called a weapon," said Shay. "She could be sketching it for some art class."

"It would certainly make me feel better," acknowledged Lucy.

"Well, okay," said Cheryl. "We don't know what the lad will be carrying or what his poor friend, coerced into helping him, will have." She checked her watch. "Time is getting close. Everyone needs to get to their places. We have someone watching the newsagent. They will let us know when they meet. There is also an officer stationed near the alley…"

At that point her radio went off, "Suspects in sight. Treeves is outside the newsagent and another lad is approaching… He is passing his accomplice a bottle. Looks like a water bottle of some type… He's showing him a blade… Looks like there is some sort of disagreement… He's threatening the other lad.

Got him up against the wall... They're moving off now, headed in your direction."

"Right, everyone, places please," Cheryl ordered.

All was still and quiet when a second message came through, "Two youths entering the alley, now. We will follow through with backup once they have entered the back garden."

The next five minutes seemed like an eternity. Lucy had put on some music, but not too loud, so that she could still hear the arrival of the young men. She poured herself a glass of wine as was her habit when home and set up her sketch pad and pastels.

She sat at the table and attempted to sketch. Her doodles became pictures of hate filled faces and boys with demonic expressions. She even had one that closely resembled James Treeves. There was a sound from the kitchen of glass cracking and the sash window sliding up. Usually, lost in her music she wouldn't have heard it but because her nerves were more tightly strung than a new violin string Lucy was aware of it. Still, she maintained her position although she wanted to leap up and confront her intruder.

James moved stealthily into the kitchen, across the floor and into the living room. He was wearing a balaclava hiding his face and clutching a deadly looking blade. He laughed in menacing glee behind her.

Lucy froze momentarily and then spun around to face her attacker. She rose from her seat. "Stay put, Miss Lucinda Wheeler." He waved the blade in front of her. "Give me the acid," he demanded of his friend.

Tommy Porter stuttered, "You don't want to do this... you really don't"

"Oh, but I do. I've had enough of authority and their bullying."

"She's never bullied you," rebuked Tommy.

"Oh, but you don't know. You don't know the half of it. Her and her do good friend."

"Please, James. Don't. Stop now and we can walk away."

James turned on his friend ferociously, "I said, no names. Are you stupid or something."

"What do you intend to do?"

"I've told you. What good's an art teacher without her eyes? Now, gimme!" Tommy lifted the bottle and slowly began unscrewing the top. He stopped. "What are you waiting for?"

"No, I can't do it. She's never done anything to me."

"Maybe, you need a little reminder, Tommy boy." James turned on his friend and slashed at his arm, making a grab for the bottle. Lucy's hand closed on the rolling pin and she threw it with force at James's head. James grabbed the bottle, which slipped and the cap came off. The acid poured over his hand and he screamed.

Cheryl Dixon had heard and seen enough. She and Shay came out from the dining room and apprehended the boy. The acid was spilling out onto the floor and melting the covering. Cheryl yelled, "Quickly get some cold water on the lad's hand and on this mess."

More officers entered through the front door and dealt with the spillage. James was now screaming hysterically. Cheryl had pulled off his balaclava and Shay was pouring cold water onto his blistering hand. James began to fight back. He shrieked at Tommy, "You! You told them. I'll get you for this."

Tommy looked frightened out of his wits. Lucy spoke with more calm than she felt, "It wasn't Tommy who informed on you, but someone else."

"Who? Who? I'll kill the bastard."

"You want to be careful where you talk and plan your foul deeds. You were heard by someone else. Tommy is not to blame."

James had now dissolved into hiccupping sobs. Shay Connor had dragged him to the kitchen and was running the cold water tap on his hand. Cheryl had called an ambulance and the others had come out from hiding. It was a chaotic scene.

Lee was comforting Lucy and had taken her by surprise with a tender kiss to which she relinquished herself utterly. Tara and Steve nudged each other and smiled. They looked on in satisfaction as the two boys were led away. Cheryl watched them go. She turned to the others, "We will keep up the pretence of Tommy Porter's compliance with Treeves but he will be released without charge. We have everything on tape. This delinquent is definitely going down."

The other police cleared from Lucy's front room leaving one man to deal with the spilled acid. Cheryl Dixon said, "We will have to take statements from everyone but we have all the evidence we need. I suggest you get on and enjoy the rest of your evening. I'll see you all in the morning." With that she radioed in and left.

The others collapsed onto the settee and arm chairs. There was a stunned silence, before Lucy announced getting everyone a drink, "Except you," she said to Tara. You can have orange juice."

The phone rang.

They all stopped and stared at the offending instrument demanding to be answered. Lucy moved tentatively toward it and cautiously picked it up, "Hello?" She sighed in relief as she heard Raymond's voice on the other end of the line and explained to him that all was well.

The school bully had been stopped once and for all and life was looking good for all of them.

Author's Acknowledgements

A HUGE thank you to Tony Rome and his company, Logyk Studios for designing Web of Fear's amazing book cover using Dreamstime images and to his ever patient partner Carole-Anne Crowhurst who endures solitude while he works on this and other projects. It is so much appreciated.

Thanks too, to my lovely husband, Andrew, without whom I would be unable to write, my lovely son, Ben Fielder, with whom I share many a creative discussion and many other dear friends who encourage me with their continued support like Hayley Raistrick Episkopos. I love you all.

Special thanks to my commissioning editor, Sarah Luddington and her excellent team at Mirador who take all the worries of publishing away allowing me to do what I do best and write.

And here's to the next!

Future titles will hopefully include, the sequel to The Electra Conspiracy and a sixth in the Detective Inspector Allison series. Please feel free to contact me on my Facebook Author's page:
https://www.facebook.com/Elizabeth-Revill-221311591283258
If you like my books please click 'Like'. Thank you.

Other books by the author

*The terrifying Inspector Allison
psychological thrillers:
Killing me Softly,
Prayer for the Dying
God only Knows
Would I Lie To You
Windows for the Dead*

*Llewellyn Family Saga:
Whispers on the Wind
Shadows on the Moon
Rainbows in the Clouds
Thunder in the Sun*

*Against the Tide
Turn of the Tide*

*Stand alone novels:
The Electra Conspiracy
Sanjukta and the Box of Souls
The Forsaken and the Damned
Web of Fear*

Lightning Source UK Ltd.
Milton Keynes UK
UKHW012010261121
394655UK00001B/115